The Edwards Brothers—Book One

Rescued

KIKI CHALUPNIK

WESTBOW
PRESS®
A DIVISION OF THOMAS NELSON
& ZONDERVAN

WestBow Press books may be ordered through booksellers or by contacting:

WestBow Press
A Division of Thomas Nelson & Zondervan
1663 Liberty Drive
Bloomington, IN 47403
www.westbowpress.com
1 (866) 928-1240

ISBN: 978-1-9736-1120-2 (sc)
ISBN: 978-1-9736-1121-9 (hc)
ISBN: 978-1-9736-1119-6 (e)

Library of Congress Control Number: 2017919353

Print information available on the last page.

WestBow Press rev. date: 01/02/2018

Contents

ACKNOWLEDGEMENTS

Thank you to the many friends and family that have encouraged and yes, even prodded me to publish my second book. To my best friend, companion for over 55 years, and love of my life, my husband Rick, who has been my greatest cheerleader and encourager, I love you.

Thank you to the friends who willingly read my manuscript from the very first writing: Di Rasmusson, Linda Van Noy, Elaine Sola, and Mary Louise Rossman.

To my dear friend, Carma Smith, who willingly edited my final manuscript, thank you. She is a teacher and librarian—and she loves books. Carma is a recent breast cancer survivor and has been an amazing example of God's love and grace. She battled this horrible disease with a happy and joyful heart. Her greeting has always been, "hey girl"; and with the biggest smile on her face and a cute scarf covering her head, she courageously faced this battle.

A special thanks to my son, Rick, and his wife, Susan, and of course Kali and Trevor, for the beautiful new computer they gave me this past Christmas. Rick said that when he was visiting Arizona with our grandson, Trevor, the spring of 2016, and saw the mini-laptop that I used to write my stories, he was convinced I needed to have a new computer with a larger monitor. It has truly been a joy to use.

To our children and their spouses, Rick and Sue; Janet and Mike; our four grandchildren, Kali, Trevor, Tyler, and Travis. You know "I love you more"— more than you know.

My prayer is that my stories express my heart and encourage the reader to know God and His great love for each of us. To Him be the glory.

Psalm 115:1 (NIV)
Not to us, LORD, NOT TO US
but to your name be the glory,
because of your love and faithfulness.

MEMORIUM

This book is dedicated to Babs Woolston who went to be with her Lord and Savior November 9, 2016. The day she was diagnosed with bone cancer she said, "I was ready to go be with Jesus when I accepted Him as my Savior at nine years old." She lived the final year of her life as she did every year…with love and joy. She loved life and she loved to laugh. She also loved to paint and was an amazing artist. She glorified God in her life and in her death.

Babs believed in me as an author. She encouraged me every step of the way as I wrote my first novel. Because of Babs and her husband Jon, my first book was published. I will be forever grateful. I miss you, Babs, but I know because of Jesus, that one day I will see you again.

Chapter 1

MOLLY SAT NERVOUSLY in front of Mrs. Harrison, anxiously waiting for her new assignment. Mrs. Harrison was the manager and owner of the Harrison Temp Agency. Molly unconsciously nibbled on her lower lip. It was something she was in the habit of doing when her nerves got the better of her. She was very aware of the scarcity of finding a permanent job since her college graduation two years ago. She had been given several temp jobs and although they never seemed to pay enough, she was thankful for anything. Seriously, she made more in tips when she waitressed back in her college days. After she received her master's degree, she was certain a job would come easy, but with the economy the way it was, it simply had not happened. She hoped for a better position every time she sat in this office. She was aware that many temp positions led to a permanent hire and that's what she hoped for with every job she accepted. Molly needed this job more than her next breath, which at the time, she did not realize she was holding.

"Well Miss Beaumont, I think we have a position for you. The position is for an executive assistant. You will be taking the place of Mrs. Larsen. It appears she will be taking an undetermined leave of absence." Mrs. Harrison slid the contract in front of Molly for her signature, and Molly nearly fell off her chair when she saw the pay she would receive. She swallowed hard, not knowing if she saw correctly or not.

"They want to pay me seventy-five thousand dollars for my yearly salary?"

"Yes, that's exactly what they want to do—including benefits. You do understand they can terminate this contract at any time if your job performance does not meet their requirements."

"I understand. Believe me: I will do all I can to keep the position." She signed the contract, shook hands with Mrs. Harrison, and thanked her for considering her for the position.

Molly left the temp agency certain her heart would explode right out of her chest. She had to call her mom immediately. She would also have to find an apartment that would be in the city. She had been taking the train from her home in Connecticut to New York City for several of her other temp jobs, knowing they were only for a matter of months. She never knew where she would be working next, yet somehow, she always managed the long commute. So much was going through her mind as it jumped from one subject to another: new job, amazing salary, finding an apartment, and calling her mom. She really wasn't a scatterbrain, but in the excitement, she certainly felt like one.

Chapter 2

FOR THE PAST two years, Molly had been helping her mom with her bills, which included her dad's nursing home expenses—something she never questioned. Molly's dad suffered from Alzheimer's, and two years ago, her mom had had no choice but to put him in a home. Insurance ran out and her dad was now getting state assistance. However, that meant the State took his pension and social security checks, leaving her mom with a stipend to live on. Fortunately, their house was paid for, and that alone brought comfort to Molly and her mother. Molly gave her mom much of her paycheck then finally had to go into her nearly depleted savings. She had saved quite a bit of money waitressing while in college. It certainly helped that she lived at home, but eventually her savings would run out.

Molly left the agency feeling as if she were floating on a cloud. As soon as she exited the building she pulled out her cell phone to call her mom. "Mom, you'll never guess this in a million years. I just signed a contract as an executive assistant for a very large corporation in downtown New York—and they will be paying me seventy-five thousand dollars a year. Yes, it's temporary, but Mom, seventy-five thousand dollars—plus benefits! Do you believe it? And it could very well lead to a permanent position. The woman I'm replacing is taking an undetermined leave of absence."

Molly could not contain her excitement—or the laughter that bubbled up from deep within. She walked with her head down as she talked excitedly to her mother. She was completely animated as she talked, and when she finally looked up, she smacked into a businessman—a very tall, handsome businessman. He was meticulously dressed in what undoubtedly was a very expensive custom-made suit—And he was carrying a large cup of Starbucks coffee. "Bye, Mom."

Ending her call abruptly, she looked up at the gorgeous creature in front of her. Coffee had splashed out of the cup and onto his suit. To her shock, he immediately snapped at her.

"What. Do you think. You're doing? If you weren't talking on that—dumb cell phone of yours, you would have seen me." It was obvious he had a few choice words he was thinking. And thankfully, he refrained from using them.

"Sir, I am so sorry. You are absolutely right. I was so excited over a job that I just had to call and tell my mother." Molly had some tissues in her purse and she immediately tried to dry the spill off his suit jacket. Of course, the lint from the tissue was getting all over his dark suit, which made it appear even worse. Molly shrugged and mindlessly began biting on her bottom lip.

"Just leave it. I'll have it cleaned!" he barked.

"I would be more than happy to pay the dry-cleaning bill, sir. I can give you my name and number where you can reach me. It's my cell phone number." Molly quickly took out a piece of paper and pen and jotted down her name and phone number. The man never even looked at the paper but stuffed it in his pocket.

"If you would, just get out of my way. I'm already late for a meeting."

Molly quickly stepped to the side, allowing the "gentleman" to walk away. *How rude. I'm probably going to miss my train and will have to wait an hour for another one.* She was embarrassed but also felt a little indignant at the way he talked to her.

Molly continued to the train station. Now that she missed her train, she had time to pick up a paper to read on her long commute. Hopefully by the weekend, she would have an apartment to rent. Since it was only Tuesday, she had the rest of the week to find one. Not even the incident with that nasty man could squelch her excitement over her new job. She felt glorious!

Douglas Edwards tried to push the incident aside but, could not get those huge aqua-blue eyes of hers out of his head. They were the biggest, bluest eyes he had ever seen in his life—like the waters of the Caribbean— and were framed by the longest lashes he had ever seen. Obviously, she was unaware of him as he turned to see her walk away from him, and not without noticing her very, very long, brunette hair. It cascaded in waves down her back almost to her waist. Thoughts of running his fingers through her gorgeous locks had him glued to the sidewalk.

When he came to his senses, he was totally unaware of all the people who were walking around him, much to their annoyance. Shaking his thoughts, he desperately tried to dismiss the incident, and the clumsy woman, when his cell phone buzzed. "Edwards here."

"Mr. Edwards, I wanted to let you know that your two o'clock appointment is here. He knows he is early, but he was hoping your meeting could be pushed up."

"I should be there shortly. I would have been there by now—" He breathed heavily into the phone.

"I hear a '"but"' coming next. What happened?"

"I had a girl—well, I guess a woman—plow right into me while on her cell phone. I'm telling you, Eleanor, they need to pass a law against talking on a cell phone while walking. It should be outlawed. Outlawed, I say."

"Hmm. Mr. Edwards, I believe that's exactly what you are doing, and you do it quite a bit I might add."

"Eleanor, I do not recall asking for your appraisal of my actions."

"Oh, okay. One more thing. They called from the temp agency and said they will have someone here Monday morning."

"Very good. I'm just crossing the street now. Tell Mr. Kingsley I will be there shortly. By the way, due to the mishap—I have a huge coffee with cream stain down the front of my suit jacket."

"I'll see what I can do, sir."

He was still in a huff when he entered the building and rode his private elevator to the top floor. Douglas Edwards was President of Edwards and Sons, Developers and Investors. Douglas's father had retired three years ago, leaving him, and his brother Jason, to run the extremely successful business.

Arriving on the top floor, he walked straight toward the executive suite and his office, rather than toward the conference room where he knew Mr. Kingsley would be waiting for him. Taking off his jacket as he walked, he quickly handed it to Eleanor. She immediately took his jacket and was prepared to try to remove the stain. "Well, she certainly did quite a number on this. I'm not sure I can get it all out, but it will have to do. At least all the white tissue flakes came off."

"Thanks, Eleanor, I can't wait any longer. After I greet Kingsley, I'll remove my jacket."

Eleanor simply rolled her eyes and wondered why he couldn't just enter the conference room without a jacket, but appearance was everything. That was what his father had instilled in his two sons.

"Is my brother in the conference room?"

"Yes, he's been entertaining Mr. Kingsley for some time now."

Jason caught his eye as soon as he entered. Noticing the stain on his jacket, he raised an eyebrow toward him. Douglas shrugged and after greeting Mr. Kingsley, he immediately removed his jacket. Mr. Kingsley happened to be one of their biggest investors, and a pain in the neck to boot. They had a very large investment they were counting on from him. They had been working on this deal for quite some time and could not afford to risk anything that would jeopardize the deal. Mr. Kingsley was known to be a very demanding and fastidious man, dotting all his "i's" and crossing all his "t's", and always impeccably dressed. He noticed the smirk on his brother's face, and knew he was in for twenty questions once the meeting ended.

Chapter 3

MOLLY WAS NEVER so happy to arrive home. The train ride was over an hour, and then the drive from the train station to her mom's house was at least another hour. Missing the train made the drive seem even longer. She was thrilled to share her good news with her mom—she still had difficulty believing it herself. She was excited that she found a couple of apartments advertised in the classified ads—Two apartments she would be able to afford. There were several one-bedroom apartments for three-thousand dollars a month which to Molly was unconscionable—but it was New York City. Two in particular sounded good and were less rent. She would call and make an appointment to see each of them. Her mom, Dolores, greeted her with such warmth, as she always did. After their embrace, her mom wanted to hear all about her new job. "Mom, you cannot believe what an amazing opportunity this is for me. It sounds absolutely perfect!"

"I am so happy for you dear, but I'm certainly going to miss having you around every night."

"I know Mom, and I'm going to miss being here, but you know what this means, don't you? I will be able to help much more with expenses. With my savings dwindling we really need this."

It always saddened Dolores to hear how committed her daughter was in helping with the expenses. Seeing the sadness in her mom's eyes, Molly knew what was coming next and she never wanted her mom to feel guilty about her willingness to help out. "Mom, we have already discussed this and you know this is what I want to do. I know I don't have to, but you and Dad have done so much for me, putting me through college and always being there for me. This is the least I can do for you.

You must believe me when I say, I want to do this. Now, when would you like to visit Daddy? I can't wait to tell him the news."

Dolores patted her daughter's hand and suggested they go visit him sometime tomorrow.

"That will work for me. I would like to call on the two apartments I found and see if I can go into the city Thursday to take a look at them. Why don't you come with me and we can make a day of it?"

"That would be lovely, dear. I'd like that a lot."

Noticing the giddiness in her mom's voice, Molly was pleased with her suggestion. Her mom never got out much except to church and the nursing home. Oh, once in a while she would meet a couple of her friends for lunch but that was about the extent of her going anywhere. Molly started to make plans that after the apartment hunting they would check out the building she would be working in. It would be good to see how long the drive would take from the new apartment to her new job. Then they could have a relaxing lunch at one of the nicer restaurants in the area. The more Molly thought of spending the day with her mom, the more excited she became. *Girls' day out, that's what we'll have. A girls' day out.*

Molly loved her mom and dad and the happy home she was privileged to grow up in. It was a modest home, and they were of simple means, and yet she never lacked for anything. Her home was always filled with so much love and laughter. She was confident that God was the center of her parents' marriage. He was the glue that gave them such a loving and committed relationship. In high school, her mom had a serious talk with her of the importance of marrying a man that loved God just as much as she did and Molly loved God with all her heart. To her dismay, that eliminated just about every boy she met in college. If they did claim to be a Christian, after one date she simply rolled her eyes and unfortunately, or fortunately, it would be their first and last date. Sometimes she wondered if a husband and children would ever happen for her. Until then, her priority was caring for her mom and helping with expenses. She believed in her heart that this new job was a gift from God.

Molly awoke the next morning to the sound of her mom humming in the kitchen. The beautiful sound along with the familiar aroma wafted its way from the kitchen. With all her mom had been through the past few years, it never ceased to amaze her how she always managed to have a sparkle in her eye and a song in her heart. She knew without a doubt it was from God and the complete trust she had in Him. This was the trust Molly sought to emulate in her life and her walk with God. She quickly showered and dressed, and warmly greeted her mom with a hug. "It smells so good in here. Are you making your famous waffles?"

"Yes I am. It looks like I won't have too many more days to spoil you with a good breakfast. After I shower perhaps we can head over to the nursing home and visit your daddy?"

"I would like that, Mom. I plan on visiting as much as possible before I move to the city." Molly helped herself to one of her mom's fluffy waffles and maple syrup. She could never stop at one. "Mom, as usual your waffles are the best, they're delicious. After our visit with Dad perhaps we can stop at the mall. I would like to find a couple of outfits for my new job. I know anything in the city would be cost prohibitive."

"You know, there's a new boutique that just opened up in town. I think we should stop there as well." Dolores loved to shop as much as Molly did.

Dolores and Molly walked into the nursing home and were pleased to see Dennis Beaumont sitting comfortably in a chair by a window in the day room. Molly thought her dad, who was only in his late sixties, still looked as handsome as ever. She had her dad's bright blue eyes but her mom's skin color and delicate features. She hoped her dad would recognize her today. It saddened her to know that he could be clear and sharp one minute and the very next had no idea who she was. "Hi Daddy, how are you today?"

To Molly's surprise, her dad looked up at her with the same sparkling blue eyes as hers and gave her a wink. "Hi Pumkin, it's so good to see you."

The tears started to well up in her eyes but she held them back. "I'm doing great, Daddy. I have a new job that I will be starting on Monday."

"On Monday. What day is today?"

"Today is Wednesday."

Molly's mom bent down to kiss her husband and was so thankful he recognized, at least for the present, who they were. When he was like this, they wanted to stay as long as possible. They talked, laughed, and even sang together. However, after about an hour they saw the veil slowly shadowing his eyes. Then he was gone, not knowing who they were and why they were there. Molly leaned down and gave him a hug and kiss. Her mom did the same, patting him on his hand and telling him how much she loved him and that she would be back soon to visit.

As they exited the nursing home, Molly leaned into her mom, "Mom, I don't know how you do it."

"Do what, dear?"

"Seeing Daddy like he is and yet you never get depressed or angry at God for what has happened to him."

"Oh, my dear, I have had many days that I have been depressed and shed many tears, but I have never been angry at God. When I promised your dad that I would love him in the good times and in the bad, in sickness and in health, I knew I was in for the long haul. My love for your dad has never wavered. In fact, I think I love him even more now."

"How can you say that, Mom?"

"I can honestly say this because the times when he is good, it's like we're together for the first time. I'm just so thankful I still have him. He is still such a handsome man, isn't he?"

"Yes Mom, he is. And when his mind is clear, I see so much love in his eyes for you."

"Well now, let's grab some lunch and do some shopping for that new job of yours before I become a blubbering fool."

Off they went arm in arm, mother and daughter, with a smile on their lips and a spring in their step. Molly was so grateful for God's amazing grace that He continually poured out on her and her precious family. Yes, she had a lot to be thankful for.

Dolores and Molly came home from their shopping spree exhausted. Molly was pleased to have found a few ideal outfits for her new job. "Mom, I love the new boutique in town. I found some beautiful clothes there, but are you sure the blue suit looks okay on me?"

"Better than okay, sweetheart, your beautiful blue eyes really pop and the pretty light pink shell underneath is perfect with it. You'll be stunning on your first day of work."

"Thanks Mom. I can't believe I was able to afford a designer suit. Of course, I wouldn't have if it wasn't on sale. I guess with the fall styles out soon, all the summer clothing will be on sale. I feel very fortunate to have found so many beautiful outfits."

"Yes, you were very fortunate and the shoes and handbags look very chic and fashionable. You will fit perfectly in your high-class downtown office."

Molly giggled, "Thanks Mom. You are always such an encouragement. How would you like a cup of tea before heading to bed? We both have a big day tomorrow. It's our "girls' day out" in the Big Apple don't forget!"

"Oh, I haven't forgotten. And a cup of tea sounds lovely."

Chapter 4

"**D**EAR, I AM so pleased that you did not take that first apartment. I hate to say this but—it was a dump, and in a very bad neighborhood. I had a feeling it wasn't good."

"I'm glad I didn't settle for it either, even if the rent was quite a bit less. I'm very happy with the second apartment, and I really like the landlady. Of course, the two flights of stairs will give me quite the workout. It will save me a gym membership." They both chuckled at that last comment.

"At least the neighborhood seems better, and yes, the landlady was very sweet. It's always best when the owner also lives on the premises."

"And it's furnished…somewhat. I think I need to get a slipcover for the couch, and I still want a new mattress for the bed. I was pleased the landlady agreed to me purchasing a new mattress. Maybe we can stop after lunch and I can pick out a mattress and have it delivered on Saturday."

"Sounds like a plan, dear. Now where can we have some lunch? I'm starving."

After lunch at an upscale restaurant, they stopped at a couple of stores and purchased a new mattress and then a slipcover for the couch. Molly was grateful the bed was queen size and not some tiny single bed, even if the mattress was somewhat higher in price. As they headed for home, Molly was pleased with how well the day had gone—thrilled with her new apartment, and her new wardrobe, but mostly her new job. She hoped her nervousness would not belie her confidence come Monday morning. She was smart and could pretty much handle anything that was thrown her way, but, a new job was always somewhat daunting.

She was determined to work on her shyness. She would be bold and assertive.

They returned home in time for a light supper. They decided on a bowl of soup, and then headed for the nursing home for a quick visit with her dad. She was determined to visit with him each day before the move on Sunday.

After breakfast, Molly told her mom she was going to the hair salon. It was a big decision, but she had made up her mind. It was time to get her hair cut! She would donate her hair to Locks-of-Love. She felt good about her decision. All through college she had so many comments about her long hair and how beautiful it was. But the more she thought about the time it took her to get ready in the morning, the more she realized, that with her new job, she would have less time. And besides, she was a twenty-six-year-old woman and this was a good reality check for her. *I'm probably too old to have such long hair anyway, and I'll look much more professional with it shorter.*

When Molly returned home, her mom was stunned as she stared at her daughter. "Molly you look more beautiful than ever. I can't believe it."

"Thanks Mom. I thought I would have some highlights added to the brunette and...Voila. I feel very sophisticated and stylish—more than I thought I would," Molly said with a giggle.

Molly's hair was still shoulder length, and not really that short at all. She wanted to be able to sweep it up in a ponytail or put it in a sophisticated "up-do"—anything would be easier than what she had to deal with when it was almost to her waist. Now she could not wait until Monday morning, confident she would make a good impression for her new job.

Molly and her mom were at her apartment bright and early on

Saturday for the delivery of her new mattress and to fit the couch with the new slipcover. Her mom was a big help in setting up her apartment. And, bless her heart, her mom had enough pots and pans, kitchen gadgets, dishes and silverware, and even a couple of lamps and bedding that she didn't have to spend any more money than was necessary. Setting up her apartment was exciting enough let alone the new job she was looking forward to on Monday. They did not have a chance on Thursday to make the drive to her new office, so after setting up her apartment, and the delivery of her new mattress, they drove downtown. She was pleased it was a Saturday so traffic was not as horrendous as it would be on a weekday. She located the parking garage for the building and wondered what floor she would be working on. The building looked like it had about twenty floors to it. Mrs. Harrison only told her it was the Edwards Building on 5th Ave. She would find out soon enough come Monday morning. With all this excitement, she doubted she would get much sleep the next couple of nights. The two-hour drive home was tiring and Molly realized there was no way she would be able to make the drive every day—it was exhausting. She was convinced that the decision to get her own apartment in the city was the best decision she could have made. She timed the trip from the apartment to the office and it took a good thirty minutes with light traffic—still better than two hours or a train ticket both ways. *Everything is going to work out just fine.*

Molly spent time with her dad each day as planned and for this she was grateful. When her dad was lucid, he was so happy to see her and always remembered her nickname, Pumkin, he had given her. This brought a smile to her face and evoked many precious memories every time he called her that. Sadly, those times would become less frequent as time went on.

On Sunday morning, Molly went with her mom to church and then out for lunch with a couple of her mom's lady friends, Clara and Alice. Molly had known these two dear ladies all of her life and was happy for her mom that they had remained such good friends for so many years. She stopped one more time to visit with her dad before heading out on her new adventure. That's exactly what it felt like to her—an adventure. It was seven o'clock when she arrived at her "new home". Pleased it was still light out. It was August, so the sun was still up for at least another

14

couple of hours. She stopped at her landlady's apartment to say hello and let her know she would finally be moving in for good. Mrs. Brackenburg always came out to say hello to Molly and her mom each day they were at the apartment. Her landlady seemed just as anxious for Molly to move in as she was.

Molly took the evening to familiarize herself with her new apartment. She was thrilled—it really was a lovely little place! It had a rather large living room, a kitchen with a table and four chairs, decent appliances, and a good size bedroom. All the furniture was used but nice and clean. As clean as the cupboards were, they still washed everything well on Saturday. They had scrubbed everything thoroughly the day before that it still smelled of Clorox. Molly noticed that Mrs. Brackenburg had hung a very pretty curtain and valance in the kitchen giving it a homey touch. She had told Molly and her mom that the living room and bedroom drapes had been cleaned along with the carpet. Molly could not have asked for anything more perfect. She had brought the TV from her room back home so she was able to sit and relax for a while before heading to bed.

There were way too many butterflies in her stomach to get to sleep and Molly was positive that she lay awake all night, but at some point, her eyes closed in a very sound sleep—startled when her alarm went off at five-thirty. In spite of her sleepiness, she managed to get to the kitchen and get the coffee pot on and then head for the shower... knowing coffee and a shower would wake her up.

Molly blow-dried her hair and was so pleased it fell right into place framing her face as it was supposed to. Her makeup was minimal but when she put on her mascara it made her eyes look bigger than ever. She dressed in her new blue suit with the pink shell underneath. She slipped on her three-inch patent heels and filled her new designer handbag with what she needed for the day. *Going to the outlet mall really paid off.* She slipped the strap over her shoulder feeling confident she looked as good as she felt.

Chapter 5

Douglas Edwards stepped out of his office at eight o'clock and asked Mrs. Larsen when the new temp assistant was to be in. "I told her to come in at nine today, sir. I thought perhaps we could get a few things taken care of before she arrived."

"Good idea. Sometimes the mornings are a bit rushed."

"Mr. Edwards, I planned a little reception for her as we have for the others in the past; giving her an opportunity to meet the officers, and some of the secretaries, before she is thrown into the job."

"That's fine. Does everyone know about the reception?"

"Yes, I sent an invitation to everyone, and the smaller conference room is cleared. They will be delivering the sweet rolls and coffee just before ten."

"Okay, good. I have a lot to catch up on in my office. Get Mr. Kingsley on the phone say about eight-thirty or even eight-forty-five. I want to give him a chance to be in his office and settled before you make the call."

"Yes sir, will do."

Mr. Edwards turned abruptly and headed for his office. His bark was always worse than his bite. Eleanor had first worked for his father, Edward Edwards Sr., and now was Douglas's assistant after the senior Edwards retired. And when Douglas spoke, everyone really did jump— except for Eleanor Larsen. He couldn't fool her for one minute. She had known the two brothers for most of their lives. They were like family to her.

Molly allowed plenty of time for her drive into the city. Traffic was horrific but she could handle it. She pulled into the underground garage and parked in a visitor parking place. Hopefully she would have an assigned parking spot after today. She walked into the lobby and was stunned to see how beautiful it was: marble floors, beautiful lighting fixtures, groupings of leather couches and chairs, it looked quite opulent for a lobby. She immediately walked over to the information counter and gave her name, explaining that she was sent by the Harrison Temp Agency. A very pleasant woman behind the desk found her name listed on a visitor sheet and asked her to fill out some information. She gave her an employee ID card and lanyard along with a garage pass. The pass identified the location of her reserved parking space. She handed her a personal elevator card, and directed her to the elevator she would be taking to the private twenty-first floor. *Wow, I can't believe I'll actually be working on the top floor. I can't wait to tell Mom!*

Molly arrived at the twenty-first floor and the receptionist directed her to the executive suite and Mr. Edwards's office. She was fifteen minutes early—better than being late. Mrs. Larsen greeted her kindly but had a quizzical expression on her face.

"I know I'm a little early and I certainly hope I'm not disrupting anything."

"Oh, no dear, you're fine. I'm somewhat surprised at your age. Oh, that didn't come out right. Mr. Edwards always requests older women, at least forty-five or older, so I'm just a little taken aback by how young you are."

"Well, I'm twenty-six and I don't consider myself that young. I'm sure you have seen my resume and educational accomplishments. I have no doubt that I'm well qualified for the job."

"I'm sure you are. I'm so sorry that I gave the impression that you may not be. That is not the issue at all. It's just that Mr. Edwards has a very strict policy on office dating and office relationships."

"Well, he will not have to worry about me. I'm here to do the job and plan on doing the best job possible."

"Eleanor!" bellowed Mr. Edwards through the intercom.

Mrs. Larsen and Molly both jumped, almost falling out of their chairs. Poor Molly stiffened and stared at Mrs. Larsen.

"Yes Mr. Edwards, what can I do for you?"

"I need you to call Kingsley. I asked that you have the call in by eight-forty-five. What's the hold up?"

"Our new assistant arrived a little early and I was greeting her. I will get the call in right away, sir. Are you planning to attend the reception for Ms. Beaumont? Remember that's at ten, sir."

"I know it's at ten, but I doubt I will be there. If I do make it, I'll be late, so you can introduce her to Jason. I'm sure he can handle the introductions. If she stays the week, we'll be lucky. She's probably no different than the others."

Molly had such a lump in her throat she could barely swallow. "What exactly did he mean? I'm no different than the others. How many others have there been?"

"Three others—but please don't let Mr. Edwards upset you. As long as you do the job, you'll be fine." Mrs. Larsen patted her hand and then gazed into her eyes. "Oh my, you have the most beautiful blue eyes I have ever seen."

Molly didn't know if she was trying to change the subject or if it was truly a compliment; she trusted it was the latter, and thanked her for her kind compliment. She hoped she could not see the tears that were welling up behind her "beautiful blue eyes". She had to have this job. Her mom and dad depended on her.

Mrs. Larsen began explaining the position to Molly and why she would be replacing her. "My daughter is expecting triplets and it won't be long before the doctor has her on complete bed rest. I will have to be there for her as long as needed, before and after the babies arrive."

"That sounds so exciting. I can't imagine having one baby let alone triplets."

"I take it, Ms. Beaumont, that you are not married."

"No, I am not. I don't even have a boyfriend, and please call me Molly."

"I can't imagine a beautiful woman such as you could still be single."

18

Molly simply shrugged her shoulders and thought perhaps she said too much. No one needed to know her personal life.

It was obvious Eleanor was stalling waiting for ten o'clock to arrive, and Molly wondered if Mrs. Larsen expected that she would not be there much past the reception planned for her.

"Well, it's almost ten. Mr. Edwards asked that I introduce you to Jason Edwards. Jason can introduce you to the other officers and their secretaries."

Eleanor walked Molly down to Jason's office and asked his secretary to announce them. When they entered his office, he was on the phone with his back to the door. After hanging up his phone, he turned in his chair, and keeping his head down, began going through some papers on his desk. "Hi Eleanor, what can I do for you?"

"Mr. Edwards, I would like to introduce Ms. Beaumont to you. Your brother's new assistant."

Jason looked up from his desk and the shock on his face was evident. "Hello there. And what did Eleanor say your name is?"

"My name is Molly Beaumont, sir."

Jason's eyes darted from Eleanor to Molly putting her in an awkward position. "You're Doug's new assistant? Why it's certainly a pleasure meeting you, Molly." He took her hand to shake and held it a little too long for Molly's comfort.

"It's very nice meeting you, Mr. Edwards. I'm looking forward to working here."

"And I'm certainly looking forward to you working here." Jason could not take his eyes off her. She was absolutely beautiful, and those eyes were amazing. They seemed to look into the depths of his soul. They were mesmerizing.

"Jason, Douglas asked that you introduce Molly to the other officers and their respective secretaries. I'm not sure if your brother will even make it to the reception." Jason gave Eleanor a puzzled look as though he was completely unaware there was even a reception. "Jason, everyone knows about the reception, and if you looked at the invitation I sent you, you would be aware of it as well."

"Sorry Eleanor. You know I never read everything that's sent to me, and I keep telling you to tell Ann. She is my secretary you know."

"Yes, I know Jason, and I did send one to Ann as well. I'm also sure she told you. You are simply choosing not to pay attention so you do not have to attend."

"I will be more than happy to escort this beautiful lady—and introduce her to the other "piranhas", I mean gentlemen, in the office."

Molly wondered what she was getting into but kept telling herself how much she needed this job. And it could be that Jason was hamming it up on her account. She hoped so.

God forgive me for not praying about this first. I was so excited about the job that I totally left you out of what this day would be like. I need your wisdom and direction Lord, and I pray this job will work out. Give me strength to withstand whatever comes my way. If this job is not for me, then help me to trust you for another.

After her brief prayer, Molly felt someone grab her elbow and began to lead her out of the office. She looked up to see Jason at her side and Mrs. Larsen following close behind. Evidently it wasn't enough to have Eleanor make all the introductions, but someone in a higher position.

All heads turned as they walked into the conference room. There wasn't a man in the room that did not come over to meet her. The secretaries seemed to be off to the side but looked very sweet and pleasant. Molly did not think there was a secretary under forty, and yet it seemed the men were all in their late twenties to mid-thirties. *What a strange place.* Jason introduced her to all the men and included each particular title that they held in the company. They shook her hand and welcomed her to the company, each with the biggest smile on their face. The women were all gracious and very welcoming. One of the men, Andrew, brought her a cup of coffee, asking if she needed cream or sugar. "No, black is fine, thank you."

The men were all warm and friendly, and several had questions as to her career. They were complete gentlemen. A few of the men appeared to be married, and after their introduction, they wandered to another part of the room. Molly had her back to the door as she was talking to a couple of the men and Jason. Eleanor was focused on the secretaries and chatted with them. It was obvious that someone had entered the room as all the heads turned towards the door. Molly turned as well, almost dropping her coffee cup, when she saw who entered. Douglas Edwards, taking notice of the young woman standing with his brother, walked over immediately and without hesitation asked who the new person was. "Why, you don't even know your new assistant, Doug? I'm surprised. I thought you knew everything that goes on in this company. Let me introduce you. Miss Beaumont, I would like to introduce my brother, and your boss, Douglas Edwards."

Jason's sarcasm was obvious, but Doug was not going to let it get the better of him. "Nice to meet you Miss Beaumont, I apologize for not coming out to meet you earlier." Doug looked into her eyes and simply shook his head. *Those eyes sure look familiar, but this can't possibly be the same woman that bumped into me last week. This woman is much more sophisticated and elegant. I'm positive it can't be the same woman. That woman was a brunette with hair down to her waist. Hair I would have loved to run my fingers through. This woman has what I think would be called auburn colored hair. It must be the eyes—they have the same eyes, if that's even possible.* Jason patted his brother on the back shaking him out of his reverie.

Molly stood frozen to the floor, her heart pounded so fast she was sure everyone around could hear. Her only hope was that he would not recognize her. After all, she had a totally different hairstyle. She could not let on that she had bumped, rather plowed, into him the week before. *Besides, he was the one that had been totally rude to me. And rude he was, even today. The way he spoke to Eleanor, berating her for not making a lousy phone call? Why did she even take that from him? I would never allow a man to talk to me like that even if he were my boss.* The faces of her mom and dad quickly flashed before her eyes and she remembered exactly why she needed this job. She would stick it out no matter how rude one man could be. Molly straightened her shoulders and extended her hand for a quick handshake.

After the brief reception, they all went to their respective offices. Jason was extremely kind to Molly and she was very grateful. She guessed he was a flirt but she thought him manageable. She had gone out with a few obnoxious guys in college and was pretty proud of the way she handled herself. After Jason told her he would see her later, she noticed that Eleanor and Mr. Edwards were waiting for her to walk her down to their office. She and Eleanor followed behind Mr. Edwards like two puppies that had been scolded for wandering away from the house. *Why was this man so intimidating?*

As soon as they entered the assistant's office, Mr. Edwards barked at Eleanor to come to his office…alone. "Why don't you have a seat at the desk, dear. I'm sure I'll be right out and then we can begin with some of the job responsibilities."

Molly simply nodded but quickly sat in one of the chairs at the desk hoping she really would have a chance to begin her job today. Maybe she would be fired before she even started. *If that's the case, so be it.* Sitting here alone meant that Molly had more time to pray, and so she did.

"Eleanor, you know the rules! No secretaries or assistants are to be under forty! I do not want my men distracted by some…beautiful young woman…especially Jason. In the past, it has always led to problems. I want to know why the agency sent such a young woman."

"Mr. Edwards, would you, for once, give a younger woman a chance. Miss Beaumont has an incredible resume. She has a BA, and her Master's. She is very qualified for this position."

"Okay, so she's smart. There are a lot of smart women over forty."

"Thank you, Douglas. I didn't think you noticed." Eleanor said this a little tongue in cheek. "I think it's you that can't handle working with a younger woman, not the other men."

"That's not true and you know it. You know my brother and the womanizer he is capable of being."

Eleanor continued her voice rising as she spoke. "And just because you had one very bad experience does not mean you should write off the entire female species."

"And I do not need any motherly advice from you! If I wanted your advice, I would go visit my own mother!"

Voices were definitely raised, and although Molly could not make out what was being said, obviously, it had to have something to do with her. She only hoped Mr. Edwards would not insist that he knew who she was. *I'm sure he thinks me a klutz and a ditz. I need to convince him I'm neither of those assessments.*

"Douglas, please give her a chance. I don't know why, but I get the feeling she desperately needs this job."

"How can anyone with all her intelligence not have had years of experience already in her field? That makes no sense to me."

"Douglas, she has worked for the temp agency since graduation and they have sent her all over creation, but each job has been a temporary position."

"That's what a temp agency does— Does it not?"

"You can be so pigheaded sometimes. What do you want me to tell her; after all, you're the boss."

"And don't you forget it—well, all right. We can give her a chance but any dating within the office and she is gone... that includes dating Jason."

Molly felt like she had been sitting on pins and needles for hours waiting for Eleanor to exit Mr. Edwards's office. If there were any chance at all of her getting a decent job some other place, she would walk out that door and never look back. With those thoughts bombarding her mind, she looked up to see Eleanor Larsen approach the desk. Molly was afraid to even look at the poor woman, who by the sound of things was getting an ear full from her boss, and all on her account.

Eleanor took the chair next to Molly, and in the kindest, most gentle tone said, "Now let's get started, shall we?"

Molly sat with her mouth agape, but quickly recovered when she realized she had the job...for now anyway. "Thank you so much, Mrs. Larsen. I really appreciate what you have done for me."

"Remember, it's Eleanor. Keeping the job will be entirely up to you."

Mrs. Larsen spent the entire day going over what would be required of her as executive assistant to the CEO of Edwards and Sons. Molly hoped she would be able to keep it all straight, and Eleanor assured her that after a week or two she would have no difficulty. It was obvious to Eleanor that Molly was an intelligent hard-working woman and wanted to do the best job possible. After hours of instruction, and being interrupted by the booming voice of Douglas Edwards, Eleanor closed her instruction for the day by telling Molly the steadfast rule: there would be no dating or any kind of relationship with any male employee in the office and that included Jason Edwards, who was COO of Edwards and Sons.

"That should be no problem. I have never made dating a priority in my life."

"Tomorrow I will have you shadow me, and you can get a first-hand feel for what my day is like. You will find that Mr. Edwards runs a fairly tight ship here. It's a huge responsibility that his father has entrusted to him and he takes it very seriously."

"I understand. I only hope I do not disappoint him, or you in any way."

"Molly, I get the sense that this job is of the utmost importance to you, and I hope I'm not prying when I ask what makes you want it so badly. You have heard Mr. Edwards on several occasions speak rather harsh and yet you seem to overlook his gruffness."

Molly began biting her lower lip, which she did out of habit when she was nervous. "Oh, Eleanor is it that obvious? I need this job more than my next breath. I have been helping my mom pay some monthly expenses. You see, my dad is in a nursing home; he has Alzheimer's and has been in a home for two years now. My mother had no choice but to put him in a home, and financially it has taken everything she has. I have gone through nearly all of my savings to help them. I feel with all the support they have given me, it is the least I can do."

"Where does your mom live?"

"They live in Connecticut. It's over a two-hour drive from here. Even by train it was a long trip, and considering the cost of a train ticket, I was fortunate enough to find an apartment over the weekend not too far from here."

"Well good for you. I certainly hope everything works out for you, and thank you for telling me. I hate to pry, but after our working together today, I felt you had a very resolute reason for seeing this job through."

"I just hope I'm able to hold my tongue when it comes to Mr. Edwards. I wonder how you put up with him."

Eleanor patted Molly's hand and told her that most of the time his bark was worse than his bite, but she still needed to tread carefully around him. At least until she figured out how to handle him in her own way. "I worked for Mr. Edwards Sr. and have known his two sons since they were young boys. They know not to mess with me." Eleanor said this with a wink and a twinkle in her eye. Molly got the feeling that Eleanor was more of a family member than an employee. No way could she assume he would treat her in the same manner as Eleanor. She would have to keep on her toes and not make any mistakes. Her mom and dad depended on her, and she depended on this job.

Chapter 6

OUGLAS SAT QUIETLY in his office and could not get Eleanor's words out of his head: "Just because you had one very bad experience does not mean you should write off the entire female species." *Bad does not describe that relationship. Being with Peggy for three years only to have her walk out on him because he didn't want to marry her at the time, was no reason to end what he thought was still okay.* However, when Douglas realized Peggy was nothing but a gold-digger, their relationship had changed. She wanted more and he kept giving it to her…whatever she wanted, until he finally came to his senses. And that only happened when she wanted a permanent ring on her finger…a four-carat diamond no less. He thought of his parents: happily married for almost forty years now. He remembered all the lectures he got from his parents about living together before marriage, and how that was not the answer to finding the right partner. At least he listened to that advice. He thought he loved Peggy in the beginning, but now that he looked back on things, he realized he never did. She was convenient and she threw herself at him every chance she had until he gave in. When she wanted to move in with him, he tried telling his parents that it was the culture today—times had changed. He grew up in a loving Christian home and his parents could not understand where they had gone wrong with their two sons. As far back as he could remember, they had stressed what the Bible said about being unequally yoked and that always niggled at the back of Doug's brain. He was grateful it kept him for doing anything he would regret. He and his brother both believed in their parents' values at one time, but when they got into college things changed. Both he and Jason got caught up in the liberal lifestyle. It didn't mean they were bad people, just liberal thinkers. Nobody really believed the way his parents did anymore. But he knew his parents had something special going for them. Not only did they love life and each other, but they both loved God and served him every chance they had; sometimes he envied them and what they had. After Peggy, he had made the decision to pour himself into the company. He certainly did not need another relationship, nor was he a frat boy any longer. Even if he did want to date there were plenty of women out there that he could go out with. Suddenly he thought of the woman with the beautiful blue eyes. But which one? The woman that spilled coffee all down the front of his suit… Or his new assistant? Funny how they both had the same eyes—they were mesmerizing, that's for sure. Shaking himself out of his reverie, he looked up at his clock on the wall. It was already six-thirty, and he wanted to get out early. At least his penthouse was not too far away.

Molly called her mom as soon as she got home. She had so much to tell her. She hesitated in telling her about last week's incident, but then realized she had nothing to lose by telling her the whole story. "Mom, remember when I abruptly hung up on you last week, the day I called to tell you about my new job?"

"Yes, I do, and I completely forgot to ask you about it."

She heard her mom gasp when she continued to tell her about the man she had bumped into, spilling his Starbucks all down his suit. When she told her that the same gentleman was now her boss, there was silence at the other end of the phone. "Mom, are you there?"

"Yes dear, I am, and I don't know if I should laugh or cry. You don't think he has recognized you?"

"No Mom, I don't think he has. At least for the time being, and I hope by the time it dawns on him, I will already be doing such a fantastic job that he can't do without me."

"Oh honey, that is pretty funny. I'm going to be praying that it will take him a very long time to figure it out."

Mother and daughter talked and laughed back and forth for some time. Dolores especially liked the part where Mr. Edwards walked into the reception and had no clue Molly was the same woman he had encountered the week before. "But Mom, the look on my face had to be priceless. I absolutely froze in place. I could not move. It was a good thing his brother Jason never noticed. He made a bigger deal out of Mr. Edwards not meeting me before the reception."

After their lengthy conversation, Molly and Dolores said their goodbyes and wished each other a good night's sleep, Molly, however, wondered if sleep would come any easier to her this night than the previous night. She had a feeling that tomorrow would be just as stressful as she shadowed Eleanor for the day. She feared she would encounter Mr. Edwards much more than she did today, as she barely saw him at all today. She prayed before drifting off to sleep that her nerves would be kept at bay tomorrow. *And please, Lord, no run-ins with Mr. Edwards. He is just a man. Well not just any man and not just my new boss. He is probably the most handsome man I have ever seen.* There was no way she would confess that to her mother.

Chapter 7

MOLLY ARRIVED AT the office at seven-forty-five per Eleanor's instructions. Eleanor said she always arrived before Mr. Edwards so she could get his office in order. He liked his blinds opened and coffee ready before he came in. The New York Times and the Wall Street Journal on his desk. Molly followed Eleanor into his office and noticed she used a remote to open the automatic blinds. His windows reached from floor to ceiling giving a breathtaking view of the city. His office was huge and this was the first Molly had seen it. His mahogany desk sat in front of the windows with two leather chairs facing it. A very plush leather chair was in place for Mr. Edwards. Molly dubbed this "the king's chair" the moment her eyes saw it. Against one of the walls was a beautiful leather couch with two matching chairs on either side, a coffee table and two side tables. Beautiful oil paintings lined the walls. Opposite the massive windows were a sink, counter, and small fridge. Molly noticed the coffee pot on one side of the counter and on the other side a tray with several coffee mugs. Eleanor immediately filled the coffee pot, put the cream in a ceramic creamer, and set out the matching sugar bowl. "I take it Mr. Edwards must get his own coffee in the morning."

"Oh no," said Eleanor. "I always pour his first cup in the morning, but after that he does help himself. However, if he is out and about he usually stops at Starbucks and brings back his large vanilla latte. Sometimes I think he's addicted to them."

Hearing the word Starbucks caught Molly by surprise and all she could do was mouth an "O". She hoped her reaction did not create any suspicion. Eleanor must have known of the incident last week. *Please don't say anything, Eleanor.* To Molly's relief nothing was said. She let out her breath that she had not realized she had been holding.

"Mr. Edwards likes one sugar and a little cream in his coffee. You will soon catch on to his peculiarities."

"With so many mugs on the counter, does he entertain in his office?"

"If there are clients or business associates meeting with him, then yes. I make sure coffee or water is served to everyone. But that isn't every day."

As Eleanor was going over everything with Molly, Mr. Edwards entered his office. He certainly could not avoid noticing the beautiful woman standing before him. She wore a simple aqua colored shirtwaist dress that seemed to accent every curve she had, no matter how modest it was supposed to be. Mr. Edwards simply nodded good morning, walked to his desk, set down his briefcase and immediately sat down in "the king's chair".

Molly observed as Eleanor prepared his coffee, walked over, and set it down. His two papers Eleanor had already set just so on his desk. "Good morning Mr. Edwards."

"Good morning, Eleanor." He looked up at Molly and simply grumbled a hardly audible good morning to her.

Molly had all she could do not to give a very rude reply but simply smiled the best she could and in a very cheerful voice said, "Good morning to you too, Mr. Edwards. It's a beautiful morning, isn't it?"

"Mm-hmm." It was definitely not much of a response, thought Molly.

Molly wondered what kind of an answer that was but dismissed his rudeness as she followed Eleanor out the door and returned to her desk.

Molly was occupied all day taking copious notes from Eleanor. She wanted everything to be clear, and tried very hard not to miss anything that may be expected of her.

Eleanor was detailed in explaining every aspect of her position. It was obvious that Molly was going to do an excellent job in filling her shoes—only time would tell.

By the end of her first week, Molly was more confident as she listened and followed Eleanor in arranging appointments. She contacted business associates per Mr. Edwards, and corresponded with several overseas developers. It was obvious that Mr. Edwards depended on Eleanor to maintain his calendar and write detailed reports, even without his input. To Eleanor's satisfaction, Molly was more than capable. However, on Friday as Eleanor was going over their overseas investments, Eleanor told her there would be overseas trips she would be expected to take.

Horror gripped Molly's chest at hearing this announcement. She tried hiding the tension tightening her chest. She was sure she was going to have a heart attack, or at least start hyperventilating. What no one, but her parents and only one other person knew, was that Molly was terrified of flying. *How in the world can I keep this job if I can't even get on an airplane?* Eleanor asked Molly if she had her passport and immediately she said no. Eleanor said Mr. Edwards had a flight to London the following week, and since she did not have her passport she would make the trip and that Molly could stay in the office. She told her she would have to apply for a passport so she would have it in time for Mr. Edwards's next trip. Molly simply nodded and said she would stop by the post office and fill out the application that weekend. She hoped her voice did not contradict her true feelings. Somehow, she would have to get up the nerve to board an airplane.

When Molly was thirteen, she went on a trip with her parents to California. It was to be a grand vacation, and one that everyone was looking forward to, especially Molly, as she had never flown before. They were going to Disneyland, Universal Studios, SeaWorld, and the beach. The excitement was more than she could contain. This had been her request for her thirteenth birthday present from her parents. Everything was perfect. The flight was smooth, until the plane had an engine fail. At that time, they discovered they had no landing gear. They had to make an emergency landing at Sky Harbor Airport in Phoenix. Everyone sat with their heads between their knees in a crash-landing position. The screams were terrifying as the plane slid off the runway. When it came to an ear shattering stop, the front of the plane burst into flames. Most of the passengers got off safely, but several perished. Molly vowed she would never step foot on another airplane. She spent a year in therapy, but the fear of flying never left her. Oh, she prayed for God to remove the fear, but the ghost reappeared at every mention of flying. *Lord, how in the world am I ever going to be able to get on a plane? There is no way I can talk to Eleanor about this, let alone Mr. Edwards. No one would understand such paralyzing fear.* Well, at least for now she did not have to worry about it, and with that, she resolved that she would apply for her passport on her next visit home—no matter what.

Eleanor called the office early Monday morning telling Molly that she would not be in. She had packing to do and several errands to run prior to their trip to London. "You know what to do, Molly, and I'm sure you won't have any problem handling the office. Tell Mr. Edwards I have arranged for the limo to pick me up in the morning."

"Okay, I will." *This should be interesting—alone with Mr. Edwards all day.* Molly entered his office and immediately opened the blinds, situated the two papers just so on his desk, and proceeded to make coffee—exactly per Eleanor's instructions. She was just finishing when Mr. Edwards entered his office. "Good morning, Mr. Edwards. How are you this morning?" Molly set his coffee on his desk.

"Where's Eleanor?"

"Excuse me?"

"You heard me, where's Eleanor?"

"Mr. Edwards, there is no need for you to me rude to me. Usually when someone says good morning to another person their response is a good morning in return. However, it's clear you were never taught such manners and I will excuse your rudeness." Molly was treading on thin ice but there was just so much she was going to take from this man. She felt her legs tremble and hoped it was not visible.

"Sorry, good morning… and I'm fine. Now where is Eleanor this morning?"

"Eleanor called requesting I give you the message that she will not be in as she has packing to do for your trip tomorrow, and several errands to run."

He harrumphed and then took a swallow of his coffee. "This is not how Eleanor makes my coffee!"

"Oh. Yes. It is. It's exactly how Eleanor makes it. I followed her instructions to the tee. If it's not to your liking, tell me what I did incorrectly and I will be happy to make another pot."

Douglas grumbled some more but then said it would be fine. He was trying desperately not to look at Molly. After just so much avoidance, he could not hold out any longer. *Why did she have such mesmerizing eyes?* He was sure he could drown in the depths of those ocean-blue eyes. And it wasn't only her eyes that were beautiful. He needed to get a hold of his thoughts and wondered how he would be able to work with her all day; let alone every day once Eleanor went to care for her daughter and new grandbabies. And if he let her go, his brother Jason would be knocking on her door; probably every single guy in the office would be at her door. He could not help but notice all the attention she received whenever he was at Eleanor's desk, soon to be her desk. One of his men always seemed to be hanging around asking for a file of some sort or another. They were like a bunch of testosterone filled teenagers. They all knew the rules. *I guess I should have had a "no looking" rule included.*

"And Eleanor said that she has arranged for a limo to pick her up in the morning."

"Excuse me?" He did not realize how taken up he was in his thoughts.

She repeated. "Eleanor said that she has arranged for a limo to pick her up in the morning."

"Fine. That will be all for now. Thank you."

Molly left his office and immediately exhaled the breath she had been holding. *I seem to be holding my breath quite a lot lately. Mr. Edwards is infuriating to say the least. How am I ever going to manage working for him when Eleanor leaves?*

The rest of the day was filled with several bellows coming from Mr. Edwards. He was always direct and to the point as to his requests. Molly was pleased that she had no difficulty completing every task. She only hoped Mr. Edwards was pleased with her performance. At five, Molly knocked on "His Highness's" door, this was a new name she dubbed him, informing him that if there was nothing else he needed for the day, she would be heading home.

"No, that will be all. Feel free to go."

"Thank you, and I hope you have a good trip sir."

"Yeah, thanks. There may be some papers to fax but Eleanor will contact you if need be."

"When will you be returning Mr. Edwards?"

"We'll be returning on Friday." *If she thinks she can slack off and not put in a full day, she's in for a surprise. She doesn't know this, but Jason will be keeping a close watch on her comings and goings.* Jason was a little too anxious to keep tabs on her but he didn't know who else to ask. He certainly did not want the employees to think this was a normal procedure and that they were all watched this closely.

"Well, goodnight, Mr. Edwards."

Just then Douglas looked up from his desk and melted into her blue eyes. "Goodnight Molly, I mean Miss Beaumont. See you next week."

Her knees were shaking as she walked out his door, closing it behind her. *"Molly", why did he call me by my first name? That was a first. It was obvious he let that slip.* Suddenly Molly wondered if he ever looked at the slip of paper she had given him with her name and phone number on it. She hoped it was still in his suit pocket, at the cleaners, or perhaps he even tossed it in the trash can after she gave it to him. *One could only hope.*

Molly finished clearing her desk. Knowing her ride home would be at least forty-five minutes in traffic, she thought she better go to the ladies' room before heading to the garage.

As Molly was heading for her car, she noticed a beautiful red Porsche a couple of spaces down from her car, it made her vehicle look pretty pathetic. Her car may have been old, but it was paid for. Before Molly had the chance to open her car door, the lock on the Porsche tweeted. When she looked up to see whose car it was, to her surprise, Mr. Edwards walked past her with his keys out and ready to get in his car. He nodded his head, trying desperately not to look into her eyes.

"Goodnight, again, Miss Beaumont."

"Goodnight, Mr. Edwards."

Douglas Edwards slid into the driver's seat of his Porsche but not without noticing the car Molly got into. *I guess she really does need this job. What in the world is she driving anyway? Her car has to be at least eight or even ten years old.*

Chapter 8

MOLLY RETURNED TO her apartment feeling drained from her long day alone with Mr. Edwards. This was not the only reason. The thought of having to fly at some point left her anxious and tense all day. As she flopped onto her couch, her head in her hands, she felt totally overwhelmed...to her dismay the tears began. She had to tell her mom; there was no point in trying to keep this information from her. She had already gone the whole week and could not keep it in any longer. *How can I keep this job if I refuse to fly?* Her mom picked up on the second ring. "Hi Mom, how are you doing? How is Daddy?"

Dolores sensed a deep sadness in her daughter's voice and immediately was aware that something was amiss. "Molly, I know something is troubling you. What is it dear?"

"Oh Mom, I haven't said anything to you, but Eleanor is flying to London with Mr. Edwards tomorrow, and I guess the next time he goes to Europe I will have to go with him. Mom, you know what that means; I just can't do it."

"Sweetie, I know what you have gone through, but I also know you are going to have to face your fears. God does not want us to fear. In fact, that is the most talked about command in the Bible."

"Mom I know all of that, but I just can't get on a plane."

"You know it isn't enough to simply believe in God, but you must believe God: believe what he says in his Word. When God says, I will never leave you or forsake you, you must know God means what he says. You know your dad and I have prayed about this for many years, and I'm going to pray that you will conquer your fear once and for all by the time you need to fly."

"Thanks for praying Mom, but I'm not sure it will make flying any easier for me. I did tell Eleanor that I would pick up an application for a passport. I couldn't bring myself to do it this past weekend, but I plan on coming to see you and Dad next weekend, and I promise I will go to the post office Saturday. Would you mind coming with me? I think I'll need all the moral support I can get."

"Of course, I will go with you, and you can be sure I will not let you back out of it."

"Okay Mom, and thanks for always being there for me. I love you and I'll see you soon."

Mom and daughter said their goodbyes, and once again Molly was so thankful for the loving mother she had. She wondered if her dad, when his mind was clear, continued to pray for her. She had a feeling he did.

Molly tossed and turned the entire night, but she still managed to arrive at the office at seven forty-five Tuesday morning. Other than making the pot of coffee for Mr. Edwards, she kept her routine the same and made the coffee for herself; then picked up the remote for the blinds. Someone was sitting in "the king's chair". To Molly's surprise, Jason looked up from the desk. "Mr. Edwards what are you doing here in Mr. Edwards's office? May I help you with something?"

"I wasn't sure when you would arrive so I thought I would wait for you. Umm yes, I need the Kingsley file."

"Not a problem, sir. I will get it for you."

"Please call me Jason."

"Yes sir—I mean Jason."

Molly felt his eyes on her the entire time she walked out of the office; how odd it seemed for him to be in the office so early. She retrieved the file and re-entered the office, placing the file on the desk. "Is there anything else sir, I mean Jason? May I get you a cup of coffee?"

"Thanks, that would be great. However, unlike my brother, I drink it black."

Molly walked to the counter picking out a mug, and poured Jason a cup of coffee. She held the mug with both hands as she was about to set it on the desk. Jason immediately reached up to take it from her, and in so doing, held both her hands in his. "Thank you, Molly. I appreciate it."

With both hands wrapped around the mug she could definitely feel the heat permeating the cup. She felt he was intentionally holding her hands a little too long. "Excuse me Mr. Edwards, but the cup is quite hot." She said this as she tried to wiggle her hands free.

"Oh, I'm so sorry, Molly. I didn't realize I was still holding your hands so long… forgive me. Yes, I can feel it's quite warm." He really did not intend to hold her hands that long, but was totally mesmerized by her beautiful blue eyes.

He took the cup from her but Molly did not believe for a minute he did not know what he was doing. She immediately excused herself stating that she had a lot of work to do.

"Before you go, how about we have lunch together today?" He was hoping that with his brother out of the country he could exercise his freedom in asking her out to lunch.

"Thank you but no. I don't think that would be a good idea, and besides I already have plans."

Jason wondered what plans she could possibly have. She just started working there a couple of weeks ago, and as far as he knew, she did not socialize with any of the secretaries or the receptionist. He would be keeping a close eye on her anyway for the rest of the week. After all, it's what Douglas asked him to do and he always did what big brother requested. Molly didn't know this, but Jason would definitely be keeping an eye on her. *She has to be one of the prettiest women I have seen in a long time and I have seen a lot of beautiful women…outside this office. Keeping an eye on her will be a pleasure.*

Molly worked diligently the entire day. She surprised herself with all she had to keep busy. She definitely wanted to familiarize herself with the files and the many accounts associated with Edwards and Sons. The more informed she was, the easier it would be for her when Eleanor left. Yes, she definitely had more than enough to keep herself busy the entire week.

Five o'clock came and Jason was back in her office returning the Kingsley file. She was not surprised by this, but it seemed odd that he would wait until five. Molly was still at her desk; however, she was in the process of putting everything to rights. She still needed to wash the coffee mugs and clean the coffee pot. Jason seemed a little taken aback that Molly was still in the office. "Oh, hi Molly, I thought you would have been gone by now."

"No. my day ends at five, and I still have some cleanup to take care of." Molly returned the Kingsley file and started walking into Douglas's office.

"How about I wait and walk you to your car?"

"That really won't be necessary. I'm sure I'll be fine, but thank you anyway."

Molly could not help but notice the disappointment on Jason's face; however, Eleanor was extremely adamant regarding any contact with any male co-worker, including Jason.

"Hey I'm not asking you to go out with me. I know my brother's rules. I simply offered to walk you to your car."

"Well then that would be fine. I do need to clean things up however, and I also need to run into the ladies' room before leaving. My drive home can be anywhere from forty-five minutes to an hour, depending on the traffic."

"That's fine. I don't mind waiting."

Molly felt somewhat awkward as she quickly ducked into the ladies' room. Jason was patiently waiting for her when she came out. "Thank you for waiting for me."

"Not a problem at all. Where do you live anyway that your drive takes you that long?"

Molly did not want to disclose her address to him but simply stated that she had an apartment in the upper eastside. Jason noticed her reluctance and asked no further questions. He did not want her to feel uncomfortable with him in any way.

Jason was polite and non-threatening as they rode the elevator down to the garage. As they walked to her car they passed a beautiful red Ferrari. Molly was sure this had to be Jason's vehicle. She noticed the uncomfortable look in his eye as she motioned to her old, but paid for car. "Thank you for walking me to my car, Jason. Have a nice evening—I'll see you tomorrow."

"Yes, thank you. You have a good evening as well. Goodnight Molly."

"Goodnight."

Walking back to his car he wondered if Molly realized that he drove the red Ferrari that they walked past. *What in the world is she driving anyway? I can just imagine where she must live. No wonder she didn't want to tell me her address.* Realizing this, Jason no longer was compelled to break the rules to try and talk her into going out with him; it would be a difficult task, but he had to try. *It's obvious she really needs this job.*

The remainder of the week went well, except for Thursday, which was a totally different story: Thursday afternoon Molly received a very disturbing phone call from Mr. Kingsley, demanding she set up a lunch date with Mr. Edwards the following week. Molly told him she would not schedule any such lunch without the approval of Mr. Edwards. Mr. Kingsley said his niece was in town and wanted to meet Douglas. She was not about to tell him that Mr. Edwards had another appointment the same morning. Not acquiescing to his demand, this did not sit well with Mr. Kingsley.

Jason always seemed to be at Molly's desk by eight every morning, and each night he offered to walk her to her car after work. Of course, his brother had been calling asking if Molly was in the office during her expected hours. Jason thought his brother was irrational to keep such strict tabs on her—she had been a dedicated employee all week. Eleanor called twice for information regarding a couple of investors for two major building projects. To Eleanor's surprise, Molly found the information in record time which left her totally impressed. Eleanor was quick to relay this information to Mr. Edwards, hoping he would realize he had a very responsible and intelligent employee... in spite of her youth. Well, in spite of being under forty. *Sometimes it's just impossible to figure out that man.* Douglas seemed indifferent to everything Eleanor was telling him, and it was making her furious. *We'll see how he feels once we are back in the office. I can't wait until my daughter needs me and he's alone with that sweet young girl.* Eleanor was beginning to think Molly would be a very good match for Douglas Edwards. Getting Douglas to realize this was not going to be easy; and before they left the airport for their return flight, Eleanor was determined to see the two together… no matter what his rules may be.

Chapter 9

FRIDAY MORNING CAME and Molly was in the office earlier than usual. She had no idea when Mr. Edwards would be returning to the office. As she did every morning, Molly made the coffee and began opening the drapes when, to her surprise, she heard a groan and a few choice words come from the couch. Almost jumping out of her skin at the shock of someone sleeping on the couch, Molly rushed over thinking it was probably Jason. "Jason, what are you doing sleeping on the couch this hour?" However, to Molly's chagrin it was not Jason. It was Douglas Edwards. "O my goodness…what are you doing here?"

"This happens to be my office—and this happens to be my couch! Now why are you here so… unbelievably early?!" His tone certainly did not sit well with Molly, or the language he chose to use.

"Excuse me, but I happen to work here, and I came in early since I had no idea when you would be returning to the office today. And kindly watch your language when addressing me. You needn't be so snappy." Molly tried being as calm as possible, however, once the words left her mouth there was no taking them back. *He'll probably fire me on the spot.*

When Molly took careful notice of him lying on the couch, all he was wearing was a white T-shirt. At least he had a throw covering him from his waist down. Glancing at the nearest chair she eyed his black suit pants, white shirt, tie, and black suit jacket. His socks and shoes were neatly on the floor in front of the overstuffed leather chair. Realizing what he was wearing, or not wearing, Molly gasped, but her feet seemed glued to the floor. She could not move for anything. Douglas stared up at her, and her amazing blue eyes were staring right back at him. The only words Molly could get out were, "Would you care for a cup of coffee?"

"What?! A cup of coffee?! I would prefer putting some clothes on first if you don't mind."

"Not at all. I'll leave you to do that sir, and you can call when you would like your coffee. Umm, do you want the drapes opened or closed?"

"Please just leave them as they are. I'll take care of that later."

"What about the light? Would you like me to turn it off or leave it on?"

"Would you mind just leaving?"

As Molly turned and walked out of the office, Douglas could not help but notice how cute she looked wearing a pair of designer jeans and an aqua silk blouse…the four-inch heels didn't look too bad either. *She's my new assistant and our relationship is strictly employer/employee. I… am…a confirmed bachelor.*

With shaky legs and trembling hands, Molly closed the door behind her and quickly went to her own desk. She sat there for a few minutes trying to gain her composure. It wasn't long before her phone rang and it was Eleanor calling. "Hi Molly, this is Eleanor. How is everything going? I wanted to tell you how much I appreciated how well you knew each of our clients I called about while in London." She jokingly asked if she had been memorizing all their accounts and to her surprise Molly told her that's exactly what she had been doing all week. Eleanor continued to tell her that because they arrived so late the night before, she would not be coming into the office.

Whispering into the phone as if Mr. Edwards could even hear her, Molly said, "Eleanor, did you know that Mr. Edwards came to the office and was sleeping on the couch when I arrived this morning? And I might add…in his underwear?"

Eleanor began to laugh which did not help Molly's disposition one bit. "Eleanor it's not funny. I walked in, made the coffee, and started to open the blinds when I woke him up. He was like a bear being awakened from his winter sleep. How can one man be so infuriating?"

"Oh Molly, I'm sorry for laughing, but I can just imagine Mr. Edwards's reaction to seeing you standing over him. I know he wanted to stop at the office and get some work done. I'm sure he was just too tired to head home. He often does that."

"Well, I was mortified. I first thought it was Jason since he has been in the office by eight and then back at five to walk me to my car."

"Molly, please do not tell me anymore. You know the rules."

"Jason only walked me to my car. He was every bit the gentleman."

"Well I'm pleased to hear that. Jason can be quite the ladies' man, and to be honest, he is the main reason Douglas has set such strict company rules."

"Believe me when I tell you, he was nothing but kind. Although I have to admit, his presence at first was a little unnerving. He always seemed to have a good reason for being in the office each morning, wanting this file or that file."

"I'm glad to hear that. Please let Douglas know that I will be late. I was not going to come in at all but now I think I will. You may need someone to run a little interference today. In fact, he probably figured it out that I won't be in. Don't tell him anything."

"Okay, if he doesn't ask, I won't tell." They both chuckled at that. "And Eleanor, I'm glad you will be coming in. I think I woke a sleeping grizzly, and I certainly do not want to "poke the bear" any more than necessary."

Eleanor could not help but chuckle and getting a rise out of Douglas like that had to be priceless. *It certainly sounds like Molly can hold her own when it comes to handling Douglas. Now if he can handle Molly, that's an entirely different story.*

Eleanor came in about eleven-thirty and neither of the women heard one peep out of Mr. Edwards. Since Eleanor came in so late, she said she was not going to have lunch, so Molly left for an early lunch. When she returned at twelve-thirty, Eleanor said she had not heard anything from Mr. Edwards. She said it was good to let him stew for a while. She was not about to tell him she had come in. It was obvious that he was keeping his distance from Molly after the morning he had.

Everything changed at one o'clock when Mr. Edwards bellowed, "Miss Beaumont! In—My—Office—NOW!!"

His thundering voice shook Molly to her core. She tried desperately to maintain her composure as she rose to go into his office. Eleanor put her hand on her arm and said she would come in shortly. "I'll try and play defense for you, hon. He may only be thirty-two but I swear he's not too young to have a heart attack."

"Thanks Eleanor, I can't imagine what I did this time." *He's only thirty-two?*

Upon entering Mr. Edwards's office, she could not help but notice how red-faced he was. She thought he was going to have a full-blown heart attack. *Eleanor was right.* "Yes Mr. Edwards, how may I help you?"

"Help me? You have got to be kidding. You think it's helping me when you tell my biggest investor, Mr. Kingsley, that I can't have lunch with him next Tuesday?"

"I'm sorry, sir, but you can't. You have a lunch appointment at eleven with the Kline brothers. When I entered the appointment in your calendar, you said that could not be changed for any reason. And besides, Mr. Kingsley only wanted you to meet his niece. He said she was in for a couple of days and wanted to meet you; said Tuesday was her only day available."

"Do you not realize that Kingsley is our biggest investor for the Hamilton project?"

"Yes, I'm very much aware of that. In fact, he made sure I was aware of it. He was extremely rude telling me I had no business telling him off, and that he would make sure I did not have a job by the end of this week."

"What exactly did you say to him, hmm?" Molly's head hung down and she began chewing on her bottom lip. "Well, tell me!" he bellowed.

"I told him he was a bully, and if he did not want to invest in the Hamilton project there were Mr. Lewis and Mr. Stevenson who would be happy to invest in the project. I told him that they could definitely make up for his part of the investment and then some."

"And how in the world do you even know this?"

"I know their portfolios and I also spoke with them earlier last week and they seemed very anxious to be a part of the Hamilton project. They know a good investment when they see one…sir. It is obvious that Mr.

Kingsley bullies his way around you and Jason all the time. I'm sorry but I was not about to let him belittle me and have me bow down to him."

"Did you tell him I had a lunch appointment?"

"No, I did not."

"And why not?"

"I was so upset with the way he talked to me, and then to threaten my job like he did; I was not about to give him the satisfaction that there was a good reason for you not to meet with him."

"Molly, I mean Miss Beaumont, you may have lost us our biggest investor."

"I'm truly sorry, sir. If you must let me go, I understand."

Hearing everything, Eleanor stepped in from behind the door. "Douglas, I have to applaud Molly for what she said to that old goat. He has given me and I might add, you and Jason, nothing but headaches. He needed someone to put him in his place. The nerve of him to think he could call and demand lunch with you and all because he wanted you to meet his niece. Who, by the sound of it; could only squeeze you in on Tuesday. She must be another gold-digger. Come on Douglas, stop letting him control you, or bully you as Molly said. You have to speak up to him, unless you want Molly to do it," she said this with a giggle and twinkle in her eye. "It's obvious she has no problem speaking up to him."

"No, I'll call him back. And thanks for letting me know you came in, Eleanor. Miss Beaumont, stay right here." Douglas pointed to a chair he wanted her to sit in.

Molly sat stiff in the chair with her hands folded on her lap, wondering exactly what her fate would be. Mr. Edwards stared at her and he was immediately drawn into those mesmerizing eyes of hers. *I refuse to fire her simply because our biggest investor tells me to. Some choice for me to make: lose Mr. Kingsley or lose Molly Beaumont.*

Molly watched as Douglas Edwards picked up his cell phone and began calling Mr. Kingsley. *No wonder Mr. Kingsley's call did not come into the office line—he called Mr. Edwards directly on his cell phone. That snake.*

"Jonathan, Douglas here. Yes, I did speak to Miss Beaumont. No

Jonathan, I have no intentions of firing her." There was a long pause and Molly could just imagine what Mr. Kingsley was telling him. "Jonathan, you may choose to take your finances and go elsewhere. I'm sure there are many institutions that would be pleased to have your business. Yes, she told me Stevenson and Lewis would be interested in investing in the Hamilton project. Well, she did her homework and had already spoken to them. We would definitely welcome them as investors in this project. I would be willing to continue having you as one of our investors however, not without an apology to Miss Beaumont. You heard me, an apology to Miss Beaumont. I will not allow anyone to threaten her in any way. She is my assistant." Suddenly Douglas's eyes brightened and a chuckle evaporated from deep within. "Yes Jonathan, she is quite the spitfire, and you better not get in her way. Good talking to you too, Jonathan—don't forget to call her or we're through."

Molly sat with bated breath and could not believe the way Mr. Edwards stood up to Mr. Kingsley on her behalf. "Thank you, Mr. Edwards. I'm sorry I put you in this position."

"You may go now, Miss Beaumont."

Molly certainly sensed the abruptness in Mr. Edwards's voice, but dismissed it as she returned to her office.

Eleanor had a questioning look as Molly returned to her desk. "I certainly hope you will not be cleaning out your desk any time soon, Molly. If he fired you, I will march right in there and give him a piece of my mind."

Molly had a stunned expression as she sat down at her desk and began telling Eleanor about Mr. Edwards's phone conversation with Mr. Kingsley. "Eleanor, I was sure he was going to fire me, but instead he defended me to Mr. Kingsley. I don't know what Mr. Kingsley told him but before he hung up he told Mr. Kingsley that before he could continue as one of his investors, he expected him to give me an apology. Do you believe it? He actually defended me and told him he would not be firing me."

Eleanor grabbed both of Molly's hands, and told her how happy she was that she would not be going anywhere. It wasn't long before the phone rang and it was Mr. Kingsley on line 2. Molly accepted the call and was surprised at how timid Mr. Kingsley sounded. She accepted his apology, and told him she hoped he continued investing in Edwards and Sons. Eleanor gave her a hug and knew without a doubt that Molly would be with Edwards and Sons for quite some time.

Molly left exhilarated as she walked to the elevator that evening. She had her job and for that she was grateful. Other than specific files and the usual cleanup Molly had at the close of the day, Mr. Edwards ignored her much of the time, and it made for an awkward afternoon. She would have loved to know what was going through his mind. He cordially said good night to her, but mentioned nothing regarding the event of the day. Perhaps for Mr. Edwards it was not a big deal, however to Molly it was huge.

Molly was elated over the outcome of the day as she walked into her apartment, even though there was a continuous dark cloud hovering over her the past two weeks. A day didn't go by that she had not felt consumed with the thought of having to fly one day. Falling onto the couch, Molly clung to one of the pillows and began to sob. Whether it was from the stress of the day, or the dread of flying, she did not know. The very thought of having to fly brought back a flood of memories. How long she sat there she did not know, but when she heard a rap on her door she wondered who it could be. How in the world could she answer looking such a mess? She brushed the tears away as best she could. Someone knocked again and she thought she better answer. Upon opening the door there stood Mrs. Brackenburg, her landlady.

"Oh, my dear, you look terrible. What's the problem? Did you lose your job today? Are you ill? Were you in an accident?" the questions kept coming without Molly able to get a word in. Mrs. Brackenburg never even took a breath as she led Molly to the couch. "Come sit down, dear. How about a glass of water?" Without a response from Molly,

Mrs. Brackenburg was off in a flash for a glass of water, as she headed to the kitchen. Watching all of this certainly took Molly's self-pity off of herself.

She was such a dear soul that Molly felt comfortable confiding in her. *She will probably think I'm overreacting or crazy, but maybe it will do me good to confide in her.*

When Mrs. Brackenburg returned with the water, Molly had pulled herself together enough to explain her shaken state. She told her of the horrific plane crash she experienced as a thirteen-year-old. Mrs. Brackenburg sat with her two hands over her mouth—her compassionate eyes told Molly all she needed to know. Her precious landlady seemed to relate to her pain.

"Oh, how terrible for you." Mrs. Brackenburg pulled Molly into a warm embrace.

"I don't know if I will ever get over it, and now I'm expected to fly… overseas. I can't lose this job, I just can't." Once again, the tears began to flow freely.

Mrs. Brackenburg looked at Molly and asked if she could tell her something.

"Of course, you can tell me anything, Mrs. Brackenburg." Molly apologized for being such a ninny as she wiped the tears and blew her nose one last time.

As Mrs. Brackenburg continued to hold Molly's hands in hers, she began to tell her of her first husband, the love of her life, and her precious little boy, Timothy. "My husband Frank and I had been married five wonderful years. Our son, Timothy, was three. Timothy was strapped into his car seat in the back seat of our car. We were coming home from my parents' home where we celebrated Timothy's third birthday." Mrs. Brackenburg's eyes began to glisten with unshed tears. "The roads were extremely icy and dangerous, and although Frank was a very good driver, it didn't matter; suddenly we hit a very icy patch of road. We started to spin out of control, and I'm sure Frank would have managed to straighten the car, except for a semi coming from the other direction. As we were spinning out of control, the truck hit the driver's side with such force causing us to tumble several times, landing us in the ditch. When everything settled, the stillness was deafening.

Frank had landed on top of me and we were trapped. I cried for my baby, and as I tried looking for him in the rear seat, I couldn't see him or his car seat at all. I held Frank closely to my chest but couldn't even feel his breath on me. Molly, they were both gone. Timothy's car seat was behind Frank's on the driver's side. When the semi hit, our baby was crushed and then thrown from the car as we tumbled over and over. I didn't want to live. Molly, they were my life."

"I am so sorry. What did you do? How did you go on?"

"For one thing, I never wanted to get in another car again, but I did. I was alive and spared for a reason. I had no idea what the purpose was, but I had to force myself to go on. Molly, I had to continue living. You're alive and your parents are alive, along with many other passengers, and you must be grateful for that. You must realize it's for a reason. After meeting your mother, you and she seem to be very godly people."

"Oh my, yes; I love God with all my heart. My parents told me about Jesus from the time I was a little girl. But it's like I can't let go of the fear I have. It has such a consuming hold on me. When I think of flying, I have all I can do not to have a panic attack in front of others. I feel like an octopus with all its tentacles is squeezing my chest. When I'm alone it's a different story—I fall apart. What is wrong with me that I can't get over this? I have had the same horrible nightmare over and over again. I wake up trembling and in a cold sweat."

"I think you're choosing not to get over it. You have to start living each day with a purpose. It isn't about you and your fears. It's about living, not about death. Perhaps if you found something you could do other than working and existing each day. Maybe volunteering someplace would help."

"I never thought about that. I know your husband died recently, and I know it wasn't Frank."

"Five years after the accident I met a wonderful man, Samuel Brackenburg. We were married and he gave me two beautiful children, a boy and a girl. They in turn have blessed me with five grandchildren. You see, in the beginning I felt much like Naomi in the Bible: bitter, alone, and forgotten. Then I met Sam, and he loved me so much. I never thought I could love again after Frank, but I was wrong. Samuel stole my heart, but God restored my heart, and if it wasn't for my Samuel,

I would never have known what it meant to be forgiven and to have a personal relationship with God through his son, Jesus. You see, Molly, God does make beautiful things out of our lives if we let him."

"Wow, Mrs. Brackenburg that's a beautiful story."

"Molly, it's more than a story. It may be my story, but it's really God's story and I happen to be in it, and he isn't finished writing it. You have a story, and I know God isn't finished writing your story either. In fact, he's just beginning." Mrs. Brackenburg asked Molly if she could pray for her. Molly nodded and bowed her head. To her amazement, she felt an unexplainable peace flood her soul. If only she were over this fear she had—only time would tell. Giving Mrs. Brackenburg a hug, she thanked her for sharing her story with her, and for praying for her.

That night Molly had the best sleep she had had in a very long time…no nightmares, no waking up drenched from sweat. She felt marvelous.

Chapter 10

MOLLY WALKED INTO her office that Monday morning feeling as if a weight had been lifted from her shoulders. Her heart was lighter...the heaviness gone. The day could not have been any better. Mr. Edwards was pleasant and even smiled at her a few times. It may have been her imagination, but she didn't think so. Molly was even looking forward to Saturday when she and her mom would go to the post office so she could pick up a passport application. She would not put it off another weekend. The real test would come when she was expected to board an airplane.

Molly had worked later than usual and her day was finally over. She cleaned off her desk, and put the files away. She had the coffee pot to clean and mugs to wash out, as Eleanor had already left for the day. Mr. Edwards was still at his desk when Molly asked if there was anything else he needed. He said goodnight to her without even looking up, this was par for the course. *How could one man be so infuriatingly handsome?* As per her routine, Molly stopped in the ladies' room and then took the elevator down to the garage. Sliding into the driver's seat of her old, but paid for car, she put her key into the ignition; completely stunned when it did not start. *Oh no, not now. I've had such a great day I can't believe my car won't even turn over.* She tried and tried but nothing. What were her options? She didn't have any—other than the bus. Taking the keys out of the ignition, she reached for her purse. When she turned to open the door, there stood Jason.

"Molly, it sounds like your battery's dead. We'll have to get a tow truck over here with a new battery tomorrow."

"Tomorrow? Well I guess that will have to do. I was going to head over to the bus stop."

"You're not going to take a bus. Not this time of the evening. I'll give you a ride home."

"Jason, I can't let you take me home. You know the rules."

"Hang the rules. Your car won't start and you need a ride. I'll call for a tow truck in the morning."

Jason took Molly's hand and helped her out of her car. He helped her into his red Ferrari. As they pulled out of the parking space and headed for the exit, neither of them noticed Douglas exiting the elevator. However, Douglas noticed them.

His blood boiled and his thoughts were racing as he saw Molly sitting next to his brother in his Ferrari. Punching his fist into his hand, he told himself his new assistant would have to go. He would not allow for the rules to be broken. *I'm sure they never expected me to witness the two of them together. I wonder how many times they went out when I was gone last week.* Come morning he would have Eleanor call the agency and let Molly, rather Miss Beaumont go. Eleanor would be leaving soon and this had to be done quickly. He shouldn't be surprised by this as he had known all along that it wouldn't take long before she was being wooed by one of his men. He thought Jason would have had more brains than that. What a shame she had to blow it. He really liked her, and he was more than impressed with her performance.

Douglas waited until later that night before calling his brother. He tried eating but only pushed his food around on his plate. He couldn't understand why this was so difficult to do. He usually had no problem taking action when the rules were broken, and that meant any rule. He had to be firm or the entire office would think he was getting soft. He picked up his phone and dialed his brother. He wasn't answering. *Well I'm not hanging up until he answers.* On the fifth ring Jason answered.

"Hey, what's up bro?" Jason had looked at his phone knowing it was his brother.

"What's up? What's up? You just blew it man, and tomorrow morning Miss Beaumont will be gone!"

"What are you talking about?"

"You heard me. Tomorrow morning… she's gone! I saw the two of you take off in your car, and I don't want to hear any excuses. Got it? Not one excuse! I'm sure you had a great time with me gone last week! It definitely was not a problem keeping an eye on her, was it?" With that Douglas slammed his phone down.

Immediately Jason called his brother back. "Doug it's not what you think, I was—"

"Forget it Jason, don't even try." He hung up once again on his brother.

Jason felt bad; somehow, he had to fix this, but how. When his brother made up his mind, there was no changing it. *How could I have messed things up so bad? Poor Molly, I know she needs this job.*

Molly took the bus to work early Tuesday morning. Jason offered to pick her up in the morning, but she declined knowing that taking the bus in the morning was not as perilous as taking the bus at night. When she entered her office, she was taken aback by the presence of Mr. Edwards. He was in earlier than expected. "Good morning, Mr. Edwards."

Molly never heard a response other than his deep baritone voice asking her to step into his office. She acquiesced to his request. As she went for her notepad on her desk, he told her it wouldn't be necessary for her to bring it in. She complied and followed him into his office.

"Have a seat, Miss Beaumont." Mr. Edwards went to the "King's chair" and Molly sat in the chair across from him. The tension was obvious, and Molly sat there in utter confusion, and out of habit began biting her lower lip. *What is going on? I can't imagine what I have done now.* "Miss Beaumont, you may not be aware of this but when I exited the elevator last night, I saw you driving away with my brother. You know the rule. There is to be no dating with any employee."

"Oh Mr. Edwards I can explain—"

"No explanation is necessary. I don't want excuses. It's obvious you and my brother got along just fine when I was gone last week. You are here in my office so I can personally terminate you. Your services will no longer be necessary."

Molly sat with her mouth agape and felt her eyes sting as the tears started to escape. "Sir, I need this job." She was not about to let him see her cry.

"You should have thought of that before you got in the car with Jason."

"But Mr. Edwards…I—"

Douglas's hand went up keeping her from any further explanation; she was dismissed. "That will be all Miss Beaumont. Your final check will be mailed to your home address."

Molly walked out his door in total shock and disbelief. She just lost her job. And all she did was allow Jason to give her a ride home after her car wouldn't start.

Molly walked to her desk. Eleanor wasn't in yet; she was sure Mr. Edwards would tell her she was terminated. Shock and bewilderment flooded her thinking. *No, I can't even think right now. I feel like I have just been run over by a bus. I still have to get my car fixed but when can I do that? I have to get out of here before I completely break down.* Feeling nauseous and confused, Molly grabbed her purse and immediately left the office. She was running down the hall when she flew past Eleanor. Eleanor tried stopping her to find out where she was going, but to no avail. When she turned around, Molly was already in the elevator. Eleanor could not imagine what had happened and hoped she did not receive bad news regarding her father. Upon entering her office, Mr. Edwards was sitting at her desk. "Douglas, do you know what happened to Molly? She just flew past me in the hall; it's obvious she was in tears. Did something happen to her father?"

"Her father, no. I had to terminate her Eleanor, and I would appreciate you getting a hold of the temp agency as soon as possible. And be sure you ask for someone in her forties this time—even fifties— or sixties. I don't care if she's eighty."

"What did she do? I can't imagine you having to terminate her over anything."

"Eleanor, she broke the rules. I saw her and Jason pull out of the parking garage in my brother's Ferrari last night. You know the rule. I'm

55

sure it's not the only time the two have been together. We were gone all last week. I knew this was going to happen."

Jason happened to be standing in the doorway listening to his brother tell Eleanor that he terminated Molly...and it was because of him. He couldn't take any more and walked to where they were standing. "Doug, listen to me."

Doug's hand went up to stop his brother from saying any more. "I told you I want no excuses. It's over and done with." Mr. Edwards stormed out of the assistant's office and into his own.

Eleanor stood in shock the entire time Mr. Edwards was ranting. "That man—what in the world has gotten into him, Jason?"

"Eleanor, will you at least listen to me?"

"I would certainly like someone to tell me what's going on. Molly flew past me in the hall, obviously in tears. I thought something may have happened to her father."

"What's wrong with her father?"

"He's in a nursing home in Connecticut and Molly has been helping her mom out with the bills. She is an amazing woman, and it's obvious she is extremely close to her parents."

Jason stood running his fingers through his hair. "I guess I messed up, and my own brother won't even hear me out."

"Tell me what happened, Jason. Even if your brother won't listen, I surely will."

Jason began to tell Eleanor how Molly's car would not start the night before, and how he offered to take her home so she wouldn't have to take the bus. "I swear all I did was to take her home. I offered to pick her up this morning but she wouldn't hear of it. She said that riding the bus in the morning wasn't as bad as at night. Her car is still in the garage. I told her I would call a tow truck this morning."

"Why didn't you tell Douglas all of this?"

"Tell him? It was impossible to get two words out last night. Yeah, he called me late last night and told me what he saw and that he would have to terminate her. He said, 'the rules are the rules'. We certainly can't have anyone break a rule, no matter how innocent. The trouble is; he now thinks we spent time together last week. That is so beyond the pale. Last week I walked her to her car after work and that was it."

Eleanor got up from her desk, straightened her shoulders, and headed for Mr. Edwards's door. "What are you doing, Eleanor? You know what he's like when he's angry. He refuses to listen to anyone. I don't want to see you out of a job as well." Jason said this a little tongue in cheek. They both knew Douglas wouldn't dare let Eleanor go.

Eleanor did not bother to knock, but entered the office ready for a fight, now that she was aware of the circumstance that brought Molly to tears. Upon entering, she noticed the drapes were not opened, coffee not made, and Douglas sat with his head in his hands. He looked up at Eleanor. "What are you doing in here, and don't try to convince me that I was wrong in letting Mol... Miss Beaumont go."

"Mr. Edwards, you can be such an unreasonable...pig-headed... man. Did you even give your brother, or Molly, for that matter, a chance to explain why she drove out of here with Jason? Wait, I can answer for you. No, you did not, because you are too stubborn, and no one dares to break one of your precious rules." Douglas tried interrupting but she pressed on. "Your brother was only being a gentleman offering her a ride home because her car would not start." Eleanor made sure to emphasize the last part of her sentence. The sheepish look on his face was priceless and Eleanor knew she was getting to him. "Jason offered to pick her up this morning but she declined his offer and took the bus instead. And for you to draw your own conclusions that they were together last week is totally absurd. You should be ashamed of yourself. Now I said my piece, and if you don't believe me, you may go down to the garage and see for yourself that her car is still sitting there. She is the best person for this job and you better get on your knees and beg her to come back." Eleanor turned and stormed out of his office knowing he could be stubborn enough to leave things as they were. Mr. Edwards never begged anyone.

Douglas Edwards sat stunned gazing at the door Eleanor stormed out of. He had his rules, and the most important one was broken. Okay, he had to admit it may be a dumb rule but he knew his brother, and wasn't it Jason that drove her home? He thought of Friday and hearing how she stood up to Kingsley; he had to admire her for that. He was keeping his distance from her, and he also knew the reason. She was beautiful and tempting, and things had to be kept strictly professional; *but did I have to fire her?* He called his brother asking him to come down to his office. *I better start with Jason and hear what he has to say.*

Jason walked into his office with anger in his eyes. "You really did it this time, brother."

"Just tell me what happened, okay?"

Jason proceeded to tell him about her car not starting when he went down to the garage after work. "She was getting out of her car to walk over to the bus stop. Doug, it was getting dark and I couldn't let her take a bus home. I dropped her off at her house and made sure she got in safely, and then I left. I offered to pick her up this morning but she refused. I told her last night that I would get a tow truck over in the morning and have a new battery installed. If that's what it needs."

"Did you call a tow?"

"No, not yet, but I will. And accusing us of being together last week was way out of line, Doug. How do you plan on fixing this?"

"Why do I have to fix anything? She broke a rule."

"I cannot believe what you're saying. She did not want to go with me for that very reason and I certainly did not want to see her take a bus at night. No, Doug, you have to fix this. I'm going down to wait for the tow truck." Jason walked out of Doug's office shaking his head at his brother's logic.

Jason called for a tow truck and then went down to the garage to wait. Surprisingly, his brother joined him before the truck pulled up. "That's some car she's driving. What year is it anyway?"

"I bet it's at least nine or ten years old. Molly keeps saying it's paid for; I think she takes pride in that."

"Have you talked to her since she left?"

Jason raised his eyebrows with that question. "Why would I have talked to her? I don't even know her phone number. You know, Doug, Eleanor told me how badly she needs this job, and not for herself. Eleanor said Molly's dad is in a nursing home, and she helps her mom with expenses. This job was very important to her."

Doug ran his fingers through his hair. "Yeah, Eleanor told me. Why don't we buy her a new car? That could be her severance pay."

"I can't believe you just said that. You're going to buy her off with a new car? You're a real... I can tell you right now she won't accept it. Doug, she needs her job more than she needs a new car."

The tow truck pulled up and the attendant asked for a key to start the car. Jason reached in his pocket and gave the driver her car key. Doug skeptically looked at his brother. "What? I had her give me her key last night. They need the key to start her car today, Doug."

The attendant slid into the driver's side of her car and turned the ignition, nothing. "You're right; it sounds like the battery is dead." The attendant popped the hood and put in a new battery. He asked Jason to try it—the car came to life immediately. Jason paid for the service, and the new battery; pleased that her car was running once again.

"Now what do we do?" asked Doug.

"Well, I think I can find her house again; I guess I could drive it over there. Then I suppose I'll take the bus back."

"No wait. I'll follow you and give you a ride."

"I think you should do more than give me a ride back. I think you know what I'm talking about, Doug."

"You're expecting me to talk to her? I suppose you want me to beg her to come back?" Doug said this sarcastically and really had no plan on talking to Molly. He made his decision and needed to abide by it.

"You got it, bro. I think that's the honorable thing to do. Your way is the coward's way." Jason knew his brother was tough and could be an unreasonable employer, but he hoped that in his heart of hearts, he would do the right thing.

Jason slid into the driver's seat and put Molly's car in reverse. "Are you going to follow me or not?"

"Yeah, I'll follow you. I have no idea where she lives, so take it easy."

"Do you think you're going to have trouble keeping up with me when I'm driving this, and you're driving a Porsche?"

"No, I guess not."

Jason waited as Doug pulled out of his parking spot to follow him.

Being in such a good mood, Molly never noticed the chill in the air when she walked to the bus stop in the morning however, now when she got off the bus, she unconsciously wrapped her sweater around her. After her talk with Mrs. Brackenburg Friday night, she felt as though a weight had been lifted from her shoulders. She was even looking forward to going to the post office with her mom this weekend to pick up the passport application. *Well, I guess now I won't have to worry about a passport. How am I going to tell my mom that I can't help her until I find another job?* The tears started to flow once again as she walked the three blocks to her apartment.

Mrs. Brackenburg was out in front sweeping her sidewalk when Molly walked up. Surprised to see Molly walking up the sidewalk, she couldn't help but notice the tears flooding her eyes. "What is it, love? Why are you home so early? Did you forget something? Why the tears? Oh, I'm sorry, I'm rambling again. Why don't you come inside to my apartment and you can tell me why the tears?" Mrs. Brackenburg was hoping Molly did not get word that something had happened to her dad. *Poor dear, she has already experienced so much in her young life. Losing her father would be so difficult for her.*

Molly sat with Mrs. Brackenburg and the words flowed freely, leading up to her termination by Mr. Edwards. "Oh, my dear, you mean he never even let you explain?"

Molly shook her head and whispered. "No, he never gave me a chance. Mrs. Brackenburg, I need to go to my apartment. I have to call my mom and give her the news. I was sure I had the perfect job…apart from the boss I had."

Mrs. Brackenburg told Molly not to worry about her rent. She believed she would soon have another job. Molly gave Mrs. Brackenburg a hug and thanked her as she left the apartment. She was grateful for such a dear landlady.

Molly sat in her apartment trying to summon the courage to call her mom and give her the news. How could everything have gone so wrong in such a short time? If only she could have worked there for a year or two before this happened, then she would have a decent amount of money saved up to help her mom. Surely her mom would understand... accepting defeat was the hard part.

Just as Molly reached for her purse to retrieve her cell phone, there was a knock on her door. Expecting to see Mrs. Brackenburg, to her surprise there stood Jason holding out her car key. "They put a new battery in your car, Molly. It should be good to go." Jason's grin was overshadowed by the obvious: Molly's red eyes and blotchy face from crying. "Molly, I'm so sorry. I'm sorry my brother is such a...an unreasonable person."

"It's not your fault, Jason. I just can't believe he never even gave me a chance to explain."

"Molly, would you mind if I called you sometime? Maybe we can do coffee, or go out for dinner." No sooner had Jason asked, there was a deep cough and a harrumph behind him. To his astonishment, there stood his brother. Doug had made it clear that he had no intention of giving Molly back her job. Jason turned and glared at his brother.

Molly looked past Jason to Mr. Edwards. "Mr. Edwards, why are you here?"

Looking sheepish and totally embarrassed, Mr. Edwards nervously answered Molly. "Umm, Miss Beaumont, I'm here to ask you to come back to Edwards and Sons."

Molly knew she could have a good time with this. "And why should I come back? You were not very kind in terminating me without even so much as an explanation."

Doug had to give her a lot of credit for her spunk and sassiness. *I can't believe how she stands up to me.* He cleared his throat to answer. However, before he did, Molly opened the door wider and invited the two men in. "May I offer you something to drink? I have soda, coffee, water—"

"No thank you, Miss Beaumont," said Doug. His tone noticeably clipped.

"Thank you, Molly. I think I would like a soda. What do you have?" Molly couldn't help but notice the glare Jason received from his brother.

"I have Dr. Pepper, Diet Coke—"

"Thanks, I'll have a Dr. Pepper."

Molly excused herself to fetch a Dr. Pepper for Jason. The brothers exchanged looks as they took in Molly's humble apartment. It was very neat and clean; the furniture sparse but decent. A few pictures sat on a couple of side tables. Douglas tried to get a better look at the pictures, but just then Molly returned with Jason's soda. Molly asked if they would like to have a seat, they both declined. Jason gave his brother a slight poke in the ribs prompting Doug to once again answer Molly's question as to why he would want her to come back to Edwards and Sons. "Jason explained the circumstance that led to him giving you a ride home—"

"However, Mr. Edwards, you would not allow me to give you an explanation." Molly felt her legs go weak and hoped they didn't notice just how badly they were shaking.

"No Mol...Miss Beaumont I did not, and I apologize for not giving you the opportunity. I was wrong. If you come back—I would like to buy you a new car." Doug had no idea where that came from. He just blurted it out. Jason gaped at him in astonishment.

"Thank you for the offer, Mr. Edwards, but that won't be necessary. I'm perfectly happy with the car I have. I do appreciate the new battery however."

"Does this mean you're willing to return to Edwards and Sons?"

"Yes I am. However, I would ask that in the future, I am given a fair chance to explain should my performance or conduct be questioned."

Never had Douglas Edwards been talked to or negotiated with in such a manner. "Well then. I expect to see you in the office tomorrow."

"What he means, Molly. He looks forward to seeing you in the office tomorrow." Jason said this with a wink. Doug nodded to Molly as he moved Jason toward the door. Both men said their goodbyes as they left. Molly stood motionless at her door. She could not believe what just happened. *I guess I have a job after all.* Relief and excitement flooded her spirit. She was very close to jumping up and down she was so excited. Suddenly she stopped dead in her tracks: the pictures. *Oh my, the pictures.* Molly could not help but wonder if Mr. Edwards recognized her in any of them. He would certainly know she was the same clumsy woman that bumped into him a couple of months ago. *Well, I'm certainly not going to say anything. He had plenty of opportunity to say something if he did recognize me.*

There was another knock on her door and Molly was pleased it was Mrs. Brackenburg. Mrs. Brackenburg had a pretty good idea who the two men were since they stopped and asked her for Molly's apartment number. The two women shared a cup of tea and chuckled over the visit Molly had. "Molly, I began praying as soon as you left my apartment this morning. I was hoping the two men were here with some good news, although, the one gentleman struck me as somewhat intimidating. He appeared slightly hesitant in heading up to your apartment."

"That was my boss, Mr. Edwards. And yes, he can be very intimidating and infuriating I might add."

"He is certainly a very handsome man and quite distinguished looking."

"Yes, he is quite handsome. To be honest, I've been more nervous about keeping my job than looking at him." Molly wasn't being entirely truthful with Mrs. Brackenburg. She had noticed how handsome he was from the first day she bumped into him—literally bumped into him. Her nervousness, and his rudeness, certainly outweighed any thoughts of how good looking he was. *Oh no, she never really noticed his sandy blond hair, gorgeous dark blue eyes, perfectly square jaw and high cheek bones— to say nothing of the way he filled out his shirts. Ha, not much.* "I still can't believe he showed up at my apartment. He practically begged me to come back to work. He even offered to buy me a new car if I returned."

"He must really appreciate you or he would not have been here."

"No, I think it was probably his brother, Jason, who talked him into coming. He did need someone to drive him back. I'm sure he and Eleanor gave him a hard time over the whole situation. Mr. Edwards can be a very unreasonable man. I don't know if I'll ever find him anything but rude and arrogant. It is a great job and I don't want to lose it. I am finding out I need to stand up to him if I'm going to work there." It was incredulous of her to think anything more could possibly become of their employer/employee relationship. She dismissed the thought as quickly as it surfaced.

Molly had the rest of the day off and did not know what she could possibly do with herself. It was only Tuesday and she would not be heading home to her mom's until after work on Friday. She put on some sweats and a T-shirt, and went for a quick run. The neighborhood was a little unsavory, but it was daylight and she did not think it would be a problem. She did some stretches before taking off. It was a beautiful fall day, and the oak and maple leaves were beginning to turn with just a hint of red, gold and orange. In a few weeks, they would be breathtaking with their vibrant colors. There was definitely a chill in the air. It never did warm up from when she walked home from the bus stop that morning. Molly ran for about twenty minutes, and in that short amount of time her lungs felt like they would explode. She knew she was out of shape however, she didn't realize by how much, she thought she had better slow to a walk. As she approached her apartment, she noticed a man leaving. She guessed he would be in his late twenties. She was positive he didn't live in her building. As he walked past her he smiled and nodded to her. *Perhaps he was visiting Mrs. Brackenburg.* She entered her building and noticed that flyers had been placed next to the mailboxes. Molly took one and glanced at the information. It was an opportunity to volunteer at the Help You Stand Homeless Shelter. With Thanksgiving just around the corner, they were looking for volunteers to help prepare and serve the Thanksgiving meal they would be providing. Molly noticed the address, and from what she could tell, it wasn't too far from where she lived. Maybe this is what Mrs. Brackenburg meant when she told her she needed to find something to do for others, to volunteer somewhere. She needed to start living, giving of her time and herself. As she climbed the stairs to her apartment, Molly thought she would give the center a call that afternoon.

After her phone call to the center, Molly quickly showered and put on a pair of fitted jeans and a blue cashmere sweater—the sweater was a gift to herself with her first paycheck. A little extravagant, but Molly had always wanted to own a cashmere sweater. She would be plenty warm, even with the early chill of fall.

Molly walked into the Help You Stand Homeless Shelter and was greeted immediately by a rather matronly older woman. She had the kindest eyes and was definitely what you might call fluffy. The woman introduced herself as Mary; she asked Molly how she may help her. "I spoke with a Kevin Jackson on the phone earlier today and he invited me to come in for a personal chat. He said he would share the volunteer opportunities that you have."

"Follow me Miss —"

"I'm sorry, it's Miss Beaumont but please call me Molly."

"It's nice to meet you Molly. Mr. Jackson is in his office. In fact, he was passing out flyers all morning and has only been back a short time."

Molly wondered if this was the man she saw leaving her building. As she entered his office, he looked up to greet her. Yes, this was the same man. He was a very good-looking man. Molly extended her hand as he rose from his chair. "It's very nice to meet you, Mr. Jackson."

"Please call me Kevin."

"Kevin this is Molly Beaumont."

"Thank you, Mary."

Mary excused herself stating she needed to get back to the kitchen. Molly thanked her for the warm welcome. Kevin pulled a chair over to the front of his desk and offered Molly a seat. "Please, have a seat Miss Beaumont. How may I help you? You mentioned on the phone that you're interested in volunteering at the center for Thanksgiving."

"Yes. I would love to see how I may help out—whatever you need me to do."

"Is it just for Thanksgiving, or would you be willing to volunteer on a regular basis? We can use volunteers throughout the year. Tell me a little about yourself."

Molly began sharing her background with Kevin. "I was raised in a small farming town in Connecticut; I graduated from the University of Maryland and then attended the Robert H. Smith School of Business for my Master's. I have been employed by a temporary agency, but now have a fulltime job in New York City." Kevin was mesmerized as he stared into Molly's eyes. *Man, she's a beautiful woman. I can't believe I could have her working for me here at the center.* She continued talking but he never heard another word she said. All his ears heard were blah, blah, blah... "and I could spend every other weekend volunteering here."

Shaken from his reverie, he only picked up on Molly saying she could come in after six and perhaps every other weekend. "What did you say about coming in?"

"I said I could come in after six and every other weekend."

"And why is that?"

"Excuse me?"

"Why after six…and every other weekend?"

Molly realized he really had not heard a word she said. *He must have a lot on his mind if he can't even pay attention to the few things I had to say.* "I happen to have a full-time job as an executive assistant and would not be able to come in until my work-day is completed."

"Right. I understand perfectly." *Does she have any idea that I have been staring at her the entire time? I need to be a little more professional.*

Kevin hoped his embarrassment was not too evident as he felt the blush rise from his neck to his face. Changing the subject, he began telling her of their center. "We feed about fifty to seventy-five people on a regular basis. We house fifty, and that includes children. Presently we have about ten children, many have single moms; however, we do have a few couples. The single men spend the nights at another facility. The adults staying here have to help out with chores such as housekeeping, washing linens, and in the kitchen. We have some permanent employees, and believe it or not, they were once homeless themselves."

"Wow, it sounds like you have quite the operation here. How may I be of service to you?"

"To be honest, I really need some office help. How are you with keeping records and paying bills? This is my downfall. I know I procrastinate when it comes to keeping books."

"I would be more than happy to help out, and I certainly wouldn't mind volunteering in the kitchen or wherever you may need me, especially when Thanksgiving is here."

"Miss Beaumont, you are a godsend. I handed out the flyers this morning and wondered if it was going to be all for naught. You have made my day. I hate to sound too eager, but when can you start?"

"Please call me Molly. I told my mom that I would visit this weekend, but I can stop by Friday evening after work and you can show me what you need done. I planned on leaving after work on Friday, however I can come in and leave early Saturday morning for my mom's."

"Are you sure? I hate to interfere with your plans." *I know she said something about her mom and dad, but I sure can't remember—why does she go to Connecticut? Is it to see her parents? I hope it comes up again or I'm really going to feel like a complete idiot.*

"I'm sure. I'm new to New York and I really have no friends here. I pretty much spend the evenings alone anyway. It will be fun to meet some new people."

Kevin stood from his desk and was very close to giving her a hug when he said goodbye; instead he extended his arm for a handshake. "Welcome to Help You Stand, Molly."

"Thank you. I'll see you Friday at about six then. Is that too late for you?"

"Not at all. I'll be sure to be here. Once you are familiar with everything, you may come in whenever you have the time." *My managers in the other two centers are going to be so jealous when they see the beautiful woman I have working for me. I can't wait to introduce her to them.* Thinking of this, Kevin remembered they had a fundraiser coming up in a few weeks. Molly would have to attend along with a few of the other employees that always accompanied him. The fundraisers were always quite the gala event, and having Molly beside him would give him great pleasure.

Chapter 11

I T WAS WEDNESDAY morning and Molly arrived at work her usual time, perhaps a little earlier. No one was in the office and for this she was grateful. She wanted to get the coffee ready and her other duties completed before she had to face Mr. Edwards. Although, she wondered why the nervousness; she had done nothing wrong. Molly no sooner opened the blinds, had the two papers just so, and was anxious to walk out when Douglas Edwards arrived. "Good morning, Miss Beaumont."

Molly was taken aback by such pleasantness coming from her boss. This certainly helped settle the butterflies in her stomach. At least Mr. Edwards wasn't abrupt or rude…so far. "Good morning, Mr. Edwards. May I get you your coffee, sir?"

"Thank you. I'd appreciate that."

Molly immediately went to the back counter and prepared his coffee. No sooner did she have it on his desk than Jason entered the office. "Good morning, Molly. How are you this morning?"

"Good morning Ja…Mr. Edwards. I'm good thank you. May I get you a cup of coffee?"

"Thank you that would be great. I haven't had my coffee this morning and I sure could use a cup."

Molly returned to the counter and poured a cup for Jason. He was already seated at his brother's desk when Molly approached with his coffee. When Jason took the cup from Molly, he gave her a thank you and a wink. He couldn't help but feel the glare and raised eyebrows coming from his brother. He didn't intend to make her blush or feel uneasy but it was obvious he did.

Molly excused herself and left the office. *Boy, that felt uncomfortable and I have no idea why.* She returned to her desk and began going over documents that were new on her desk. It wasn't long before Eleanor walked in; she lit up when she saw Molly. Her excitement was evident. "Molly I am so happy to see you in today. I missed you. Jason filled me in on what transpired yesterday morning. I can't tell you how livid I was after Jason told me his reason for driving you home Tuesday night."

"I have you to thank for sticking up for me."

"From what I heard from Jason yesterday, you had no problem sticking up for yourself. I'm really proud of you. As far as I'm concerned you are the best thing that's happened to this office."

"You're very kind Eleanor. To be honest, I was shocked when Mr. Edwards showed up at my door. I should say, both the Edwards brothers."

"Believe me, there is nothing going on between Molly and me." Jason sat in front of his older brother and did not appreciate what he had implied. "I got to know her a little better the week you were gone. And since you were the one who asked me to keep an eye on her, I was at your desk every morning to see what time she would arrive for work, and then I walked her to her car each night. I'm guessing you're wondering how she knew I took my coffee black? Well, there you have it. She made me coffee each morning you were gone. Nothing else going on, believe me."

"Be sure and keep it that way. Don't think I didn't hear you ask if you could call her sometime."

"I only did that when I thought she would no longer be working here. I won't do anything that could jeopardize her employment. You saw for yourself how much she needs this job."

"Yeah, I did."

"I need to speak with Mr. Edwards, Molly. Has he come in yet?"

"Yes, he is, and Jason is with him."

"Good, I can hit two birds with one stone."

Molly wondered what she needed to talk to the Edwards brothers about, but felt it was none of her business to pry. If she wanted her to know, she would tell her. Eleanor knocked lightly on the executive's door and walked in. Molly hoped that one day she would have that much courage to simply walk right in. So far, she waited until Mr. Edwards called her to come in unless she had a very pressing matter and then she called him first. Twenty minutes later Eleanor returned and told Molly that Douglas wanted to talk to her. "Oh no, what did I do now?"

"You did nothing. I feel it's important that Mr. Edwards gives you the news."

Molly's knees began to shake as she walked into the office. Jason was still seated at the desk. There was another chair next to him and Mr. Edwards motioned for Molly to take a seat. "Miss Beaumont, Eleanor has just informed us that tomorrow will be her last day. Her daughter will be placed on complete bed rest next Monday. She told us it would not be a temporary leave as was understood at the onset. She will be retiring. She assured me that you are more than capable of doing everything she does in this office, and that you are quite the asset to Edwards and Sons. We bought out your contract with the temp agency and now you will officially be employed by Edwards and Sons. Starting next Monday, I would like to give you a pay increase of fifteen hundred dollars a month."

Molly sat speechless. Was she hearing correctly? She was already making way more than she ever imagined. The office went silent and you could hear a pin drop. Molly was certain they could hear her heart thumping. "Umm, thank you very much, sir. I certainly hope I meet your expectations."

"Have you applied for your passport? We'll be heading for London in a couple of weeks."

Jason could not help but notice how Molly sat wringing her hands, and unconsciously biting her lower lip, when his brother asked this.

"I planned on applying for one this weekend when I visit my parents. I'm going to the post office back home."

"That's fine. We will pay for the application, and be sure to have it expedited."

"Thank you but that won't be necessary. I can take care of that."

"Very well… and Molly?"

"Yes sir."

"Welcome once again to Edwards and Sons."

"Thank you, sir." *Once again—he never welcomed me the first time.* However, when she extended her hand, Mr. Edwards reached out, shook it, and gave her a wink. This was the first time she had ever taken his hand and she had to admit a pleasant shiver went up her arm and reached all the way to her toes. This man that intimidated her actually seemed kind and caring. *What a change in character.* She would definitely keep her guard up because someone such as Mr. Edwards could very easily become the rude and intimidating boss once again. Especially, if he ever realized she was the woman who, no doubt, ruined a perfectly good and very expensive suit.

When Molly reentered her office, Eleanor was seated and waited for her with bated breath. "How did it go, Molly?"

"He gave me a raise, Eleanor. I can't believe it. I really don't deserve it."

"Nonsense. Molly, don't ever say that. You're already doing a fantastic job and you know more than I ever did even after I worked here for a year. It won't be long and you'll be well over six figures."

"You're very kind, Eleanor. I am going to miss you terribly, but I know your daughter needs you. Will you keep in touch with me? I'd appreciate that."

"I will do more than keep in touch. I'll probably be a pest. With nothing much to do, I'll be stopping by so we can have lunch together sometime. I'm going to give you my cell phone number."

"I would like that, and I will give you mine as well, although, I most likely will be at my desk most of the day." The two women giggled. They would miss each other terribly.

Molly stepped into the executive office, but not without knocking. Mr. Edwards looked up from his desk with a questioning look. "Mr. Edwards, have you and Jason thought about a little farewell party for Eleanor tomorrow?"

Douglas was pleased with her suggestion and no way would he admit that that was the furthest thing from his mind. "Yes, I've been wondering how we could pull something like that off. Do you have any suggestions?"

"Why don't you let me take care of it, sir? Perhaps I could call a caterer this afternoon and we can have the party in the large conference room. We can have fancy finger sandwiches, a cake, and whatever they may suggest that would be appropriate with such a short notice."

"Take care of it then, Molly." He took out his company credit card and gave it to her. "I will have to get you your own company card."

This was the second time he called her Molly. Either he was forgetting his formalities with her, or because she was replacing Eleanor and this was common practice for him. She never dreamed that she would one day have a company credit card. Her head was spinning; all this was so unexpected.

Surprisingly everything fell into place for the caterers and the party planner. Molly was extremely pleased with herself. Confident she would have Mr. Edwards's permission, she stopped and purchased a Rolex watch for Eleanor. She had it engraved with her initials and years of service on the back cover of the watch. Of course, she used Mr. Edwards's credit card. When she returned to work Friday morning, after giving Mr. Edwards his coffee, she told him how well the farewell party for Eleanor was coming along. Last night she had sent out announcements via email to the company employees; the party planners would arrive at ten, the caterers at eleven; the luncheon would be served at twelve-thirty. "Sounds perfect, Molly. It sounds like you haven't missed a thing."

"Sir, I know you have been quite busy and Eleanor's retirement has taken you by surprise. I took the liberty of stopping by the jewelers and purchased a parting gift for her."

Mr. Edwards cleared his throat looking embarrassed. He would have to admit that was something he never gave consideration to. "I'm sorry. I have not given any thought to that."

"If you don't mind, sir, I stopped at the jewelers last night and they were gracious enough to open early for me today." Molly took the gift out of the bag; however, it was already wrapped beautifully so she had to describe what she purchased to Mr. Edwards. "It's a Rolex watch with her initials and years of service engraved on the back cover. It's quite lovely. I hope you approve."

"Yes of course. Thank you for thinking of it." He could feel the rise of embarrassment flush his face and hoped Molly did not notice. This would not sit well for his image.

"I have a lovely gift bag to put it in. I think it would be appropriate for you to present it to her. I'm sure a few words from you would be fitting as well."

"Yes, happy to do it." He was so pleased with all that Molly was doing for his assistant and friend. His dad would be so proud. Thinking of his dad and mom, he wondered if Molly had thought to invite them. "Did you happen to give any thought to inviting my mom and dad for Eleanor's party? I really don't expect you to have thought of them."

"I did call your father and he said they are leaving for Ireland tomorrow afternoon and had too much to do. They were surprised to hear the sudden change in her plans to actually retire. He said they would definitely take Eleanor out to dinner when they returned in two weeks." She refrained from telling Mr. Edwards that his parents were sending flowers over for her. She arranged to have them delivered to the conference room at twelve-forty-five.

Douglas was very impressed that Molly had even thought of his parents. She was turning out to be quite the assistant. "Eleanor certainly did not give us much time to arrange anything for her, and probably for that very reason. She will definitely be surprised."

"Everyone will be in the conference room at twelve-fifteen. I plan on bringing her down at twelve-thirty; it would be good for you and Jason to be there before she arrives."

"Not a problem. Umm, thank you, Molly."

"You're welcome, sir."

Sir, I wish she would stop calling me that. It makes me sound so old; my dad is sir. I'm only thirty-two—do I really seem that old to her?

Chapter 12

MOLLY WAS EXHAUSTED when she pulled into the parking space at Help You Stand. Everything turned out perfect for Eleanor's farewell party and she could not have been more pleased. Eleanor was so surprised and that alone made everything worthwhile. She only hoped her first night volunteering at Help You Stand would not require too many brain cells because she certainly did not have many to spare at this point.

Six o'clock and Molly had not arrived; six-five; six-ten. *I knew she was too good to be true. She's not coming. What did I say? I need to stop pacing and think about heading out of here.* Straightening up his desk to leave, Kevin looked up excited to see Molly walk through the front door. In fact, he was beyond excited. He had his doubts that she would even show up. Molly quickly apologized for being so late and explained that she had a farewell luncheon that she had to clean up from. Kevin was just happy to have her there. They immediately got to work with Kevin showing Molly the paperwork and bills that he needed help with. Sitting so close to her as he went over the bills and spreadsheets, was a little unnerving and he hoped he could keep it together. Molly was anxious to learn all she could and had no problem understanding what he wanted her to do. The time went by quickly and before she knew it, it was almost ten o'clock. Even the two cups of coffee Kevin brought for her did not abate her weariness. "Molly I'm sorry it's so late. I didn't think we would spend so much time on all of this. I told you bookkeeping and bill paying was not my forte. We can call it a night."

"I believe I have a pretty good handle on things, and when I come in Monday night I can get the bills paid. You weren't kidding when you said paperwork was not your strength. It shouldn't take me too long to get things organized, and once that is done it won't take me long at all to keep up. I think I'm going to head home if that's okay with you."

"Molly, remember you're a volunteer here. I have no say in when you choose to come in and when you choose to leave. I just appreciate having someone willing to help out."

"Well, I'll see you Monday night. Even with such leeway, I would like to come in around six."

"Goodnight Molly." As she began walking toward the front door, Kevin jumped up to follow her. He was torn between inviting her to their fundraiser or not. *Shoot, if I don't ask, I'll never know if she would like to attend.* "Say Molly." She turned quickly just before she exited. "I know this is a short notice, but a week from this Saturday we will be having our fundraiser for Help You Stand. Several of us will be attending and I was wondering if this would be something you may be interested in. It's quite the gala event, held at one of the swankiest hotels in New York. In fact, it's at the Ritz."

"When is it, and at what time?"

"It's a week from tomorrow at six pm. They call it a black-tie event." Kevin was holding his breath as he waited for her reply. He really had no business asking her on such short notice, but he would love to have her sitting beside him. *Yeah, I would love having her on my arm.*

"Thank you, Kevin. I think I would like that."

Kevin could not hide his excitement no matter how hard he tried. "Great, Molly, that's just great! Well, have a good weekend and I look forward to seeing you Monday." Molly could not help but chuckle to herself. Kevin was cute, even if he seemed a little awkward. He reminded her of a seventeen-year-old that was too embarrassed to ask a girl to the prom. She figured Kevin was her age or perhaps older by only a couple of years. She would go to the fundraiser, and she would have a good time.

Chapter 13

MOLLY'S SATURDAY WAS bittersweet. She was excited to tell her mom about her week. Now that all the drama had passed, she could laugh it off. Her mom sat with her hand over her mouth much of the time. She was thankful Molly did not lose her job, and laughed at the surprise visit she had from Mr. Edwards and his brother Jason. She was astonished to hear of the fifteen hundred dollar a month increase her daughter would be receiving. "Molly, that is so unbelievable and totally a gift from God. You must have impressed Mr. Edwards for him to give you such a huge raise."

"Mom, I think it was more Eleanor and Jason. They are the two people that went to bat for me. I'm not quite sure how Mr. Edwards feels about me. I really think I'm a thorn in his side— and as long as I get the job done to his satisfaction, he'll be happy."

Molly began to tell her mom about her conversation with Mrs. Brackenburg. "I know so much of what Mrs. Brackenburg said I have heard from you and Dad, however, there is always something different hearing it from someone else. Of course, her story was one of sadness, but then great joy. Kind of like the verse that says what man intended for evil, God intended for good. I am trusting God to get me through the whole flying trauma. I know it won't be easy but after talking to Mrs. Brackenburg I was encouraged. Why, the next day I felt like nothing could go wrong. It was like a weight had been lifted off of my shoulders. Of course, once I got to the office I felt so defeated, but even that God worked out in a way I could never have imagined." Molly's mom looked lovingly at her daughter, admiring her for the godly woman she had become. "Now I have to take the first step, and that's going to the post office to pick up my passport application. Mr. Edwards wants me to have it expedited, so make sure I don't forget that."

"Molly, if you take the first step I know God will get you through the rest. You will see that getting on that plane is not as bad as you expect it to be." Her mom said this knowing that getting on a plane would be the greatest challenge in her daughter's life.

"Mrs. Brackenburg told me I need to get involved in giving back to the community and not focus so much on myself and my fears. When I was off that Tuesday, we had flyers by our mailbox. The flyer was for a center seeking volunteers for their Thanksgiving dinner. I went in that afternoon for an interview and found out the director needs a lot of help in his office. I went in last night to see what needed to be done. I told him I could come in every other weekend and in the evenings."

"That's wonderful, dear. You are so gifted. I know you will be a huge asset to a place like that. Will it only be office help?"

"Oh no, I'm going to help in the kitchen serving the food when they need me, especially when it gets closer to Thanksgiving." Molly did not want her mother to feel sad because she would not be visiting as often, but hoped she would understand her need to give back, and be involved in others. She was taking Mrs. Brackenburg's suggestion seriously.

"Perhaps I could come in and help out for Thanksgiving. I would love to be used somehow."

"That would be great, Mom. I'm sure they can use all the help they can get. You can stay with me. It would be loads of fun, mom. Kevin, the director, invited me to attend the fundraiser they will be having next Saturday. He said it's a black-tie event with dinner at the Ritz Carlton. He said it's quite the gala affair."

"Then I think we better include a shopping trip after we hit the post office."

Chapter 14

MOLLY RETURNED TO work Monday morning floating on air. She had a glorious weekend with her mom, and was so thankful she had a chance to visit with her dad on Sunday before leaving. She found a beautiful dress for the fundraiser on Saturday. *I guess it is actually a gown. I have never owned a gown before. I'm so excited.*

Reality set in once she realized this would be her first day without Eleanor. She wondered what Mr. Edwards would be like being alone with her in the office. As far as Molly was concerned, she was sure he merely tolerated her.

No sooner had Molly finished her morning routine than Mr. Edwards greeted her. She was still in his office when he arrived and she politely brought his coffee to him. His greeting was extremely pleasant for which she was thankful. As soon as she was leaving his office he stopped her. "Molly, how was your weekend?"

Taken aback by his question since he never once asked her how any of her previous weekends had been. "It was very good, sir, and how was your weekend?" This was the first time he ever initiated a conversation with her, and Molly had to admit she was a little flustered.

"My weekend was good thank you. I understand you went to visit your parents in Connecticut. Jason mentioned that they live there."

"Umm, yes they do. It's where I grew up. It's just a small farming town in the north-west corner of the state."

"Were you able to apply for your passport?"

"Yes, and they will be expediting it. It should take about two weeks."

"Very good. I need to be in London in three weeks, so hopefully you will have it by then, or I will have to push the meetings back a week."

Molly stood wringing her hands as her heart fell about two feet. *Oh dear, what am I going to do if I have to fly to London with him.* "If my passport isn't here by then I'm sure you would be able to make the trip without me, sir."

"No, I wouldn't. Eleanor always accompanied me on business trips. I definitely need an assistant when I'm in these meetings."

"Well then, let's just hope my passport is here by then. Will you be meeting with Mr. Schuster and Mr. Jewels?"

"Why yes I will. It sounds like you're familiar with them. They are two of our biggest investors in Europe. We will have two separate meetings while there. I'm impressed, Molly, it's obvious you've been doing your homework." *Yes, I'm very impressed with her.*

"Do you need me for anything else, sir?"

"No, not at the moment, and Molly… please stop calling me sir. You may call my father sir."

"Yes sir… I mean yes Mr. Edwards."

"Molly, just call me Doug or Douglas, unless there is a client, or we are out on business."

"Yes Mr. Ed… I mean Doug. Thank you." Why did she feel so flustered talking to this man? Yes, he was intimidating and bellowed when he called for her, but she could not help but notice how handsome he was, and that made talking to him even more difficult. Maybe he was really trying to be kinder to her.

Molly spent every night that week at Help You Stand. She was pleased that she was able to straighten out the spreadsheets and get all the bills paid. It was a big accomplishment, and Kevin was a pleasure to work for. He was extremely considerate of her time, and twice that week they had dinner together. Molly tried to pay for her meal each time, however, Kevin insisted that since she was a volunteer, he could easily pay for her. The excitement over the fundraiser event was building with each day. Molly could not wait to wear her new gown.

"Molly, is it okay that I pick you up Saturday evening—say six o'clock? I know I told you it starts at six, but that's when the doors open.

They actually won't begin serving dinner until seven." Kevin was so nervous Friday night and waited until Molly was ready to leave before asking her. He should have asked her sooner, but he felt like a sixteen-year-old on his first date. *What if she hadn't come in tonight? I really would have been in a pickle.*

"That would be fine, thank you. Will Mary and Alice be driving with us as well?" The two women would be attending but Molly had no idea if Kevin was providing transportation for everyone.

"Mary will be with her husband Harold. You know Harold, he heads up maintenance. And I'm not sure about Alice."

"Alice lives alone, doesn't she? She could certainly drive with us."

Kevin did not take kindly to her suggestion. That would certainly put a crimp in the evening and the time he wanted to spend with her. "Ah yeah, I guess she could… unless she goes with Mary and Harold." *Boy that would work out so much better for me. I better get to Mary and ask if they would take Alice with them.* "I'll pick you up at six tomorrow evening then."

Molly started out Saturday morning with a quick run for about thirty minutes and spent the rest of her time cleaning house. She was excited and anxious for this gala affair. She didn't know if it was due to her not getting out much or because it was such a formal event, the likes of which she had never experienced. She thought probably the latter.

"Thank you for helping me with my dress, Mrs. Brackenburg. I certainly appreciate it. I don't think I could have zipped this dress up by myself."

"My pleasure, Molly. I'm pleased you asked me. What a beautiful gown and it fits you perfectly."

"I hope it's not too revealing. I'm not used to anything this low cut." She had chosen a strapless, duchesse satin gown. Yes strapless, but she had to admit it was the color that convinced her. It was a deep aqua blue, the exact color of her eyes. And although her mom questioned her decision when she picked out a strapless dress, it was the color and how it molded to her daughter's figure that convinced her mom that it was the right dress.

"Oh Molly, it is absolutely perfect. You will be the belle of the ball! I love the way you pulled back your hair in this beautiful sweep. Why dear, you have a beautiful neck. Wait right here. I'll be right back." Mrs. Brackenburg took off and Molly couldn't help but wonder what that sweet woman was up to. As Molly looked at herself once again, she was thankful she had enough on top to hold up such a dress, and as far as she could tell, nothing showed that would be embarrassing for her, since she always thought of herself as being quite modest. Before long, Mrs. Brackenburg was huffing and puffing as she walked into her apartment.

"Mrs. Brackenburg, I feel badly seeing you running up and down all those stairs. You must sit down and catch your breath."

"I'm fine. I think I'm as excited as you are. I feel like I will be attending this extravagant event with you." She opened a beautiful black velvet jewelry clutch and took out an exquisite diamond necklace and matching earrings. "Turn around my dear and let me put this on you, and take off the earrings you have on. They're beautiful but these do match the necklace." She was being kind and Molly quickly acquiesced to Mrs. Brackenburg's request. As Molly's dear landlady slipped the delicate diamond necklace around her neck, she noticed a few glistening tears slipping down her cheeks.

"Oh Mrs. Brackenburg, I'm so sorry. You're crying. This necklace must be very special to you. Are you sure you want me to wear it?"

"Absolutely sure. They are tears of a fond memory. My husband gave this to me on our 25th wedding anniversary. Isn't it lovely? It lays perfectly on you, just below your collarbone as it should. Now put the earrings on, dear." She watched as Molly put the diamond earrings in. The way her hair was pulled back in an upsweep, the earrings were stunning. Molly was sure she would be in tears along with Mrs. Brackenburg as she looked at herself in the mirror. She wished her mom were there to see her, although Mrs. Brackenburg was a wonderful substitute. As if this dear lady could read her mind, "My dear, let me get a picture of you. I'm sure your mom would love to see how beautiful you look tonight. Your mom and dad must be so proud of you."

"Thank you so much. I was thinking how much I wished my mom

could see me tonight. But I'm so very grateful to have you here." Molly looked at her watch and realized she had ten minutes before Kevin would be picking her up. "Oh my, I better be ready when Kevin gets here."

"Now I am going to sound like your mom. Who is this Kevin who is picking you up? Are you sure he's a respectable young man?"

"He's the director of Help You Stand. It's the homeless shelter where I have volunteered the past two weeks. They have three such facilities and Kevin is the head director. And yes, I think he is respectable. However, if he is a Christian or not I couldn't tell you. He is however a very nice man. I'm sure I can trust him, so don't you worry. From what I understand, they plan on about three hundred people attending and several employees from the facility will be there as well." Molly went to the coat rack to retrieve her winter coat. However, Mrs. Brackenburg put her hand on her arm to stop her. Her landlady went to the chair in the living room and picked up a beautiful silver fox fur jacket. Molly's mouth dropped, and her eyes looked like two huge saucers. "Oh my goodness, Mrs. Brackenburg that is absolutely gorgeous. You really want me to wear this tonight?"

"Absolutely. I would not have brought it if I did not want you to wear it. Please put it on so I can see how you look in it." With Mrs. Brackenburg's assistance she put the beautiful jacket on.

"It's absolutely elegant. What do you think?" Very often Molly was mistaken to be much younger than her 26 years. But tonight—she felt exquisite and classy. She had more confidence than she thought capable of. She was going to have a grand time.

"I think you look like a princess. And it is way more than the dress and the jacket; it's the beautiful woman wearing it. Molly, you are just as beautiful on the inside, and that is why whatever you wear will look beautiful on you. It's you, not the wrapping, that is beautiful."

Just as Molly wiped a couple of tears, her door buzzer went off. "It's Kevin. Thank you so much Mrs. Brackenburg. I'll tell you all about the fundraiser later."

Kevin could not take his eyes off of Molly as he escorted her into the ballroom of the Ritz Carlton. Adding to the elegance of the room was a four-string quartet playing as the guests entered. The chandeliers sparkled like diamonds casting a beautiful glow to the room; the centerpieces were extravagant beyond words; every guest was dressed 'to the nines'. Seeing all the tuxedoed men, and the women in the most beautiful gowns she had ever seen, helped ease the apprehension Molly had earlier of being overdressed. She had to admit she had wondered if her strapless gown was a little over the top. That notion was dismissed as soon as she saw the elegant gowns worn by the elite. She couldn't help but notice the looks and stares from both the men and women as she walked through the room. She really did feel like a beautiful princess. Kevin found their table and Molly thought their seats were fabulous. Their table was down in front and to the right of the stage. Mary and Harold were already seated along with Alice. Alice was not alone after all and introduced them to her date, James. Molly knew a little about Alice's background. She was in her early twenties and homeless when she first came to Help You Stand. She was now a permanent employee and oversees the three kitchens. Now in her thirties, Alice was a beautiful confident woman and Molly could not help but admire how far she had come. Both Mary and Alice wore lovely dresses and their men looked so proud in their fitted tuxes. It wasn't long before they were joined by four other guests. Kevin introduced Molly to Sam and Glen, directors of the two other Help You Stand Shelters. It was obvious that Sam and Glen were single as they both were eager to impress Molly. They introduced two other guests with them: a once homeless woman, Carol, and a once homeless man, Benjamin. They would be telling their story and what the shelter had meant to them.

Dinner was absolutely fabulous. Molly did not think she ever in her life had a five-course meal. Once the plates were removed and guests served their dessert, Mary asked Molly if she would like to accompany her to the ladies' room. "Great idea, I would love to." It was always best to use the facility before it was crowded with too many women.

Mary and Molly had to wind their way around the tables as they returned to their seats. They found themselves directly in front of the stage. Mary turned heading to their table, but before Molly turned to follow, she looked up. Her eyes took one look at Douglas Edwards standing at the podium. They locked eyes for an instant before Molly quickly turned to follow Mary. *Why would Mr. Edwards be on the stage? He didn't tell me he would be attending tonight—but then I guess he wouldn't have to.*

Mr. Edwards had just begun to greet the guests when his eyes met Molly's. He was sure it had to be her but when he shook his head, blinked, and then opened his eyes again, she was gone. *Maybe it isn't her but someone that looks a lot like her.* Wondering where he was in his speech, he fumbled for something to say. He never had to write anything down. He was passionate about his foundation that he had begun eight years ago. Never at a loss for words, had he now found himself speechless? Running his fingers through his hair, he began to mumble something. "Umm, ladies and gentlemen I know you have deep pockets and I look forward to how generous you will be tonight." *That was dumb. Telling everyone they had deep pockets. Just because I know the portfolios of most everyone here, there's no need to point it out. Maybe it isn't her anyway, but I would sure love to meet that gorgeous woman with Mary.* Because of the bright lights, it was almost impossible to make out the faces in the audience. He finally found Kevin's table and noticed the woman seated next to him. *If it is Molly, why is she with him?* Doug continued talking but had little sense of what he was saying. He introduced Kevin Jackson, Director of Operations for the three Help You Stand facilities, and asked him to come on stage and introduce those seated at his table.

Kevin was happy to oblige as he bounced up the stairs to the podium. He asked his directors to stand as he introduced them. First Mary, the facility manager of his shelter, Mary's husband, Henry, the head custodian; and Alice, head of the kitchen staff. He introduced their special guests, Benjamin and Carol, who would be sharing what the shelter had meant to them. The applause was held until all were introduced. Doug asked Kevin who the other guest was at their table. "Oh, James is a guest of Alice's this evening."

Doug felt himself getting a little tight jawed with Kevin. He was aware that Kevin knew exactly who he meant. His cousin always gave him a hard time. "I would like to introduce the newest addition to our team at Help You Stand…Molly Beaumont. Molly volunteers in the office at our headquarters on Joshua Street. Molly, please won't you stand? And I might add that she has been an amazing addition."

"I'm sure she is." Doug did not know exactly what to think but was shocked to hear that his assistant was volunteering at one of his Help You Stand shelters.

Kevin asked Benjamin and Carol to come up and share a brief testimonial as to what the shelter had meant to them. It was very touching to hear the stories these individuals shared. Both had been on the streets for several months, but now were back on their feet. Thanks to the shelter, they were given the skills and education needed to get decent paying jobs. There were very few dry eyes in the crowd and Molly was so pleased to be a part of this amazing organization. She didn't feel like she contributed very much, but she was still a part of it.

After the introductions and speeches concluded, Mr. Edwards announced that the bar and the dance floor were open for all to enjoy. Molly felt a little uncomfortable as this was something she was not accustomed to—perhaps no one would notice her visiting with Mary and Alice. That thought did not last for long as Kevin asked what he could bring her from the bar and Molly asked for a Diet Coke. "Are you sure I can't bring you a glass of Champaign or wine, Molly?"

"No thank you. I'm fine with a Diet Coke."

Kevin headed for the bar returning with her Coke and his glass of wine. After placing the two glasses on the table, Kevin offered his hand to Molly. "Molly, may I have this dance?"

"Thank you, that would be lovely." Her stomach knotted as she slipped her hand into Kevin's. It had been a long time since she danced. She remembered how much she loved it in high school but rarely did she ever dance while in college. At least the dance was slow.

Jason was anxious to find his brother. That *was* Molly that he saw and all doubt was removed when Kevin introduced her. "I've been looking for you, bro. I had no idea that Molly was volunteering at the center. Did you know?"

Doug scowled at his brother. "Of course, I didn't know. How would

I? And wouldn't it be a conflict of interest, or something like that, for her to work at the center? She would've told Kevin where she was employed...wouldn't she?"

"I don't know how volunteering some place could be a conflict of interest. All I'm going to say is, I really don't care what your rules are. I intend to have at least one dance with her."

"Jason...never mind. Go ahead I can't think straight right now. It sure looks like there are plenty of guys lined up to dance with her." With that he stormed to the bar. Never did he think seeing Molly like this would stir the feelings it did in him. She certainly didn't look like some poor woman that needed a job as badly as Eleanor and Jason claimed. She looked elegant, and no different than the million-dollar women that were there.

Douglas had no problem talking to people. He was always popular especially among the women. In fact, there were many times he had been called a "babe magnet". He chuckled to himself thinking of that one. He wished his mom and dad were there tonight. No not really. They always left before the open bar and dancing started. He loved his parents but they needed to get into the 21ˢᵗ century. He looked up to see Jason with his arms around Molly dancing a slow number and his stomach roiled. *She's my assistant for crying out loud and I have every right to dance with her along with anyone else in this room.* It was obvious Kevin was fuming, and that gave him some satisfaction.

Douglas watched Kevin start to rise from his chair on his way to cut in to Jason and Molly's second dance of the night. He quickly made his way over before another tune began and tapped Jason on the shoulder. "Molly, may I have the next dance."

"Why of course, Mr. Ed...I mean Douglas." The band began to play "Somewhere My Love"—probably one of the most romantic tunes of all times as far as Molly was concerned. As soon as Douglas held her in his arms, she was certain she would melt. She wondered if he felt the electricity that flowed between them. *It's the song, that's all it is. It's so romantic. I'm sure I would feel this way no matter who was holding me.*

"You look beautiful, Molly."

"Thank you. I have to admit I was quite surprised to see you here."

"Help You Stand happens to be the foundation I started eight years ago. How did you end up volunteering for them?"

Molly went into her explanation of how she was led to volunteer after reading a flyer that Kevin had passed out.

"Did you disclose that you worked for Edwards and Sons?"

"Yes, I did. I told him I was your assistant. But to be honest, I don't think he paid any attention to what I was telling him."

Douglas knew what it was like to be captivated by Molly's unbelievably blue eyes and mind-boggling looks. He was doing everything he could not to fall into that trap. "He may have had a lot on his mind at the time."

The song ended and Douglas's arms felt empty. Molly thanked him for the dance as he walked her to her table. Kevin stood with her fur jacket over his arm waiting for her to return. As Douglas stood shaking his head and running his fingers through his hair, the thought occurred to him: either his brother or his cousin would do all they could to win the prize. The prize of course...was his assistant.

Chapter 15

MOLLY TOOK OFF running early Monday morning. Daylight had not broken so the sky had that grey ominous look. She had time for a quick run, and could still make it home for a shower before she had to leave for the office. About four blocks from her apartment, she noticed several guys on the sidewalk. Molly ran into the street to get around them, when to her astonishment three of the guys stopped dead in front of her, not allowing her to pass. She stopped, and as she turned around to head back the way she came, two more guys stood directly behind her—not allowing her to go past them. "Excuse me," said Molly. "Just let me go back the way I came. I won't bother you guys." Fear began to rise along with the bile. *What is happening?* She remembered hearing that if you were ever attacked, you do not allow anyone to take you to another location. She stood her ground as she looked for a way of escape.

One of the guys, named Joey, pulled out a switchblade knife; her heart almost stopped when she saw the knife appear. Then to her relief, he cut off the fanny pack that was around her waist. Unzipping it, he took out her driver's license and held it up with a five-dollar bill. "Hey lady, is this all the money you carry? Don't you have a debit or credit card?" She was barely able to shake her head no. "Tommy, this is all she got on her."

"That's all I ever carry." Molly tried with all her might to keep calm. She saw a way around the guys that stood behind her and started to make her move. Whack. A hand or a board struck her in the head and immediately her world went black. Falling to the ground, Tommy picked her up telling the others that they needed to take her to his basement. Tommy threw her over his shoulder like a sack of potatoes.

"Tommy, you said we only wanted her money. What ya plan on doing to her?"

"We can't take any chances. She saw every one of us and can identify us with no problem."

"You said nobody would get hurt."

"Shut up, Carlos. I'm not taking any chances."

The four guys followed Tommy to his house. Molly was starting to come to as Tommy sat her in a splintered kitchen chair. Coming to, she heard the names of the other two guys, one called Kye and another they called Jake. It was important that she try and remember each of their names...if she lived to tell anyone. Thankfully she heard the names Tommy, Joey, and Carlos before completely passing out. *Pray Molly, pray.* She closed her eyes asking God to give her peace and strength to get through this. *What is going to happen to me?*

Before her eyes could even adjust to where she was, they had put a bandana over her eyes, tied up her hands and feet, and duct taped her mouth. Molly realized this Tommy was not only the oldest of the guys but the ringleader. "I'm not taking any chances...she knows us now." He pulled Molly's ponytail back and unzipped her sweat jacket. Noticing her tank-top underneath, his mouth began to drool. "Hey, I'm not giving up that easy. Look at her. She's a sweet thing."

"Come on Tommy. You said you would take me and Joey to school before going to work. We gotta go... now!"

"Okay, okay, gimme a minute; just go wait outside for me guys." She heard the others walk up some stairs and a door open. She could still feel heavy breathing on her face and chest. *Oh God, what's he going to do to me? Lord, whatever it is, I know it's nothing that you don't already know about. Please help me bear this.* The verse that came to her mind was Isaiah 26:3: *"You will keep him in perfect peace, whose mind is stayed on you, because he trusts in you."* God help me to keep my focus on you no matter what, and to trust you with my whole heart...and my life. Just then her tormentor, straddling the front of her chair, ripped the tape off her mouth. Molly gasped—glad her eyes were covered. The stale cigarette odor and sweat invading her senses gagged her so much she was sure she was going to vomit.

"Tommy, come on! We're waiting already!"

"Baby you're gonna have to stay put until I get back from work tonight." He kissed her hard, biting down on her lower lip, and then taped her mouth shut again. Looking at her driver's license he said, "Goodbye Molly. I'll be back later."

Calling her Molly sent a shiver up her spine. *He knows my name, how?* Just then she remembered the guy taking her driver's license out of her fanny pack. *Not only does he know my name but he knows where I live.* Praying was all she could do as she sat on this hard-wooden chair. The oily and damp smell, combined with the chill, made it obvious she was locked in a basement. *Lord, I have no idea what you have planned for me in all of this but I know I belong to you, and I know you will not allow anything to happen to me without your permission. I pray if he is going kill me, maybe torture me, then please let me pass out...just keep me unconscious until you take me home to heaven.* She tried working the ropes loose around her wrists but to no avail. *I can't keep this up...it's hopeless to try and loosen these ropes.* Weary and exhausted, Molly felt herself drift into sleep.

Mr. Edwards walked into his office. The quiet was deafening. Where was Molly? The blinds were closed, there was no coffee made. It was obvious she was late coming into the office today—so unlike her. He called his brother and asked if he had heard from her and he hadn't. "It's not like her not to let someone know. I called security and they said her car was not in the garage and no one saw her come in."

"Why don't you call Kevin? Maybe she stayed the weekend with him."

Just that thought alone infuriated him. "Why on earth would she spend the weekend with Kevin? That makes no sense." Molly certainly did not seem like that kind of a woman. He did call Kevin anyway and found out that he had dropped her off at her apartment Saturday night.

"I walked her to her door and then left. Why are you asking?"

"She hasn't come into work and it's not like her not to let anyone know. I checked with the receptionist and no one has seen her this morning." They hung up their respective phones and Douglas was more unsettled than ever. He had an overwhelming suspicion in his gut that something was wrong. He called his brother back relating his concern. "Do you remember how to get to her house?"

"Yeah, I do. Want me to drive there with you?"

"Would you mind? I have a sick feeling about this. Maybe her landlady knows something."

The two men got in Doug's Porsche and peeled out of the garage. They arrived at Molly's house in record time. No sooner did they knock on Mrs. Brackenburg's door when she opened it. "Come in please. You're Molly's boss, aren't you?"

Doug gave a quick nod. "We're concerned about Molly. Mrs. Brackenburg, is that correct?"

"Yes, that's right. What's happened to Molly?" Mrs. Brackenburg held her hand over her chest, her face ashen. "Sorry, but she's become like a daughter to me."

"Did you see her leave for work this morning?"

"Well, let me think. She stopped by to drop off the necklace and fur jacket I had insisted she wear Saturday night. She was in her running clothes and was on her way out. She knows I'm up early. I would say it was about 5:30 or 5:45 when she stopped by. I can't say I noticed when she came back. I was baking all morning so I was in the kitchen. Oh no, I certainly hope nothing happened to her."

"Do you think we could look around her apartment and see if anything is out of place?"

"Why of course. I'll get the key."

Upon entering her apartment, it was evident that she never returned after her run. Her purse was sitting on the couch and her car keys on one of the side tables. They walked into her kitchen and noticed her phone charger was plugged into the wall but no phone. "Hey Doug, go through her purse and see if her phone is in there."

Doug felt like an intruder as he rummaged through her purse. "No phone, Jason. I think we should call the police and hopefully they can locate her cell phone."

"Good idea. I've heard they can locate the ping as long as the phone is on."

"Well then, I'm going to pray her cell phone is on," said Mrs. Brackenburg.

"She belongs to Jesus and he knows exactly where she is. We must trust him to keep her safe."

Both men rolled their eyes and gave a look that said, "You sound just like our mother" but neither said anything. Doug quickly called the police and they said they would call the phone company and get back to him.

"Shoot," being careful with their language in front of the landlady, "we can't just wait here. Do you have any idea where Molly runs?"

"Oh dear, no I don't. But every time I have seen her leave, she always runs in front of my living room window…so I guess she would run north."

"Let's hope she's a creature of habit and we can track her steps."

The two men thanked Mrs. Brackenburg. Doug had given the police his cell phone number expecting the cops to call when they had something. "Come on brother let's go for a walk." Doug patted his brother on the back as they quickly left the apartment.

They walked north several blocks but then decided she would have to have turned down one of the east-west streets. "Why don't you take this street and I'll go up one more," said Doug. "If you see anything, send me a text. I want my phone open in case the police call."

The two brothers continued on alone, Jason taking his street, and Doug walking on ahead to the next. As Doug continued down his street he spotted a fanny pack lying on the ground up ahead. He immediately ran over to it but wasn't sure if he should pick it up or not. He pulled out his handkerchief and carefully picked it up. Funny, it was a very pretty shade of blue. That in and of itself reminded him of something Molly would have. He began texting his brother when his phone rang. "Douglas Edwards here."

"Mr. Edwards, this is Sergeant Malone. The phone company was able to locate a ping coming from Ms. Beaumont's cell. It's somewhere on Lancaster Drive. We are heading that way and we'll meet you there."

"I'm already here, Sergeant. Give me the address."

"Afraid not Mr. Edwards. We're coming with a warrant. You can't simply barge into someone's house. We had to get a judge to expedite a search warrant. Hopefully someone is home."

"But I know she has to be in there. We have to get to her. Who knows what someone could be doing to her."

"I know your concern and we'll be there soon. Our ETA is about ten minutes. Just sit tight."

"I have no choice since you won't give me the address." Aware he was being sarcastic, but time was of the essence. He immediately called Jason and updated him on his call from the police. "I'm on Lancaster now, one street up from where you are. Get over here as soon as you can."

The ten minutes felt like an hour before the cops pulled up. The two cops introduced themselves, and Doug showed them the fanny pack that he had picked up off the street; he was positive it had to be Molly's. The cops were pleased he had it wrapped in his handkerchief and they immediately placed it in a clear plastic bag.

They located the house...a two-story frame house; it was in a block of old framed houses. This one was in worse shape than any of the others. The paint was peeling, the wooden stairs splintered and breaking apart. It was obvious the house was in disrepair. Doug and Jason insisted on following the officers inside. "You follow, do you understand? Don't go off on your own or ahead of us...or you'll both be waiting outside." Officer Malone was more than persuasive in his tone.

They both nodded and stood behind as Malone rang the doorbell. No answer. He rang again and knocked. Still no answer. Doug was getting impatient as the officers looked in windows and then went to the rear of the house. "Looks like no one's home," said Malone.

"You have to get in there. If this is where the ping is coming from, she has to be in there." Jason had no more patience than his brother.

"Not necessarily, they may have stolen her phone and she's not even in there," said Officer McPherson. "No doubt they moved her to some other location or even k—"

"I can't and won't believe that. You have a warrant, right? Then break the doggone door down." Doug was getting more unnerved by the minute; trying desperately to keep calm. "I'll pay for any damages."

The two officers went off to the side and returned agreeing they would break in. "Don't forget when we get in there…you follow, understood?" Malone and McPherson put on latex gloves before forcing entry into the house.

The door broke open with no problem. One kick and they were inside. They quickly scanned the living room and dining area—it was messy, but nothing looked that out of place. Heading for the kitchen, they saw dishes in the sink and dirty dishes on the table, someone had cereal for breakfast. "Upstairs," said Malone. The two officers took the lead but it didn't mean Doug and Jason weren't right behind.

Looking in the first bedroom, it was no doubt the master. The bed was partially made. Checking the closet, they noticed there were only women's clothes hanging in there and only women's shoes. It appeared to be the home of a single mom. They went into another bedroom; messy and obvious that it belonged to a teenager—they checked another closet, but saw nothing unusual. "Hey," said Malone. "In here."

Upon entering the third bedroom, their stomachs turned as they looked at the filth in the room. "Are those…what I think they are on the floor?" asked Doug. *What could he have done to her already? No, I can't and won't think the worst.*

"Yep, this is definitely the room of a pervert," said Malone.

They found nothing in the room or closet that even hinted of Molly being there. "It's pretty disgusting but there's nothing that proves she's been here."

Doug's stomach was churning and he had no doubt in his mind that Molly was somewhere in this house. "I feel it, man. She's here I just know it. Let's go back downstairs."

"I'm telling you there's nothing here. We're in deep trouble breaking and entering and not coming up with anything." Sergeant Malone was looking anxious to get out of there.

Heading back down the stairs, Doug was led to return to the kitchen. "Did we even open the doors in here?"

Officer McPherson opened the first door and it was a small pantry.

"Maybe the other door leads to the basement." He tried it but it was locked. All four of the men exchanged looks.

Molly awoke to footsteps upstairs. *Oh no, he's back.* Being blindfolded, she had no idea if it was still daylight or nighttime. She only knew she had fallen asleep. She tried again to loosen the ropes around her wrists… they would not budge. Bile rose in her throat, she heard her heart pounding in her chest. Footsteps. Someone was coming down the stairs. *Jesus, please protect me. I know you're with me no matter what happens to me. I'm yours, Lord. I'm yours.* Molly stiffened as she waited for the worse.

"She's here in the corner. She's tied up. Oh, thank God, it's you Molly." Doug and Jason kneeled on the floor beside her chair while Sergeant Malone cut the ropes around her wrists and untied her blindfold. They saw the wound on the side of her head. She looked up and saw the two brothers and the tears flowed like water over a dam. Officer McPherson untied her ankles and apologized before proceeding to pull back the duct tape from her mouth. Molly collapsed and Doug instinctively reached out and caught her in his arms. "We need to get her to a hospital. She looks pretty beat up," said Doug. He picked her up and carried her up the stairs.

"She's coming to," Jason told him she needed some fresh air and that there was a lawn chair on the back porch. Holding the door open for his brother, Doug managed to carry Molly out and gently placed her in a filthy, beat-up plastic lawn chair.

She began to shiver uncontrollably. Doug didn't know if it was from shock or the chilly fall day. He hoped it was the latter but feared it was from both. Taking his suit jacket off, he immediately wrapped her in it. "Mr. Edwards, you found me. Thank you." The tears continued to flow, but she insisted she was okay. They all thought otherwise as the fear in her eyes took on an alarming sadness. Her beautiful blue eyes looked dull and expressionless.

The officers convinced her she needed to go to the hospital and said they could get her statement there. She insisted that she did not want an ambulance. "We can take you in the police car. I think the less attention we draw the better." Sergeant Malone was so gentle and considerate he sounded like a completely different person.

Noticing the change in demeanor the officer showed, Doug wanted to take her himself to the hospital. "Can I take her in my car?"

"Sorry, can't do. If you want to drive along you can. You're welcome to ride with her in the backseat."

Doug took one look at Molly and agreed to ride along. He told Jason to take his car and go back to the house and let Mrs. Brackenburg know that Molly was found and that they would be at the hospital. "Are we going to Mercy?"

"Yeah, it's the closest and really the best," answered Malone.

Jason agreed to meet them there after he stopped by Mrs. Brackenburg's.

Molly was quickly whisked into a private ER room. Doctors and nurses were at her bedside in no time. They were concerned about the blow to her head but there did not seem to be any serious damage, however, a portable CT scan was ordered immediately and would be done in the privacy of her room. The cuts on her wrists were carefully cleaned and wound cream applied and bandaged. The doctor asked the others to leave and he privately questioned her if she had been violated in any way. "No nothing like that." She began to tremble and once again the tears flowed. "I'm sorry. He threatened that he was going to take care of that when he returned from work."

"We need to get Sergeant Malone in here and you can tell him what you have been telling me. In fact, say no more to me. I want the Sergeant in here."

Molly nodded as the doctor left to bring in the officers.

Sergeant Malone and McPherson sat with Molly for much of the time and were impressed with the details she was able to give them. Identifying the men and remembering their names came easily to her. She made it clear that Tommy was her tormentor and threatened to not only defile her but had every intention of killing her because she could identify each of them.

Jason stopped at Mrs. Brackenburg's house and told her the good news. The joy on her face was priceless. "Thank you, Jesus. Thank you, Jesus. God is good. I knew he would protect her. He sent you and your brother to look for her. I just know it."

Jason told her that the police insisted Molly go to Mercy Hospital, and of course Mrs. Brackenburg begged to go with him to the hospital. He acquiesced to her pleading; there was no way he could ask her to stay at home. "Do you mind riding in a Porsche, Mrs. Brackenburg?" Jason was impressed with how spunky this little lady was. He couldn't help but notice the twinkle in her eye. That was her answer.

Once at the hospital, they saw Doug in the waiting area outside the ER. He sat with his head in his hands waiting for any word at all as to how Molly was. Mrs. Brackenburg knew that look anywhere but kept her thoughts to herself. The three sat patiently waiting for the doctor, Sergeant Malone, or anyone to come out with word as to how Molly was. They saw a special x-ray machine being rolled into the ER and expected it to be for her. Time seemed to stand still as they continued to wait.

Sergeant Malone and Officer McPherson were the first to exit the ER. They immediately walked over to the three anxious companions. "She's going to be fine. We can't disclose anything until the trial or we would compromise the case. A defense attorney would be salivating at that. I'm sure they'll lawyer up but I think we have an ironclad case. Of course, she will have to testify. We'll make sure she is protected until arrests have been made. A big concern of hers, and ours, is that they have her driver's license and we don't want to waste any time in getting arrest warrants. Let me just say, there is one really bad dude out there and we gotta get him before he runs." He watched as they processed this information. "Do any of you need a ride or will you be okay?"

Doug extended his hand. "We'll be fine, Sergeant. Thank you for all you've done. We appreciate it." Doug had no idea how the four of them would fit in his Porsche but they would figure something out. He would call a cab if need be. No sooner did the thought enter his mind that his phone vibrated. "Edwards" It was Kevin calling to see if they had any news on Molly. He had called earlier so he knew she had been found and was at the hospital. Doug filled him in and Kevin said he would be at the hospital right away.

The doctor came out with an update and the results of the scan. "Molly gave me permission to fill you in on her prognosis. The scan shows a slight concussion. We can be thankful he didn't hit the very back of her head or even the front with the same extreme force. She is fortunate it didn't damage her eardrum or fracture her eye socket. She is a very lucky lady. She will no doubt be somewhat dizzy for a couple of days but this will pass. Just keep an eye on her the next twenty-four hours." They nodded and thanked the doctor for telling them her condition.

It wasn't long before a nurse wheeled Molly out of ER. She was so happy to see her landlady sitting with the three men. Mrs. Brackenburg, with tears flooding her eyes, came over and gave Molly a huge motherly hug. "What a scare you gave us, love."

"Mrs. Brackenburg, you can't imagine how happy I am to see you. Thank you for coming."

The three men seemed to clamor around her making it difficult for her to breathe but she didn't care. They had saved her life and she would be eternally grateful. She was warned by the police not to talk about what happened, especially in a hospital waiting room. "Mr. Edwards, how did you even think to look for me?"

"Well Molly," he began clearing the lump in his throat trying to keep his own emotions at bay, "it certainly wasn't like you to not show up for work ahead of me this morning, and to be honest... I missed my coffee." A chuckle went up from all. "When no one remembered seeing you come in, I had a feeling something was wrong."

"I can't thank you enough. Sergeant Malone said if I didn't have my phone on and in my pocket, they probably would not have found me. I can't believe those guys never even checked my pockets." Before she could stop herself, the tears began to escape. "I'm sorry but when I think of what could have happened—"

"Let's get you home." Doug relieved the nurse and said he would wheel her out. He handed Jason his keys and told him to bring his car around.

The nurse said she was sorry but she had to do the wheeling. "It's my job, and I have to make sure she gets in the car."

When Doug walked out to the parking lot, to his relief he noticed a police cruiser off to the side. Pulling out from the parking lot, he glanced in his rearview mirror to see the cruiser pull out right behind him. This gave Doug some relief, but he wasn't about to bring attention to it and cause alarm as far as Molly was concerned. He had no doubt that Malone would keep his word and have around-the-clock surveillance at her apartment. Kevin had plenty of room in his car for Mrs. Brackenburg and Jason who followed behind the police car.

Chapter 16

Doug walked into his office on Tuesday. He definitely had to control the feelings he was having for his assistant. *I don't know what has gotten into me. She's my assistant; I did what any boss would have done.* Molly had insisted on coming in, but Doug would not hear of it. He wanted her to be home and watched at least for the twenty-four hours. He really didn't feel like working anyway so he sat alone in his office, never opening the blinds. He had stopped at Starbucks for his coffee and had to chuckle as he thought of the woman with the most beautiful eyes and long flowing hair bumping into him just a few months previously. For some reason, he couldn't shake the feeling that somehow, he knew this woman. *I wish I had gotten a better look at her.* Now she was like an apparition that he couldn't shake. He never realized he was sitting in the dark when Jason came in. "Hey bro, what's with the darkness? You do know you have no lights on in here?"

"Yeah I know—just don't feel like working today. I'm counting on you to hold down the fort."

"Nothing happening that the rest of us can't handle. Have you talked to Molly today?"

"No, I guess I should call to see how she is. Mrs. Brackenburg said she would be staying with her the night. She insisted on coming in to work tomorrow. What do you think of me having a car pick her up in the morning and take her back home after work?"

"It's a great idea if she goes along with it. I wouldn't be surprised if Kevin wants to pick her up after work. After all, she's doing volunteer work for him."

"I'll talk to Kevin. I don't think Molly needs to be there the rest of the week. I called Malone and they still haven't taken in this Tommy character. They think he skipped. I have a meeting in London in two weeks and Molly will be coming with me. I hope she's good by then. At least it will get her out of here for a few days."

"Yeah that should work out. Do you need me to come along?"

"Thanks for the offer...but NO." Why he answered his brother so abruptly he had no idea.

Doug called and talked to Mrs. Brackenburg. She filled him in on Molly's progress and how pleased she was. She told him that Molly sounded like she was planning on going into work on Wednesday. Doug said he would give her a call later as she was napping at the time.

Molly agreed to have a car pick her up on Wednesday morning. In fact, Doug was quite surprised to how agreeable she was. He was certain she had to be aware of the situation that continued to threaten her. Tommy McGee was still not apprehended. The others were, and the police hoped one of them would talk. They didn't think his brother would squeal on him, but surely one of the other guys would. However, until he was picked up the threat was very real. Too bad McGee's mother was of no help; she completely broke down when questioned. Of course, she insisted that she had no idea where her son was, and claimed he was always such a good boy.

When Doug arrived Wednesday morning, Molly was completing her morning routine. "Good morning, Molly, how are you feeling today?"

"I'm much better thank you. And thank you for the limo you sent to pick me up."

"Good. I'm much more comfortable with you having a ride. We can't take any chances."

"Mr. Edwards, I am quite aware that there is a police car sitting outside my window 24/7. I feel like I'm in the witness protection program. I have to admit it is a little unnerving. What am I going to do if they never catch this guy? I can't live in fear the rest of my life."

It was a little unsettling to be called Mr. Edwards once again but perhaps this was for the best. He needed to be on an employer/employee relationship. He had to admit that he was getting a little too emotionally involved with his assistant. And he didn't know why. It was incredulous to think anything could come of it. He took the hint that she wanted to have a strictly business relationship. *Fine by me.* "Molly, I'm sure they will have him picked up in no time." Doug questioned his own statement as he sat comfortably behind his desk.

As Molly came with his coffee, she started feeling dizzy, and never realized she was not capable of walking in a straight line. Doug was up immediately circling his arm around her waist. "Whoa Molly, come sit down. You're still a little shaky. The doctor said you may feel dizzy for a couple of days." Putting his arm around her stirred all kinds of feelings in him that he was trying very hard to avoid. Not sure if Molly felt the same tingle as he did, he sat her down like she was a hot potato. "Sit here while I get you a glass of water."

"Thanks, I think I turned too quickly. I've noticed I have to get up a little slower or I find myself feeling dizzy. I guess I need to be careful in turning as well."

Molly sipped her water and then began to get up out of the chair. Doug stood beside her and offered his arm as he walked her out to her desk. "I'm fine now, thank you." She had plenty of work to catch up on and thought if she stayed at her desk she would be fine.

Not moving much in the afternoon helped a lot. Jason brought her lunch so she would not have to go anywhere, and for this she was grateful. When Doug heard, what Jason had done, he had mixed emotions. *I guess that's something I should have thought of. Na, if Jason wants to take care of her that's fine by me. The less I think about her, the better off I'll be.*

Kevin called late that afternoon offering to come by to pick Molly up and take her to the shelter if she wanted to get some work done. Doug was adamant that she should not go in the rest of the week. "I planned on calling you. Kevin, it's too much for her. She had a dizzy spell this morning and I'm worried she's going to fall if she's alone."

"She won't be alone. I can easily look after her."

"No. She's not doing it. I have a car picking her up at five."

"Man, you don't have to be so possessive of her. I'll give her a call when she gets home."

The two men hung up. *Is that what I am, possessive? I'm only looking out for my assistant.* It was Jason that walked Molly down to the limo at five. Why Doug was feeling jealous, he had no idea. His brother and his cousin were only trying to help Molly. Yes, she is beautiful, and no doubt they had ulterior motives, but he put those thoughts aside.

The limo driver had instructions to make sure he walked Molly to the door. Mrs. Brackenburg, bless her heart, was waiting for Molly as she walked up the stairs. "Come sit down, Molly. I'll bring you a cup of tea. How did your day go, dear?"

"It went well thank you, although, I did have a dizzy spell this morning...but my afternoon went well. Has the police car been out in front all day?"

"Yes, they have and I'm sure they will continue to be there as long as they believe you to be in danger. After all, that criminal has your driver's license, and I must admit I feel much safer having the police outside my door."

Molly's eyes went wide and she immediately let out a moan. "What have I done? Oh, Mrs. Brackenburg, the address on my license is my Connecticut address. My mom, oh no, my mom; she's up there all alone. She's in danger. Who can I call? I must call the police!" The tears began to flow and panic gripped her chest. "I can't believe I never gave it a thought." Just then her cell phone rang. Molly searched Mrs. Brackenburg's face for answers. Reluctantly, and with trembling hands, she answered her phone. Her voice shaky, "hello."

"Molly is that you? What's wrong?"

"Mr. Edwards?"

"Yes, it's me. I called to see that you made it home okay. Molly what's going on? You sound upset."

"Mr. Edwards, I just realized the address on my driver's license is my Connecticut address. I have not gotten a New York driver's license since moving here." Panic set in as she began gasping into the phone. "My...mom...is all alone. He's going to go after her." The tears began to flow uncontrollably.

"Molly, I'm going to call Sergeant Malone as soon as we hang up. You call your mom and tell her what's going on. Does she know what happened to you Monday morning?"

"No, I didn't want to alarm her. She would just be worried sick. I have to call her. And Mr. Edwards, thank you for calling Sergeant Malone."

Chapter 17

Tommy McGee pulled in front of the address shown on Molly's driver's license. After knocking on the door, it was evident no one was home. *Plan B would have to do.* McGee moved his truck and parked down the block. He made sure no one was out of their house, even to walk a dog. He walked casually down the sidewalk, up the drive, and to a side door. Tossing his cigarette on the sidewalk so he could get to the task at hand, he took out his handy tool to pick the lock; something he had a lot of experience with. The door opened with no problem. *Now all that's left for me to do is wait.* A diabolical laugh escaped from his throat. If he could just find an address book, the worse would not have to take place. If that didn't happen he had no problem taking care of things. He immediately started tearing apart drawers and cabinets...nothing.

Tommy McGee was getting impatient as he waited for someone, anyone, to come through that side door. Sitting at the kitchen table, he had a perfect view of the driveway. He was on his fifth cigarette and his nerves were getting the better of him. He hated waiting...for anything.

Finally, a car pulled into the drive. Tommy slowly got up from his seat and walked to the kitchen sink, peering out the window where he could get a better look at the car and its driver and maybe a passenger. He watched as an old lady got out of the driver's side of the car and opened the rear door. She took out a bag of groceries and started walking to the side door. *Why is she stopping? She's going back to her car. What the?*

Dolores Beaumont arrived home with her groceries and after they were put away she would visit her husband at the nursing home. As she approached the side door, she noticed a cigarette butt on the sidewalk.

Also, something was amiss as she looked at her kitchen door; it wasn't closed all the way and she was certain she had locked it. Taking all of this in, Dolores hastily turned to get back into her car. She quickly opened the rear door to put her groceries back in…she had to get to Clara's house. She would call the police from there. Maybe it was nothing but she had an uneasy feeling. Her legs were shaking like a leaf as she backed out of the car. To her shock and horror, a hand came over her mouth. She tried to scream but couldn't. She wanted to turn to see who was there, but whoever it was grabbed her arm and held it behind her. Her keys fell out of her hand hitting the driveway. Tommy McGee had what he came for: someone to tell him where Molly was. Once he had that information, whoever he had, would be no more. Tommy McGee did not believe in sparing anyone that could identify him. "Let's get in the house, shall we?"

Dolores Beaumont couldn't speak with this filthy hand over her mouth. She certainly didn't think her legs could move they shook so badly. She was forced to walk to the door and Tommy shoved her into her kitchen. She gasped when she saw the disarray of her kitchen: the cabinets were torn apart and contents strewn on the floor. McGee continued to shove Dolores from the kitchen into the living room. Going through her dining room, she glanced at her pretty china cabinet and saw broken dishes and drawers pulled out. He pushed her into a living room chair; she fell with a thud. Dolores clutched her stomach convinced she was going to hurl.

"Okay lady, where's Molly?"

"Molly? What do you want with my daughter?"

"Does she live here, or doesn't she? Lady, I'm not about to play games with you."

Dolores did not know how to answer his question. She had to protect her daughter no matter the cost. She would sacrifice her own life to protect her little girl. Her voice trembled as she repeated his question, "Does she live here?"

"That's what I asked. Does she live here, or doesn't she? A simple yes or no answer will do."

Her arms were wrapped around her stomach as she looked directly into the evilest eyes she ever had seen. "I'm going to throw up. I need to run to the bathroom first."

McGee saw panic in her eyes and had no doubt she was serious. "Okay, but I'm going with you. Don't try anything funny, you understand?"

Reluctantly she nodded her head and agreed to his doggedness in following her. Deep down she was hoping to buy some time to figure out a way of escape. She quickly ran to the bathroom holding her hand over her mouth. He followed. It wasn't hard for the contents in her stomach to escape as she leaned over the toilet. "I need a glass of water...please."

"Lady, I'm not here to wait on you. Get it yourself." He followed her back to the kitchen where she retrieved a small glass and poured herself some water.

Grabbing her upper arm in an excruciating grip, he pushed her back into the living room and shoved her into the chair. "Answer me... NOW! Does Molly live here or not?!"

Molly sat in her landlady's apartment, wringing her hands and trembling as she ended the call to her mom. She could not think of anything but her mother being home alone. "Mrs. Brackenburg, she's not answering her home phone or her cell phone. I just know something is terribly wrong. I'm afraid my mother is in great danger."

Mrs. Brackenburg reached over and took both of Molly's hands in hers. "Dear, let's pray together right now. I do my best praying on my knees, and I believe this is definitely a time for us to get on our knees before God."

Both women slipped to the floor and Mrs. Brackenburg began to pray: "Heavenly Father, we come to you on bended knee asking you to protect Dolores right now. She belongs to you and we know that you know exactly where she is and what is happening. She may be completely safe or she may be in grave danger...you know all things. I ask that you give Molly peace and comfort right now as we trust you. We know the man the police are in pursuit of is dangerous and evil. This young man is not beyond your reach, Father. He is lost and capable of doing vile things, but you will not allow anything to happen to Dolores that you have not already approved of. Give her your peace that passes all understanding. Your Word says that you hold us in the very palm of your hand. Help us to rest in that promise, Lord. I pray this in your Son's Name, the Name of Jesus."

Doug hung up with Sergeant Malone more disturbed than he thought possible. Malone delivered the news that McGee's DNA proved he was responsible for at least three rape cases and a homicide involving an eighteen-year-old girl in Jersey. Knowing the obvious source of McGee's DNA made Doug cringe. There was no way he would tell Molly what he just heard. Malone assured him that he would be calling the local Connecticut police department. He no sooner hung up the phone when Jason walked into his office.

"What's up, bro? You look plain scared."

Doug began telling his brother about his phone call to Sergeant Malone finding it difficult to believe himself.

"Man, this guy is a real piece of…work."

"You got that right. There is no way I can disclose this information to Molly."

"Where is she now?"

"She's home with her landlady, but I wish she were here." He noticed his brother giving him a questioning look. "Umm, I have a lot of work that I need done and without her I can't handle everything."

"Sure you do. That makes a lot of sense. Why don't you drive over there and see how she is or…I could run over there?" Goading him on he said, "Maybe Kevin would be willing to check up on her. After all, if he's at the shelter he's only a few blocks away."

The heated look Doug gave his brother could thaw an ice cube. "That won't be necessary. I'll give her a call in a bit. I certainly don't want to be tempted to say more to her than necessary."

Dolores Beaumont sat trembling in her living room chair. *How do I answer this evil man? If I tell him she lives in New York, he'll want her address. If I tell him she lives here and then never shows up, he'll probably kill me just as easily as he can blink an eye. Lord, what do you want me to say?*

"You know what, lady? I have really had it with you and I am not waiting any longer. You have no idea what I'm capable of." McGee backhanded Dolores across her face. "Hurts, doesn't it?"

Her face stung so badly and Dolores had to give some sort of answer. "Okay, wait, I'll tell you. Molly no longer lives here but lives someplace in New York. She never told me where."

"You really expect me to believe..." He lifted his hand to give her another slap – BAM – CRUNCH. McGee found himself face down on the floor. "What the?" All he knew was some big guy, a cop, had tackled him to the floor. The wind was completely knocked out of him. He tried fighting back but the big cop punched him in the gut and then an uppercut to the jaw before cuffs could be put on him.

"Consider us even" said the big cop, "We heard your plans for Mrs. Beaumont and nobody gets away with talk like that. Take him out to the car, Mike."

Dolores Beaumont looked up. "George, I can't believe you're here. It's so good to see you. I didn't think I would be seeing anyone again. Why would this man want Molly?"

"All I know Mrs. Beaumont is that we received a call from a Sergeant Malone in New York, and they feared this McGee character may be at or coming to your house. We know they have an APB out on him. Did you say Molly's in New York?"

George Bradley started out as a Shepherd police officer and had grown up in the town. He was promoted to Chief of Police a year ago. Although he was a couple of years older than Molly, he had known her since high school. He had dated her many times. He knew her well.

"George, I need to call my daughter. How did you ever know that man was in here with me?"

"Ma'am, when we came down your street we noticed a truck with a New York license plate. We called in the plate and found out it was registered to our perp. Walking up your drive we spied your keys laying in the driveway. We knew it couldn't be good. Good thing the side door was open so we could sneak in without any noise. Once we knew he had no weapon on you, we could make our move. I'm just sorry it wasn't any sooner for you, but we needed to be sure."

Dolores's hand reached up to her stinging cheek. "I'm just so thankful you came at all, George. You are an answer to prayer. I need to call Molly." Dolores stood to get her phone in the kitchen, however, she felt a little woozy when she began to walk. "Oh dear, I think this was a little too much for me." George helped her return to the chair and offered to get her phone for her. Handing Dolores her phone, he waited until she made her call. "There's no dial tone. I think my cell phone is in my car."

"Mrs. Beaumont, I believe your phone line has been cut. That creep thought of everything. I'll get your cell phone and I'll make sure the phone company comes out. Ma'am, why don't I send one of my deputies out here to help clean up this place? You have a lot of drawers to lift and put back in."

Tears flowed as Molly heard her mom's voice on the other end of her cell phone. "Mom, I'm so sorry I never told you. I never wanted to worry you. I can't believe I never gave it a thought that the address on my license was my old address."

"Molly, I'm just so thankful that you're all right. I was so worried when that man kept asking where you were. He had such evil in his eyes. I knew he was up to no good. I am so thankful the police got here in time. Molly, do you remember George Bradley?"

"Yes. I went to high school with him. You remember that I dated him for a short time. Why?"

"He is now police chief here in Shepherd. He really saved my life, Molly. What a nice young man he turned out to be. He is right here and I believe he would like to say hello to you." Dolores handed her cell phone to George. The last thing Molly wanted was to talk to George Bradley.

"Hello, Molly?"

"Hello, George. I can't thank you enough for coming to the aid of my mom. I was so terrified for her I couldn't think straight."

"She's fine now. I told her I would send a deputy over to clean up the place. I'm just glad we caught the perpetrator—definitely not a nice guy."

"What's going to happen to him?"

"Well for one thing, we'll be extraditing him back to New York so he can stand trial. I'm sure he'll be put away for a very long time. Are you sure you're okay? I saw what the APB said about him."

"Yes, I'm good now, but I have to admit it's been a couple of very rough days. Please don't tell my mom any more than she already knows. She'll be worried even more about me."

"No, I won't. I'm just glad I was here in time. Umm…Molly, it would be great to see you. It's been a long time."

"Yes, it has George. I live in New York now, but I do try and get back home on weekends."

"Perhaps we could have dinner one of those weekends."

"I guess we could. That would be…lovely."

"I'll check with your mom the next time you come up."

"Okay, and thanks again, George." What could she say but acquiesce to his request. After all, he saved her mother's life and she was grateful for that. Just hearing her mom's voice and knowing she would be okay gave her such relief. Her heart was filled with much joy. *But did she really want to re-kindle that old friendship with George?*

George returned the phone to Dolores to say goodbye to her daughter, but before they ended the call Dolores told Molly that her passport had arrived. The silence was deadening on the other end. "Molly, everything will work out. You must trust God to see you through. Look at what God just brought us through? Surely you can trust him to keep you safe on an airplane."

Chapter 18

MOLLY WAS GRATEFUL that Mr. Edwards had a limo waiting for her the following morning. He insisted that he was not taking any chances until he knew for sure Tommy McGee was locked up. She entered the office anxious to put the past week behind her. It was easy to fall back into her old routine, and by the time her boss came in she was ready to serve him his morning coffee. Suddenly her nerves became more than she could handle as she backed away from Mr. Edwards's desk. She backed into the chair; quickly shifting her weight so she would not fall completely backward. She grabbed the arm of the chair, and was able to compose herself. "Sorry, I forgot about the chair. Is there anything else you need, Mr. Edwards?"

"Umm, no I think I'm good. Thank you, Molly." He could not help the smile that claimed his lips. *Man, she was cute when she was flustered. But what on earth caused that?* There was nothing unusual to the morning: his blinds were opened, his papers on his desk, his coffee made and served exactly as he liked it. Douglas sat there for a few minutes in utter bewilderment, surprised at her sudden clumsiness. He watched as she exited the office; *why was she so flustered?*

Molly stepped into her office hyperventilating and totally shaken. *I can't believe it; I absolutely cannot believe this. I'm totally busted. I'm sure Mr. Edwards is wearing the suit I spilled coffee on months ago.* She wondered what happened to the paper she wrote her name and number on. She could only hope the dry cleaners found it and threw it away or…*what if they never found it and it's still in his jacket pocket?* The wheels started to turn as she began to think of a way she could check his jacket pockets. He usually had his jacket off before he sat down for his morning coffee, except this morning he had a meeting with a Mr. Barlow. He would be in shortly and hopefully after the meeting, Mr. Edwards would remove his suit jacket. She would make sure that she would be in the office the moment Mr. Barlow left. But how could she discreetly check each of the pockets with him sitting right there? *Somehow, I have to think of something. I absolutely cannot lose this job. But seeing how kind he had been to me this past week…how could he be so cruel and unforgiving over something as insignificant as bumping into him? Okay, maybe it was more like crashing into him. But how long could he hold that against me?*

When Mr. Barlow walked into her office she directed him to the couch in her office. "Mr. Edwards will be right with you. I know he is expecting you." Molly dialed Mr. Edwards to let him know Mr. Barlow was there. She had memorized all of their business associates and clients but could not place a Mr. Barlow. She thought perhaps he was a new client. Mr. Edwards told her to show him in immediately.

Once Mr. Barlow was seated, Molly offered him coffee or water. He accepted her offer of coffee, and after telling her how he liked it, she was quick to serve it. She asked Mr. Edwards if he would care for another cup of coffee. "Thank you, Miss Beaumont. I think I will have another." Molly took his cup and returned to place it on his desk. Her hands shook so badly that when she set his cup on the desk, the coffee splashed out of the cup. Both men looked at her wryly. Mr. Edwards wondered what her problem was and why she was so frazzled.

"Oh no, I am so sorry, Mr. Edwards. I'll get this cleaned up immediately." Molly just about ran to the counter for some paper toweling and had the spill cleaned up quickly. She immediately exited, but not before walking into the planter before finding the door. She collapsed into her chair feeling like her whole world was about to collapse. *I don't know what has gotten into me. It's that suit. I know he is soon to discover who I am. Now I have removed any doubt from his mind that I am the clumsy girl that walked into him, spilling his coffee all down his beautiful custom-tailored suit.*

Molly walked out leaving the two men staring at the door. This was so unlike her and it puzzled Doug as to what could be troubling her. He didn't have time to dwell on it with the detective sitting right in front of him.

"Detective Barlow, I want to thank you for keeping your visit discreet."

"Not a problem. I take it that's... Molly Beaumont...our victim and star witness?" Doug read the obvious expression on the detective's face. Molly was not some flake or a clumsy twit. She was extremely intelligent, controlled, organized—shoot she was everything in one complete package. He couldn't imagine why the overwhelming protectiveness of her and the strong urge to plant a fist in this guy's face, but it was there just the same.

"Yes, one and the same, and I have no idea why she is so shaken and frazzled. This is a side of her I have never seen. Are you sure she has no idea who you are?"

"I'm sure. I only introduced myself as Mr. Barlow. So, do you think she will testify when Tommy McGee is up for trial? If not, we have a big problem."

"How so? And by the way, why isn't Sergeant Malone with you? I thought he was the lead detective in this?"

"Um, yeah, he was the lead detective. That's one of the problems." He emphasized was.

"What do you mean was and what's the problem?" Doug's stomach twisted hoping there was no way this Tommy McGee could get off. What would that do to Molly if that happened to be a possibility? It sickened him to even think of it.

"You know about the girl they found dead in Jersey?" Doug nodded. "Well Malone was the one that discovered the body a few months back. All of this re-kindled much of the anger and grief he went through then. He asked for a personal leave for a couple of months. In fact, they put him on paid leave, but not for that reason."

"How is that? Why would the department put him on paid leave if he requested a personal leave due to extenuating circumstances?"

"That's one of the reasons for my visit. You, and Jason Edwards—I understand he's your brother?" Again, Doug nodded. "I understand the two of you entered the house with the officers."

"Yes, we did. They had a search warrant and we followed them in."

"You can't do that."

"What do you mean we couldn't do that? I'm the one that found Mol…Miss Beaumont. The two officers were ready to leave the house believing she wasn't there. They never bothered to check the two doors in the kitchen. I hate to think what would have happened to her had we not found her. A sight I will never be able to forget. And now you're telling me we should not have been there? Incredulous." Doug felt his anger surfacing. "I can't believe this. And who even knew we had followed them in?"

"I guess neighbors were watching and they spoke to Mrs. McGee. She was all mad for the breaking and entering."

"She was mad? When her son had a woman tied up and locked in the basement? I can't believe you're telling me this."

"I'm sure we can get this charge dismissed. I don't think they'll throw the case out for it, but we have another problem."

"I'm sure you do." Doug could not keep the cynical tone from his voice. "What's the other problem? We sat in her broken-down lawn chair on the back porch?"

"Look, I'm only the messenger here. I understand your frustration. Believe me, we are all frustrated. There's nothing we want more than to put this guy away for good, but somehow, he has one of the best defense attorneys around. He's defended a lot of big drug dealers, and I'm sure that's how he got him. Somebody's paying the bill for McGee."

Doug ran his fingers through his hair and rubbed his face in frustration. "Okay, what's this other problem you have?"

"You're not going to like this one at all. When he was taken down at Mrs. Beaumont's house in Shepherd, the chief of police and another deputy seemed to think it wasn't enough to just slap the cuffs on him. No, the police chief picked him up by the collar and punched him in the gut and then planted his fist in his face. So, the kids claiming police brutality."

"You have got to be kidding me. A police chief should have known better than that when taking a criminal down. What reason did he give for that?" Doug's stomach twisted as he thought of what all of this was going to do for the case.

"I guess the chief knows the family. Went to high school with Beaumont and took his anger out on the perp. Sounds like she must have dated him a few times."

Doug certainly didn't like the sound of that. He wondered if this police chief was a former or even current boyfriend of hers. That thought left him cold. "Okay, but what about the DNA matching the other rape victims…and the DNA on the dead girl? Isn't that enough evidence?" Doug was getting more frustrated by the minute.

"We're hoping, but right now we need one of the rape victims to come forward and identify McGee, and from our understanding, they're scared to death. We think the gang has already reached them. And as far as the dead girl…McGee has an ironclad alibi."

"I thought positive DNA was enough to put someone away."

"It should, but a crooked lawyer and a lot of money can get just about anyone off. Even if he's sent away, it probably won't be long enough."

Doug hated to hear that bit of news. *What would this do to Molly?* It sickened him to even think about it. "Tell me what I can do to help? This guy has to be put away…and for a long time."

"I totally agree. We will have to call Miss Beaumont in and explain all of this to her. The defense attorney will do all he can to rip her testimony apart. We have a strong enough case, but it has to be foolproof. We must have a united front on this and we all need to be in agreement how everything went down."

"If McGee thinks he has a good attorney, believe me, I'll get one better. Money is no object and I want Mol…my assistant to have the best."

"Since you and your brother found her, would you be willing to take the stand as well?"

"You bet I'll take the stand, and I know Jason won't have a problem with it either."

"Now if her mother would testify that McGee was resisting arrest, we can get police brutality dismissed." Detective Barlow stood and shook Doug's hand. "Mr. Edwards, it was a pleasure meeting you. I will keep in touch and together we can come up with a time to meet with Miss Beaumont."

"That sounds good. I have a meeting in Europe next week and my assistant always travels with me. I'm hoping that getting her away for a few days will take her mind off of the recent trauma she experienced. Believe me when I tell you it is not at all like her to be this nervous—and well…ditzy. I think it may be the effects from the concussion she received from the blow to her head last week." Doug couldn't keep the smile off his face as he thought about her clumsiness all morning. Something warmed in his heart as he thought about her smile and her huge beautiful aqua eyes. Barlow held his hand out again shaking Doug from his reverie. Doug shook his hand once again as he opened his door. "Thanks again for coming in, Mr. Barlow."

Barlow nodded to Molly as he exited her office. All she could think of was how she could check Doug's suit pockets. She was up immediately and followed Doug into his office. She was so close that when he quickly turned, he almost bumped into her. He reached out and grabbed her shoulders. "Molly is there anything I can do for you?"

"Oh. Sorry. No. I just wanted to see if there was anything you needed me to do for you… right now." She continued to follow Doug into his office.

"Thanks Molly. I'm good for now. Oh, wait, I do have something to discuss with you, please sit down."

Molly was sure that this was it. *I just know he found that slip of paper. I'm going to be fired. Why did I even give him my name and number? And why hasn't he taken that jacket off?* So much was fogging her thinking; she only hoped he would quickly get it over with. Doug could not help but notice her nervousness as she took a seat—wringing her hands and nibbling her lower lip was really not that unusual. He noticed she bit her lip quite often when she was nervous. *But why, what had her this uncomfortable? Was it him? What did I say? What did I do?* "Molly—Miss Beaumont, are you okay?"

"Yes, I'm fine. Would you like me to hang up your suit jacket, Mr. Edwards?"

"No. I'll hang it over my chair in a minute. Thank you. Molly, do you know the status of your passport?"

"Umm, yes I do. My mother told me it arrived, and I thought I would take a drive up there this weekend. I'm anxious to see my mom anyway."

"That's good. We will be leaving for London next week. I'll need you to confirm my meetings with Schuster and Jewels."

"Yes, sir. I'll confirm your meetings."

"We'll take the corporate jet. However, you'll still need your passport."

"I understand, Mr. Edwards." Now she was more fidgety than ever. Doug thought for sure she would bite her lip clear off if she didn't stop. He stood to remove his suit jacket. Molly was up in a flash and practically tripped over the desk as she came around to take his jacket from him. "Allow me, Mr. Edwards." She quickly took his jacket from him and began placing it over his chair. She stood behind him as she slid her hand down to the pocket. First the right pocket, nothing there. Then she started to slide her hand down toward the left pocket. She never made it to the left pocket as Mr. Edwards quickly turned his chair. Her hands were beyond sweaty as she looked straight into his eyes. "Umm, I'm just wiping some crumbs off the lapel of your jacket. My goodness, I have no idea what you had for breakfast this morning but you have a lot of crumbs on your jacket." Molly continued with the motion of wiping off his jacket.

"Really. I had nothing for breakfast this morning." He grabbed her two hands in his. Molly, what is going on with you this morning?"

"I think it must be from the concussion, Mr. Edwards. I have not been myself lately. I think I'm a little paranoid. I get the feeling my attackers are going to show up at any time and it's made me a little… rattled." Molly felt bad for lying, but what could she say? *Oh, no problem. I'm checking your jacket to see if the paper I gave you with my name and number is still in a pocket…mind if I check the left pocket so you can fire me? Oh, and in case you don't remember, I just happen to be the woman that spilled Starbucks coffee all down the front of you.*

"Molly, I'm so sorry. I never gave that a thought. You have to know those guys are not going to hurt you again. You're the last person they would want to see. Now take care of the meetings for me and I'll show you how to make the flight arrangements for us." He gave her a wink and she was sure her toes curled.

Molly left his office. His little talk and wink did nothing to dispel her anxiousness, not only for her job, but flying to Europe. *I really can't wait.*

It was Friday and Molly thought she would get some work done at Help You Stand. Doug had asked that she not go but she had a lot of catching up to do. She was pleased to see Kevin in the office and it was obvious that he was more than pleased to see her. He stood immediately upon her entrance, and raced over to take her arm. "Molly, are you feeling up to working tonight? I certainly didn't expect to see you."

"I'm perfectly fine, Kevin. I know Mr. Edwards did not want me to come in all week but I do have a lot to do. I had planned on leaving for Connecticut in the morning anyway. I should only be here a couple of hours."

"Well then, I shall stay as long as you do." Kevin cleared his throat. He did not want Molly to think they would be alone in the building for the night. "Mary and Harold are still here as well."

They began to walk towards the office when suddenly the entrance door opened. Molly and Kevin exchanged looks as Kevin quickly spoke up, "I can't imagine who would be coming in this late."

They both heard the uncontrollable sobs and the moment they turned to look, a body crumbled to the floor. Molly gasped and her hand quickly covered her mouth lest she scream. Together they ran to the form that was now lying lifeless on the floor. Kevin knelt beside her and rolled her over. Molly cautiously lowered herself to the floor kneeling beside Kevin. The young woman that lay there had been beaten quite badly. It was more than Molly could bear to look at. "Oh Kevin, the poor thing. She definitely needs a doctor. Should I call 9-1-1?"

The woman opened her one eye and shook her head. "Fhlees, no rucshtor, no 9-1-1, fhlees."

"Well, at least she's conscious, and she definitely does not want a doctor, but Kevin, she is in bad shape. Perhaps we can try to care for her ourselves. At least find out who she is."

Harold and Mary came running when they heard the commotion. Mary stepped in immediately. "Kevin, we have an extra bed in the dorm. Why don't we get her cleaned up? If she has no other injuries maybe we can keep her here tonight."

Harold seemed to know exactly what to do when he saw the condition the young woman was in. He came in quickly with a pan of warm water, some soap, antiseptic, and even bandages. Molly was totally impressed as she looked at him with her mouth agape. "Molly, I was a medic in Iraq for two tours. I'll do my best to clean her up. We need to make sure she has no other injuries…no broken bones or even internal bleeding. Looks like some guy beat her up pretty bad."

They moved the woman to a cot that was in the back of a storage room before taking her to the dorm. She winced and moaned as Harold began to clean her wounds. He was so gentle. Molly could see him working on the battlefield. She wondered if that was how he became homeless when he returned from combat and suffered with PTSD. After he had cleaned her up and applied antiseptic to some nasty cuts, he began to check for any broken bones. Mary brought him an ice pack for her swollen eye which he gently placed on her face. Kevin had pulled up a couple of chairs for him and Molly so they could talk to her when she was ready to talk. After what looked like a thorough examination, Harold spoke up. "I can't feel any broken bones but I can't say for sure if she has any internal bleeding. It looks like she may have been punched in the stomach but for now it doesn't seem too severe. Miss, are you able to talk to us and tell us what happened? Do you have any stomach pain?" The woman shook her head and mumbled. "No."

Kevin began questioning her; asking for her name and where she lived. "Bef, my name's Bef."

"And where do you live Beth? Are you from around here?"

"No. Tommy shed I could lib with him. He shed he would take good care of me." The tears began to flow as she lay trembling on the cot.

Hearing the name Tommy caused Molly to shutter and freeze right where she sat. "Beth, does Tommy have a last name?' Molly waited with baited breath for Tommy's last name.

"It's McGee, I think."

The panic in Molly's eyes was unavoidable. Kevin reached over and held her hand. Molly began to rock back and forth unable to control the shaking and fear that washed over her. The only words she could get out were, "please call Mr. Edwards." He was her lifeline.

Kevin took out his cell phone and pressed the number for his cousin. When Doug answered, Kevin told him what had taken place and the young woman that obviously had been beaten up by Tommy McGee. "Doug what do you want us to do?"

Doug did not have to even think about it. "I'm on my way. I'll call Barlow when I'm in the car. Doug didn't even realize how much he was trembling until he tried to call Barlow. "Barlow, this is Doug Edwards. What in the world is going on with McGee?! How can that scumbag be out?! Yeah, he's out and torturing women."

"Take it easy Edwards. I'll find out and call you right back."

Doug hung up but his blood was boiling. *What kind of a judicial system do we have anyway? The guys a murderer and they let him out? Unbelievable.* He put his phone to hands-free and almost immediately his cell buzzed. "Yeah, this is Edwards."

"McGee has an electronic ankle bracelet and is under house arrest; he's confined to his house. He can't go anywhere."

"How did he get out of jail anyway?"

"Some high-powered drug attorney paid the bail for him."

"Unbelievable. I'll talk to you later."

"Where are you? Tell me what's going on man."

"I'm losing my connection—talk to you later." For some reason, Doug was not feeling comfortable with Barlow. *Call it intuition but something doesn't feel right.*

Doug pulled up in front of Help You Stand and then thought he had better park in the lot so he did not look so conspicuous. He jumped out of his car and bolted for the front door. It was locked. *Good thinking on their part.* He began to bang on the door and ring the bell. Kevin quickly opened the door for him. Doug rushed past Kevin asking where Molly was.

"She's sitting in the storage room in the back. She's pretty shaken up, Doug."

"I can imagine. You think your tormentor is going to be put away for a long time and then you find out he's still in his house? That would have me pretty shaken up too!" He saw Molly rocking back and forth in her chair. He ran to her and kneeled in front of her. "Molly, trust me. He has no hold on you. I am going to make sure he is locked up for good. Everything will be okay." He grabbed her shoulders and forced her to look directly into his eyes. "Did you hear what I said, Molly? Everything will be okay. You have to trust me." She nodded and reached for his hand. He only hoped that he was convinced himself.

"Thank you for coming, Mr. Edwards. I don't know what came over me, but hearing McGee is not in jail was too much to bear. How did he even get out?"

"Some high-powered attorney bailed him out and they have him on house arrest. He's wearing an ankle bracelet and is confined to his house." He tried to make it sound like there was no way the guy could go anywhere but Doug knew better. Guys like him cut the ankle and walked free. He was not about to tell Molly that.

Doug, for the first time, noticed the beat-up girl on the cot. Her face looked pretty bad. Her one eye was open and she was staring at him. Her eyes were questioning what was going on. Surely, she was wondering if Doug was a cop. She looked fearful that maybe he was. "Hi, this is my building so I thought I better get over here and see what the problem is." The girl nodded but did not say anything. Doug did not want to give her any more information than that. He looked at the others and they seemed to get the message. Doug motioned for Kevin to step out into the hall with him. "Kev, do you know her name or what happened to her?"

"Her name is Beth. We think she's a runaway. As you can tell, it's a little difficult understanding her but we have been able to piece things together. She said she met Carlos on the street and he told her she could live with them. Said his mother is gone all the time anyway, and his brother is a really nice guy. She fell for it. It sounds like she's lived there for only a few days and look where that got her. She said that neither Carlos, nor their mother, was home. If you ask me, he made sure no one was home so he could do what he wanted to her. Of course, the kid could have been at school and the mother at work. I wonder about the other two days though."

"We'll have to tell the cops, but right now I have a funny feeling about Lieutenant Barlow. If I could only get a hold of Sgt. Malone. He was the first detective on the case. I feel like I could trust him a whole lot more than this other guy."

"You said he's under house arrest? I don't understand our judicial system at all. The guy's as guilty as sin."

"Barlow said it's all circumstantial. Can you believe it? I told Molly there is no way McGee could ever leave his house, but we both know that never stops a criminal that wants to get away, especially a rapist and murderer. As far as we know, he doesn't know where Molly lives, only that she must live somewhere in the neighborhood. I think I'll hire my own surveillance for her. The question is…do I tell her, or don't I?"

"I know what you mean. Hey, aren't you going to London next week?"

"Yes, Wednesday or Thursday."

"Good. That will get her away for a couple of days. Let's get back in there or she'll think something's up. You can keep Beth here until she has recovered…then contact the police and her family."

"You know Molly's driving to Connecticut to visit her mom tomorrow. That's a long trip for her to take by herself."

"Yeah, I'll hire someone to follow her up there."

Chapter 19

THE PREVIOUS NIGHT was difficult, but once Mr. Edwards showed up her fears abated. It was much safer to drive up Saturday morning instead of Friday night, and Molly was so happy to see her mom. The tears were bound to flow as they held each other close. Molly buried her head on her mother's shoulder. She never realized how tight she held onto her mom until her mother gave a little moan. "Sweetheart, you're crushing me."

"Sorry Mom. I was just so afraid I was going to lose you and it would have all been my fault. I can't believe I never gave my driver's license a thought. Mr. Edwards made sure I went to the DMV and had it changed."

"I'm so thankful that you're doing okay. Let's not dwell on that dreadful day. God has seen us both through a horrible experience and we can only be grateful for his protection and grace. Now, what would you like to do this weekend?"

The previous night had only heightened her awareness of how dangerous the situation continued to be, and she struggled with the decision to tell her mom about it. Driving up she had convinced herself it was best not to say anything. She would have to do all she could not to show her fear or concern. As much as she wanted to remain in her mom's house and not go anywhere, without a doubt her mom would suspect something. "Of course, we have to visit Dad. I also came to help clean up the mess that was left but it looks like you have everything under control."

"I do. That wonderful police chief that we have, George Bradley, sent a couple of deputies over to help me. He asked to see you when you come for a visit. I thought perhaps he could come over for dinner tonight."

"Tonight? Mom, you didn't. Did you invite him for dinner... tonight?" The tension did not waste any time gripping Molly's heart. *George is in the past, and I have let go of any feelings I once had for him. Lord, he certainly did not know you then and I'm sure he hasn't changed in that department.*

"Why yes, I did, and he was so pleased I invited him. He will be here at six o'clock, dear."

"Well then, why don't we go visit Dad and then go out for some lunch. And before I forget, you can give me my passport...now."

Dolores couldn't imagine the sudden iciness in her daughter. This was certainly not like her. Molly was always so warm and caring. She pulled out a drawer in the kitchen desk and handed Molly her passport. "I don't think it's something I would have neglected to give you, but then you never know."

Molly took it but not before realizing how abrupt she had been with her mom. "I'm sorry, Mom. I didn't intend to sound so snarky. I guess it's all the tension I've been under. And now having to fly to London next week has me on edge. You know this will be my first flight since the accident."

"Yes dear, I know. I also know that the God who has been so faithful to us in the past is the same God today. He is faithful and good and he cannot deny Himself. He will never change, and you must believe that."

"I know that Mom. It's just so much easier to say it than live it. But I'll be okay. Why with you and Mrs. Brackenburg praying, I know I'll make it. Now let's go see my daddy."

Dennis Beaumont was sitting in the dayroom. His hair was trimmed, his face shaved, and best of all, he had that sparkle in his eyes that Molly loved so much. Without a doubt, her dad would recognize her. "How are my two favorite girls today?"

"Oh Daddy, we're fine. It's so good to see you sitting up today." Molly leaned in and gave her dad a kiss on the cheek. Her mom followed giving him more than a peck on the cheek, but a tender kiss on her husband's beautiful lips. She ran her fingers through his thick head of hair. Their time together was sweet and lasted much longer than either of them could have hoped for. However, when the sparkle left his eyes, he was back in his own world not knowing who they were or if they stayed for their visit or left. It didn't matter to him. Molly knew that times like this would become less frequent as time went on. And finally, he would not know them at all. She would not allow herself to dwell on that thought, but would cherish each moment she had with her dad.

Mother and daughter had such a wonderful time together at lunch that Molly forgot that in just a few hours George would be over for dinner. Her stomach clenched at the thought of seeing George again. *Why did my mom have to invite him now? I don't know if I'm up for this tonight.* Molly had dated George several times in high school. She was a sophomore and he a senior. It seemed so long ago and yet like yesterday. Why, it had to be almost ten years since she had seen him last. Just thinking of George stirred all kinds of feelings that she once had for him. However, she was confident those same feelings no longer had a hold on her. She recalled the last words he said to her: "Molly, I know I love you and I always will." The words stung as she thought of them. *What is wrong with me? It's over, totally over. I can't be with someone who does not share my faith.* She wished she could tell her mom but it was too painful, and there was no way she would relive the past. She would do her best to be pleasant and treat George as an old friend. That's all he could be.

Molly kept busy in the kitchen helping her mom prepare dinner. It also helped to keep her mind off the evening to come. She wondered why her mom made such fanfare over the evening. The roast was out of the oven and Molly offered to mash the potatoes while her mom made the gravy. The dining room table was set with her mom's finest china. All the fuss was almost too much for Molly, and she hoped George would not get the wrong idea. The doorbell rang at five fifty-five and Molly stiffened.

"Please get the door, Molly. I need to finish up in here." *Mom how can you do this to me?* With legs trembling, and hands sweaty, Molly went to the door to greet George.

Oh my, ten years had made a big difference in how George looked. He wasn't the shy lanky kid with the most beautiful brown eyes. His eyes were the same, only a deeper, chocolate brown. He was tall and very well built with bulging biceps. "Hello George. How are you? It's been a long time, hasn't it?"

George took one look at Molly and forgot about the flowers he was holding in his hand. She was more beautiful than he remembered with curves in all the right places. "Wow, Molly, you look great. It has been a long time…too long. I brought some flowers. For your mom."

"She will be thrilled. Thank you. Come in. My mom is finishing up in the kitchen." *And where in the world is she? She should be out here greeting George, not me. She invited him.*

George wanted to put his arms around her and hold her close. He had a feeling that would not be welcomed. It was going to be a long night, and keeping his hands off of her was not going to be easy…it never was.

Their dinner was delicious—the conversation was beyond strained. Dolores kept a watchful eye on Molly and their guest. It was easy talking about Mr. Beaumont and his health, but as soon as the subject changed to Molly or George, she noticed her daughter stiffened. "Molly, you do remember George, don't you?" Her mother asked.

When Molly looked up to respond to her mom's question, George's eyes were fixed on her. He never took his eyes off her while he was eating, and Molly sat with hooded eyes the entire meal. "Yes, of course I remember George." How could she not remember him? Her mind was taken back to her sophomore year when she first met George. She was a cheerleader and he the varsity quarterback and team captain. All her friends told her they were the perfect couple. It started out as innocent dating, but before long their relationship started to intensify. She remembered well the night they left a football party to go look at the stars. George conveniently had blankets that he laid out in the bed of his truck. It was the most romantic evening as they lay together under the stars. It wasn't long before George wanted more than a cozy night in the back of his pickup truck. His hands started to get way too familiar with her, and Molly's body froze. "I'm not ready for this, George. Let's stop before it goes too far." George was quick to stop and did show some restraint but not before telling her he was not about to wait much longer.

"Molly, dear, did you hear anything that I said?"

Her mom's question shook her out of her reverie. "Oh sorry, Mother. I was thinking of work and my trip to London next week." Another lie but what could she say? *I was thinking about George and how close I came to making the biggest mistake of my life?* "What did you say, Mom?"

"I was saying how wonderful it was to have George here to rescue me that horrible day."

"Yes, George, I am grateful that you were here to catch that evil man. I shudder every time I think of what could have happened. We know without a doubt God was protecting Mom."

There she goes again with her God malarkey, giving him all the credit. I'm the one that made the arrest, not God. "I don't mind telling you I was scared stiff when the call came in and I heard it was your mom." His eyes bore into Molly and she could feel the heat rise from her chest, up her neck, and settle in her face. *I'm so enjoying watching her. I bet she's remembering everything I'm remembering. We were really good together.* George licked his lips and winked at her. Molly gave him a disgusted look and turned away.

Her mind drifted back ten years remembering a most amazing week. After her Saturday in the back of George's pickup truck, she left that Sunday for a week of high school church camp. Since she was a little girl, she always thought she was a Christian. She went to Sunday school and church, but that week she realized she never truly committed her life to God. She went forward at the bonfire one night making the life changing decision to follow Jesus. She had never regretted that decision. Remembering this gave her a new resolve to not be afraid of sitting here with George. He had no hold on her anymore. The past was exactly that…the past. His tempting looks and what he used to do to her meant nothing now.

"You say you're going to London? Who do you work for anyway?" George looked at Molly expecting her to answer. She was not about to tell him where she worked, however, before she could give him a nondescript answer her mother answered for her.

"Molly works for Edwards and Sons in New York. She has a wonderful job as assistant to the President."

Molly gave her mom a very disconcerting look but Dolores was oblivious to it.

"So, when are you going to London? And you're actually going to fly?" George's remark was filled with cynicism. He knew about the plane accident and Molly's horrific fear of flying. "You must have gotten over all your...fears."

She picked up on the double entendre. *Why was he sounding so nasty?* No doubt he was still angry with her for breaking up with him, but that was so long ago. *How could he possibly have so much disdain for me now?* Keeping her composure Molly answered before her mother said something. "Yes, I should be fine. We will be taking the corporate jet; that way our time is more flexible." She knew what he was implying by the plural fears. *Did he actually think she ended their relationship because she was afraid of him, or afraid of yielding to his demands?*

"Molly, I didn't know you would be flying in a private jet. How wonderful! They have certainly been treating Molly well—" Dolores was talking to George her excitement obvious.

"Mother, there are some things that we need not discuss right now." There was no way she wanted anything more disclosed to George, and Molly was certain her mother would freely tell him about her boss— even what her salary was. Dolores got the message when she heard the sternness in her daughter's voice.

George noticed the threat in Molly's voice and remembered what a spit-fire she could be when she was ticked. He had dated a lot of women, but right now, she was the one he always wanted. *Why she had to break up with me because of a God thing, I'll never understand. Maybe if I schmoozed her mother enough... she would put in a good word for me. Then Molly would once again be in my arms. I need to play my cards right.* "Dinner was wonderful Mrs. Beaumont. I better think about heading home. Molly, it was good seeing you again. I hope you have a safe trip to London and great success in your job."

Both women stood as George got up from the table. Molly was relieved that he did not want to sit on the couch in the living room— the less time spent with him the better. *But why the sudden change in his behavior?* "Thank you again for saving my mother, George." It was very difficult for her to say it was good seeing him too. That would be a lie.

Her mother was way more generous in her reply as she reached up to give George a kiss on the cheek. "Thank you again, George. And please don't stay away. You can stop by anytime."

"Thank you, Mrs. Beaumont, that's very kind of you." *Just what he was hoping she would say. And stop by he would.*

Chapter 20

B Y MONDAY MORNING Molly was her normal, well-controlled self. Molly greeted Douglas as he entered his office. Mr. Edwards was thankful to see her back to normal—he couldn't help but wonder what had gotten into her last Friday. The blinds were open, the papers perfect, and the coffee smelled good. And also, Molly. Doug never missed the opportunity to draw in a deep breath when he walked into his office. Whatever perfume she wore, she smelled heavenly.

"How was your weekend, Molly?" On his way to the office, Doug had spoken to one of the private security men he had hired to follow her. He already knew Molly had a safe trip, however, she didn't know that he had full knowledge that Chief George Bradley happened to be present at her mom's house for dinner Saturday night.

"It was very nice. I spent the weekend with my mom."

It was obvious she was not about to disclose anything, and Doug felt it best to not ask what she did on the weekend. *Would she tell him anything about the weekend? …Probably not.*

Doug was discouraged in his efforts to reach Sergeant Malone, the lead detective on the scene, and until he did, he would have to go along with Barlow. He could not explain how wary he had become of this detective but something niggled at his core. Barlow's rank was Lieutenant so he outranked Malone. Lieutenant Steven Barlow had contacted him on Saturday and they discussed a time that would be good for everyone to meet. He stressed the importance of meeting prior to their London trip. The sooner he could get everyone to meet the better it would be. He wanted the events to be fresh in everyone's mind, so he said. Doug agreed to have Barlow come in Monday morning and he hoped they could set up a time for Mrs. Beaumont and Chief Bradley to also attend. Doug offered the conference room, expressing the fact that it would be less threatening than the precinct. Their London flight was scheduled for Wednesday, and Doug hoped that making it a morning flight would not be too much for Molly. If her mom and the Chief could come in Tuesday morning or afternoon everything would work out fine. Detective Barlow said he would contact the Chief in Shepherd and perhaps he and Mrs. Beaumont would be able to drive down together. It all sounded fine but Doug wondered what Molly's reaction would be to having the Chief there. *I guess I'll soon find out.* Lieutenant Barlow would be in shortly and Doug wanted to soften the meeting they would have with him. "Molly, would you mind having a seat. I need to discuss something with you. First off, do you have your passport?"

"Yes, I got it from my mom this weekend. I confirmed your meetings with Mr. Schuster and Mr. Jewels for Thursday and Friday."

"Thank you, Molly. About that, I think we will be leaving sometime Wednesday morning. We'll be able to sleep on the plane going over."

"All right." *If you think I'll get any sleep on a plane, think again.*

"Molly, there is something else I need to talk to you about. Do you recall a Mr. Barlow that I met with last Friday?"

"Yes, and I know he has another appointment with you in an hour."

"That's right, and I have to be perfectly honest with you Molly. He is actually the lead detective on your case now."

Molly's eyes went larger than Doug thought possible—the look of betrayal and fear evident. He felt responsible for the anguish it was causing her. He should have told her right away. He thought he was protecting her; this was the last thing he wanted to do to her. "What exactly does that mean? I know Tommy McGee was arrested and is under house arrest. I don't understand at all."

"That's correct. He was picked up and extradited to New York from Connecticut, and he is under house arrest," his voice hesitating, — "it's become kind of complicated."

"What do you mean by, kind of complicated?" Douglas could not help but notice her nibbling on her bottom lip and wringing her hands. Something she most definitely did when she was nervous. "And what happened to Sergeant Malone? I thought he was the lead detective?" Molly had felt very comfortable with Sgt. Malone. He was extremely kind when he interviewed her after the horrible incident she experienced. She loved the compassion he expressed when she disclosed some of the most intimate answers to his questions. He was a big comfort to her in the ER.

"You don't know this, but Tommy McGee's DNA matches two rape victims and…it was found on the body of a young girl they found dead in Jersey."

Molly's face went ashen and she began to tremble. Doug could see that she was doing all she could to hold herself together but her watery eyes were beginning to crest. *I won't cry in front of my boss, I just won't…I can't.*

"Sergeant Malone was the officer that found the girl's body. This ignited a ton of emotions and Malone asked for a leave of absence."

"Oh, I can understand that. I can't imagine how difficult that had to be for him. But I still don't see the problem—all the more reason for that evil man to be locked up." A little of her composure was beginning to return. "And the two rape victims, they will certainly testify. Won't they?"

"Well, that's what Lieutenant Barlow came and talked to me about. The two women won't testify. It seems that McGee got himself one of the best attorneys; a high-powered attorney that the drug gangs have used. Barlow seems to think they got to the girls before they could testify.

"Tommy McGee has an ironclad alibi. It'll be up to you to put him away, Molly." It didn't take long for the fidgeting to return. My goodness, Doug thought for sure she would bite off her lower lip. "Molly, if that scumbag has a great lawyer, I'll have one better. However, this isn't the only problem."

"You're telling me there's more?" Her heart was pounding so fast she thought it would explode from her chest.

"You remember how Jason and I found you at his house?" She nodded. "We went in with Malone and his partner. Mrs. McGee is threatening to sue because we went in with the police, even though they had a warrant. Some neighbors were watching and saw us go in with them."

"But it was you who found me…not the police. You said they were ready to leave after they checked the upstairs."

"That's right. And we would do it all again. My attorney is sure that won't be a problem. However, there's another issue that's a little more disturbing."

"What else could there possibly be?" Molly's hands were sweaty and she feared she would hyperventilate.

Doug noticed her stress, but he had to press on. "From what Barlow said, when McGee was at your mom's, the chief, after cuffing McGee, picked him up by the shirt collar and punched him in the face, and in the gut. Molly, he and his attorney are claiming police brutality… especially since he was unarmed."

Molly clasped her hand to her mouth. "Oh, no, what's going to happen? He can't get off! He just can't! I saw the bruise on my mom's face from him hitting her." She now sat motionless. She had to be in some sort of shock.

"I certainly hope that incident was recorded by the police. Lieutenant Barlow is coming in to talk to us about getting our stories straight. He's hoping that George Bradley and your mom will be able to come in and meet with him. We can't believe that a police chief wouldn't have enough sense not to beat up an unarmed perpetrator. It's obvious he was protecting your mom…or you. How close is your relationship with the police chief?" He may be pushing it, and it was none of his business, but for some unexplainable reason he needed to know what kind of a relationship Molly had with this guy. *Would she even be honest with him?*

"Mr. Edwards, there is NO relationship with George Bradley."

Doug was having a difficult time believing her but for now he thought it best to let it go. "Molly, do you mind calling your mom to see if it would be possible for her to come down? I believe Barlow will be contacting the police chief to schedule a time. Would your mom be willing to drive down with him?"

"I'm sure my mother would be more than happy to drive down with George Bradley."

Doug made no mistake of noticing the sting and cynicism in her voice. *There was something off and he would definitely find out what it was...just not now.* "Since we'll be taking off Wednesday, perhaps we can all meet with Lieutenant Barlow sometime tomorrow or Wednesday morning. If it's Wednesday morning, we would have to change our flight to late afternoon. I offered our conference room instead of the police station. I think your mom would feel more at ease here. She'll even have an opportunity to see where her daughter works." Doug wanted to lighten the mood as best he could.

"I'm sure she would like that. Thank you."

It was almost time for Sergeant Barlow's appointment when Jason walked into the office. "Hey Doug, oh sorry, I didn't realize Molly was in here. Hi there, Molly." She nodded her acknowledgement and it was obvious to Jason that Molly was upset over something—he had a pretty good idea what. "Thought I would give you a heads-up. Mom and Dad are stopping by this afternoon."

"Okay thanks. I won't be going anywhere."

As Jason started to walk out the door, the Lieutenant had entered Molly's office. "Doug, Sergeant Barlow is here, do you want me to send him in?"

"Yes, and I would like you to stay as well."

"Not a problem."

Molly composed herself and quickly began serving coffee to each of them. She hoped that if she kept busy doing something she would forget her looming fear of flying.

The meeting with Lieutenant Barlow went well and Molly phoned her mom asking if it was possible for her to drive into New York Tuesday or Wednesday. Chief Bradley had already spoken to her mother and invited her to drive with him into the city. This was both good and bad news as far as Molly was concerned. No doubt George would definitely take that opportunity to sweet talk her mother, convincing her as to what a great guy he was. Dolores could easily be blinded by his smooth talk, but fortunately Molly knew otherwise. She asked her mom if she would be willing to stay in her apartment while she was gone and her mother gleefully accepted the invitation. At least George would only have her mother trapped for one way. With the decision made, they would be arriving Tuesday morning, and for this, Molly was grateful.

So much was spinning in Molly's head when a very handsome couple walked into her office: Mr. and Mrs. Edward Edwards. They were two of the kindest people, and after chatting with them for a brief time, Molly immediately felt a kindred spirit with them. She wasn't sure why. They told Molly how much they appreciated her phone call inviting them to Eleanor's surprise farewell party and how sorry they were to have missed it, however, they did have an opportunity to take Eleanor out for a private farewell dinner.

"Molly, the Rolex watch was magnificent and I'm quite sure neither of my boys thought of it, much less purchased the perfect farewell gift for her." Mrs. Edwards made this comment with the warmest eyes she had ever seen. Before Molly could protest or show any embarrassment, Mrs. Edwards continued. "Now there is no need to be humble about it. I know my boys and I'm sure you had everything to do with planning the entire farewell party."

"Well, I did ask Mr. Edwards if he had thought of a gift. You know he is quite busy and always has a lot on his mind. I'm just pleased it all worked out so well. It was my pleasure to do that for Eleanor."

"Dear, there is no need to make excuses for my son. He allows himself to get buried in his work. Eleanor told us what a dear you are and quite the asset to the company. You know Eleanor has been part of our family for many years and I hope you will be as well."

Molly was a little flustered and taken aback by Mrs. Edwards's kind and heartfelt words. "Thank you. I am so grateful to be working here and I look forward to seeing more of you and Mr. Edwards. I'm sure you would like to visit with your son."

She escorted them to their son's office and showed them in. Molly hoped that in time she would get to know this couple more intimately. She also wondered how this sweet couple could have such an intimidating and infuriating son.

Chapter 21

MOLLY WAS LOOKING forward to seeing her mom, but was not looking forward to seeing George, or the reason for their meeting. They were to arrive at nine-thirty which meant they left Shepherd about six or six-thirty. She had coffee and sweet rolls sent to the conference room per Douglas's suggestion. Jack Thatcher, Douglas's attorney arrived early and the two men had been meeting for the past hour. When Lieutenant Barlow arrived, Doug suggested they go to the conference room. He asked the receptionist to escort Mrs. Beaumont and Chief Bradley to the conference room when they arrived.

It wasn't long before Mrs. Beaumont and Chief Bradley entered the conference room. Molly's eyes lit up upon seeing her mother and she immediately rushed over to give her a big hug. After greeting her mother, Molly extended her hand to George. He not only took her hand but immediately pulled her to himself with every intention of kissing her on the lips. She quickly turned her head leaving George to brush a kiss on her cheek. Noticing this, the two brothers glowered at this assuming man giving him an imposing glare. Molly quickly stepped back, face flushed, but quite composed as she introduced her mother to everyone in the room. Next, she introduced George, only as the Chief of Police of Shepherd, Connecticut.

There was no doubt in Doug's mind that Molly knew George as more than the Chief of Police. *Was she too embarrassed to acknowledge him as a romantic interest? Was this the reason she did not want to kiss him in front of everyone, or was there a past history between them?* Doug determined that on the trip to London he would get an answer. *But what difference should that make to him? It shouldn't make a bit of difference. Was it jealousy he was feeling? He didn't think he had a jealous bone in his body. So why were his blood boiling and his stomach in such a knot?* He immediately asked that everyone be seated.

Doug was grateful Lieutenant Barlow proceeded to take over the meeting. He would have a difficult time when it came to Bradley's excuses for what transpired between him and McGee. His attorney and longtime friend, Jack Thatcher, sat unmoved and took copious notes as events were recalled. Molly was first in recalling her morning on that fateful day, starting with her dropping off Mrs. Brackenburg's fur jacket and necklace. She spoke unwavering and in complete detail about her confrontation with the five young men. However, as she spoke of her time in McGee's basement and his forcefulness, she hesitated to share the pain that once again surfaced. It was like removing a scab that had become quite comfortable until removed. She worked so hard to keep the tears at bay. They all understood. Doug noticed the pain in her mother's eyes as she reached for her daughter's hand. As Molly spoke, Doug remembered how comfortably she fit in his arms as he carried her out of that dank, oily smelling basement. Chief Bradley had a relentless stare the whole time he sat listening to her testimony. Doug was overwhelmed with a protectiveness he could not explain; he wanted to reach over and hold her tight in his arms. She had felt good then and she would feel just as good now. Obviously, it was embarrassing for her to share in detail what transpired that fateful day. He was thankful that nothing worse took place. When it was time for him and Jason to recall their story, they did not hesitate to include that they would take the same action if they had to do it over again. They spoke in detail of what McGee's room looked like and the disgust and fear that gripped them. Lieutenant Barlow interjected the lawsuit filed by Mrs. McGee. Thatcher, who now sat with his hands folded on the table, nodded as he looked to Doug and Jason. "That's the least of our problems. She doesn't have a case. I believe the two officers invited you to enter with them since you had knowledge of Molly's whereabouts."

"Okay", said Doug as he and Jason continued with their account. Doug could feel Chief Bradley's eyes penetrating right through him. *No way was this guy going to get to him. He had no idea what he had said or done to make him this wary.* Doug told them how he and Jason found Molly.

He hated to tell the whole account as he looked into Mrs. Beaumont's tearful eyes. It was certainly evident how close mother and daughter were as he observed their tender love and concern for one another. Mrs. Beaumont reminded him so much of his own mother—only in a simpler way. His parents were wealthy and yet his mother never misused her station in life. For a brief moment, Doug felt a bond with Molly's mom. There was something about her that warmed his heart. He went for the tissue box, quietly placing it on the table in front of her. She thanked him as she reached for a tissue. Collecting the tears in her tissue, she once again grasped Molly's hand in both of hers. Doug sensed that they were all intruding on a very special moment between mother and daughter. Jason had finished their account with the decision to take her to the hospital. Lieutenant Barlow said he had all the statements that were given at the hospital and had copies for Thatcher.

The Lieutenant continued with the more perplexing situation before them. Doug got the feeling that Bradley was aware as to what was coming as he saw him stiffen and appear even more guarded. As Barlow continued, he asked Mrs. Beaumont for her account of the breaking and entering that took place. "Let's start from the beginning when you returned home."

Mrs. Beaumont nodded and in a very controlled voice began her account, starting with her return from the grocery store and her plan to put her groceries away, and then go to the nursing home to visit her husband. It was at this time that Molly reciprocated as she reached for her mom's hand giving her the courage to carry on. She gave a precise account of the events. The anguish was undeniable in her voice as she continued, however, she never sounded confused or questioned anything she told them; her face was flushed as she gave her account of events. She told them how he slapped her hard across the face when she refused to tell him where Molly lived. Now Molly could not keep the tears at bay as she reached for her own tissue.

"Sorry for all the blubbering we seem to be doing." Molly said as she tried desperately to hold back her tears.

"Please don't apologize." Doug was the one that spoke up but all the men agreed...all but the chief. Doug was having a difficult time trying to read this guy. Chief Bradley just stared with his eyes fixated on Molly. He was definitely arrogant and aloof, in a crass sort of way.

Just then, Lieutenant Barlow called on Chief Bradley to give his account of the events that took place on his watch. He was quite thorough until he came to the part where his deputy cuffed Tommy McGee. It was obvious that he intentionally left out the part where he pulled McGee by his shirt collar, punched him in the gut, and then in the jaw. "Are you forgetting something, Bradley?" asked the Sergeant.

"No, I don't think so." But when it dawned on him that the Lieutenant realized exactly what he purposely had left out, he looked stunned. "Oh, you're referring to my actions when we took him down. Yeah, I was a little rough on the perp but he certainly deserved it, and I would do it all over again. Mike and I saw and heard from the kitchen how he was treating Mrs. Beaumont. My anger got the better of me and I couldn't take it. Like I said, I would do it all again. McGee resisted arrest so I punched him and accidentally clipped his jaw."

"I hope you have it in your report how Mrs. Beaumont here was treated. That she was threatened and then slapped across the face. You may not be aware of this but McGee is claiming police brutality." A few choice cuss words spewed from Bradley's mouth. Clutching his head and running his fingers through his wavy golden hair the chief mumbled a barely audible, I can't remember, but yeah, I'm sure it's all in the report.

Attorney, Jack Thatcher, immediately spoke up. "What about your deputy?"

"What about my deputy?" Bradley's sudden tone and demeanor became defensive.

"Is there a possibility your deputy gave a more accurate account in his report?"

It was obvious the words struck a chord as the chief began to turn a crimson red and the veins in his neck bulged. George Bradley had an anger problem and he would not allow the comment to rile him. "Could be. I haven't read his report."

Jack Thatcher didn't waste any time jumping into the conversation. "Do you know if there were any witnesses or friends that saw Mrs. Beaumont immediately after the event?"

Dolores Beaumont spoke up. "My friend Clara came over

immediately after the police left my house. She saw the bruise... and my eye swollen shut."

"Good. We can get a statement from her. Can you think of anyone else?"

George Bradley had calmed down considerably since his sudden display of anger. "I sent a couple of officers over to help put Mrs. Beaumont's house in order. I'm sure they saw how she looked along with the disarray her house was in."

Jack Thatcher continued, "We have to build a convincing case proving Mrs. Beaumont's life was not only threatened but that she was a victim of McGee's physical abuse. We have to prove to the court that McGee was more than deserving of the action Bradley took. And if McGee was resisting arrest there was a definite call for such action to restrain him. I'm determined to do all I can to get this dirt-bag off the street. Mrs. Beaumont, are you certain the chief here punched him before he was handcuffed?"

"Well, it all happened so fast. I did see him try and fight back after he was taken down. And I am quite sure he was not handcuffed." Dolores looked puzzled the more she thought about the incident. "I was so scared there's no telling how the events took place, but I am quite sure he was not handcuffed." Doug and Sergeant Barlow didn't know if Mrs. Beaumont was totally shrewd or really questioning herself. They both hoped it was the former. And yet there was something about Lieutenant Barlow that did not sit well with Doug. He seemed awfully anxious to twist the facts that Chief Bradley punched him after the cuffs were put on him.

Molly spoke up. "What about what he did to me? That alone should put him away."

"Yes, Molly, it should. But you will have to testify and there's no telling how his attorney is going to twist the story to his client's benefit. You will have to be prepared for any kind of character assassination and accusations imaginable. Will you be able to handle this?" Jack Thatcher showed a lot of respect and concern for Molly. For this Doug was grateful.

"I will do whatever I have to do."

Douglas Edwards was impressed with the resolve and strength

this woman had. His jaw tightened when he saw George Bradley reach over and hold her hand, but was relieved to see Molly had immediately withdrawn from his grip. Their relationship was a complete puzzle to him.

After a grueling three hours, Doug offered to have a lunch brought in for everyone. He wanted to be considerate of Mrs. Beaumont and not rush her time with her daughter. Jack Thatcher and Lieutenant Barlow said it was not necessary for them to have lunch as they would be heading out. Barlow nodded to everyone and then left the conference room. Doug asked Jack if he could have a word with him before he took off.

Doug gave a nod to Molly and then met his attorney's eyes, "Just so you know, Jason and I have no problem testifying." Doug wanted his attorney to know how willing they were to defend Miss. Beaumont.

Chapter 22

George Bradley stood with his eyes riveted on Molly as her boss talked to her about leaving for London. He definitely had to control the jealousy that was surfacing. Molly belonged to him…always had and always would as far as he was concerned. Looking at his watch Doug said, "I'll come by and pick you up about ten tomorrow morning, Molly. Will this give you enough time? The plane is scheduled to leave around noon."

Jason could not help but watch Molly's reaction as Doug talked about the flight. Once again, he noticed her fidgeting as she stood wringing her hands together and biting her lip. He wondered if this was something Doug was aware of. He would bet anything that she had a fear of flying.

"Yes, ten o'clock will be fine. I'm almost packed and being gone for just a couple of days I certainly do not have much. Mom, I'm so pleased you will be able to stay in my apartment while I'm gone. Did you bring your suitcase up with you?"

"Yes dear, I did. George was so kind to bring it in when we arrived. I believe it is at the receptionist's desk. Is that where you set it down, George?"

George had to clear his throat before answering. Taking his eyes off of Molly, he nodded and addressed Mrs. Beaumont. "Yes, it's at the desk. I'll be happy to take it down to Molly's car for you. Mrs. Beaumont, perhaps you and Molly would like to join me for some lunch before I head back?"

Not trying to look annoyed, Doug said that would not be necessary as he had planned to have lunch delivered, and Molly immediately agreed. "Thanks for the offer but having lunch here will be just fine." Doug was pleased it was Molly that answered him.

"Suit yourselves." George sat down in one of the conference room chairs looking as if he had no intentions of leaving anytime soon. Doug left the conference room with his attorney and Jason, but not before telling Molly that he would have lunch delivered and would be joining them. She looked relieved to hear that he would not be leaving her alone with her mom and George.

"Mr. Edwards, if you don't mind I'd like to show my mom around the office."

"Go right ahead, Molly. It will be a while before lunch arrives. George, feel free to help yourself to coffee or water. We'll join you in a little while." He gave Molly a wink before leaving, knowing this would get George's attention.

Molly took her mother's arm to give her a quick tour of her office—pleased this would take her mind off of her flying…and George. As they walked down the hall Dolores spoke up, "You never told me what a handsome man Mr. Edwards is. He is extremely good looking, Molly. And his brother is very handsome as well. I can't imagine Mr. Edwards being such a difficult man to work for. He seems quite nice, and I might add, concerned about you."

"Yes, he can be very nice, but he is also insufferable at times."

Mrs. Beaumont was extremely impressed with Molly's office. "Dear, I am so happy for you. I couldn't be more pleased with how well you are doing."

"Thanks Mom. Now if I can just get on that plane tomorrow, without falling completely apart, I'll be okay."

Jack and Doug stood at the elevator giving Doug a chance to tell him how he felt about the Lieutenant. "Something is not right with him, Jack. I just can't seem to put my finger on it though. I only wish I could get a hold of Sergeant Malone. I can't seem to locate him."

"I'll see what I can do, and I won't go through Barlow."

Doug patted Jack on the back thanking him for coming in and for his willingness to follow through in locating Malone. "If you could find something out, before our return from London that would be great."

"Don't worry. I'll see what I can do."

Jack left, and Doug walked down to his office. He needed to call in their lunch order. Usually Molly did this so he had to wing it.

When Jason met up with his brother in his office, he had to tell him what was obvious: "Doug, have you taken notice of Molly's response every time you mention flying?"

"No, not really. Why?"

"She's a nervous wreck whenever you mention your trip to London and the flight. I'll bet money that she's scared stiff of flying."

"Jason, a lot of people have a fear of flying, but once they board the plane and get over the jitters, they're fine. I'm sure she'll do all right once we board. I think she would have said something by now if it was that big of a deal."

"Yeah probably, but if I were you I'd keep a close eye on her, at least until you're in the air."

Doug shrugged his shoulders as if this was not going to be anything for him to be concerned about, but he did promise his brother that he would keep an eye on her. That definitely was not going to be a problem for him.

As Molly walked her mom out of her office, Mr. Edwards approached them. "Mrs. Beaumont, it was very nice meeting you. I wish it had been under better circumstances. I want to thank you for making the trip to the city. I'm sure you are very proud of your daughter; she is quite the asset to our company."

"Why yes, I am extremely proud of her, and I know her father is as well." He could not help but notice her eyes begin to glisten with unshed tears. "I should be the one thanking you. After all, you have been so kind in helping Molly and me in this horrible situation. I can't wait until this is all over. Thanks for inviting me to your office. I am pleased to have met you and your brother as well."

"Lunch should be arriving soon and Jason and I will meet you in the conference room."

Lunch arrived and the five sat quietly around the conference table. Doug had ordered chicken salad on croissants and fruit. This would certainly not be the meal George Bradley had in mind and that brought a smile to Doug's face.

After lunch, George saw that it was obvious that Doug and Jason were not about to let him out of their sight, he thought he might as well head home. "Well, thanks for the lunch. I think I better head out before the traffic builds up." He stood along with the others. Shaking Doug's hand and then Jason's, George leaned down and gave Mrs. Beaumont a kiss on the cheek. Molly reached out her hand to say goodbye but George pulled her to him with all intentions of covering her mouth with his. Once again Molly turned her head allowing him to only brush a kiss on her cheek. "Goodbye George, and thanks so much for driving my mom down."

"You're welcome, Molly. Have a safe flight and I hope to see you when you get back."

It was not without notice that Molly had not replied to George's statement. And this definitely, pleased Doug.

Molly began to clean up the trash from lunch and told her mom she needed to clean up some things in her office. "Mother, we better head home so I can do some last-minute packing. Mr. Edwards, is it okay with you if I leave early?"

"Absolutely, Molly. I will see you in the morning."

As they walked to the reception desk to retrieve Mrs. Beaumont's suitcase, Jason was there and quickly offered to take her suitcase down to the car. Dolores Beaumont was impressed with his kindness.

Chapter 23

Mr. Edwards arrived promptly at ten o'clock in a limo. Molly was waiting for his arrival and was stunned to have Mr. Edwards knock on her apartment door, not the limo driver. He stepped in and warmly greeted her mom and then carried her suitcase and garment bag down to the car. Mr. Edwards was out the door when Mrs. Beaumont hugged her daughter goodbye and told her she would be praying for her. Molly gave her mom an affectionate squeeze and told her she would call when she arrived in London.

The ride to the airport was extremely quiet and Doug did not know if it was because of him sitting beside her or if she was actually nervous about the flight. Every question she answered without hesitation, but then silence until he asked her another. He thought it incredulous to think it was all due to a fear of flying—he could not get his brother's observation and words out of his head.

When they arrived at the airport, they immediately went to the private terminal and VIP lounge. Molly took a seat and sat quietly while Mr. Edwards greeted the crew that was waiting for their arrival. The pilot, Captain Troy Alexander, and copilot, Captain Chip Hunt, greeted Molly. Their flight attendant, Lisa, was already on board getting their meals and supplies secured for the flight. The crew boarded the plane first taking the baggage that Mr. Edwards and Molly brought with them.

As Molly walked onto the tarmac her heart began to sputter and beat rapidly. With each step, it felt as if she were walking through cement about to set, and once it did, she would not be able to move at all. She froze when she got to the stairs...the cement had surely set. *Lord, please give me the strength and courage to walk up these stairs.* The mantra she kept repeating from the time she left her apartment: "I can do this", "I can do this", seemed to fade from her thoughts as she looked up at the plane. Before she took the first stair, she felt a strong hand grab her elbow; it was Mr. Edwards. Her legs trembled. *Oh no, Mr. Edwards will for sure know my fear.* However, his touch brought such warmth and electricity radiating through her entire body that it gave her the courage to walk up the stairs. Molly could not keep herself from looking up into his warm comforting eyes. When she reached the top, and looked into the cabin, the beautiful cream-colored leather chairs began to blur and spin in every direction—then utter blackness.

Thankful he was right beside her, Mr. Edwards caught her before she fell completely to the ground. He scooped her up and once again enjoyed the feel of her in his arms. Too bad it was always at a time when she was vulnerable and in desperate need of his strong arms. Carrying her to his bedroom at the rear of the plane, he lay her down on his bed. Lisa followed immediately behind them asking what she could do. "Lisa, bring us a glass of water, please." She was gone in an instant and when she returned with the water Doug dismissed her not wanting Molly to be any more embarrassed than she would be once she came to.

The moment Molly opened her eyes, humiliation set in as she realized what had happened...but where was she? She was lying on a bed. Was she in a hotel room? Her eyes focused on Mr. Edwards. "Mr. Edwards, where am I? The last thing I remember was standing in the doorway to your plane. Did you take me to a hotel room?" Feeling totally disoriented, and with shaky fingers, Molly rubbed her temples trying desperately to concentrate on where she was and what had happened to her.

"You're on my plane...in my bed. You fainted before we entered the cabin. Molly, are you afraid of flying? If you are, as much as I need you with me, I can have someone drive you home."

"No...please don't do that. I'm sure I'll be fine."

Doug noticed that she never answered his question. Something was drastically wrong with her that she would not admit. Yes, he was irritated and annoyed that this adult woman could have such a fear of flying that she couldn't even talk about it. As she spoke her lips quivered and her hands twisted so much he thought they would fall off. "Please tell me what is wrong then. We'll be up in the air for a very long time and I can't have you passed out on my bed for the entire flight. We're scheduled to take off in about thirty minutes."

Molly sat on the side of the bed. She took a deep breath and began to relate her horrific experience as a thirteen-year-old girl. She trembled beside him as the unforgettable and horrifying experience tumbled from her quivering lips. "My birthday wish was to go to Disneyland, SeaWorld, Universal, and see the Pacific Ocean. I had never flown before so that alone was a special treat. Our plane lost an engine and then crash landed when the wheels never came down. It was terrifying. We had to make an emergency landing at Phoenix Sky Harbor Airport." When she finally looked up at him, her eyes glistened with tears on the verge of spilling over. She felt vulnerable and embarrassed but Mr. Edwards would not allow her to do her job if she did not confess to him the whole truth of her fear. "My father kept hollering, 'Molly, do not look back, keep going with Mom.' Of course, as a thirteen-year-old and thinking I could handle anything, what is the one thing you do when you are told not to? You disobey and you look. The rear chute had deployed and that was how we got off the plane. We had to slide down. My mom made sure I went first and then she followed."

"Why was your father not with you and your mom?"

"My father went to the front of the plane to help as many people get out as possible. When the smoke got too heavy and he and the other men could no longer see, they came down the chute. I was never so happy to see anyone in my life. I clung to my dad with everything I had. I could not, and would not, let him go. For years, the memory has surfaced, and believe me it's been often and especially at night."

"Did you get on another flight and go on to Disneyland?" Doug was hoping that changing the conversation to Disneyland would lighten Molly's spirit.

"Are you kidding? I screamed so much when they tried to board another plane to return home that my dad had to rent a car and we drove home. I never did make it to Disneyland or SeaWorld. I guess the best

149

thing would have been to get right back on a plane but I just couldn't." She whispered, "I haven't been on a plane since."

With Molly sitting so close, the vanilla scent he had become so familiar with assaulted his senses that caused a stirring within that he could not refute. Doug wanted so bad to hold her in his arms and comfort her. However, this would not bode well in their boss/employee relationship but he felt so protective of her—and again he wondered why. Without even thinking, he grabbed both her hands in his, hoping she would look at him. Finally, her beautiful Caribbean blue eyes looked up at him. *I could drown in those eyes.* He thought this more than once in the months she had worked for him. "Molly, I am so sorry this happened to you. I can't imagine what you went through. If you don't think you can make the trip, I'll gladly have someone take you home. I can always Skype our meetings."

Suddenly Molly was more uncomfortable with the closeness of Mr. Edwards. His clean manly smell of musk and the north woods was intoxicating. As he sat beside her, she could not help but notice his broad shoulders and bulging muscles stretching out his white dress shirt. *Oh my, why have I never noticed? Mr. Edwards isn't just handsome—he is extremely handsome and very well built.* Putting the awkwardness aside, Molly spoke up. "Mr. Edwards, I appreciate your offer but I think it's time I really got over this. Mrs. Brackenburg knows of my fear and she, along with my mom, are praying for me. In fact, after Eleanor told me that I would be expected to fly to Europe, I was such a horrible basket case that Mrs. Brackenburg noticed my anxiety and immediately prayed for me. I don't know how you feel about prayer, Mr. Edwards, but when she finished praying, I had such peace. It was the first good night of sleep I had in over thirteen years. I was so confident that I would be okay today, unfortunately, I think I began to once again focus on my fear rather than trusting in a God who gives me the strength and courage to face my fear."

All of this talk of God and trusting him brought a lot of memories to the fore of Doug's mind and heart. *So, Molly is a Christian. This explains her sweet spirit and her gracious heart.* Doug remembered how happy she was to be working at Help You Stand.

The copilot ducked his head in the bedroom and announced that if all was well they had clearance to take off in fifteen minutes. "Sir, you know you will have to take your seats in the cabin when we take off."

"Yes, thank you Captain Hunt. We'll be right up." He looked into Molly's eyes and held her hand as he stood up; taking her elbow he helped her up beside him. "Molly, you understand we have to sit in the seats at takeoff and I might add, also at landing." Molly nodded her head understanding what he was saying.

Lisa stood at the doorway to the bedroom. "Mr. Edwards, I have a couple of Xanax here that may help your assistant relax."

"Thank you, Lisa. Allow me to introduce you to my assistant. Lisa, this is Molly Beaumont. Lisa will be our flight attendant for this trip." The two women nodded in greeting.

"It's very nice meeting you, Lisa. And thank you so much for the meds." With that Molly accepted the medication and the glass of water Doug held out to her.

When they returned to the cabin, Doug, wanting to go over some paperwork, took his seat at a desk on the opposite side Molly sat on. Doug sensed an urgency of having to sit as far from her as possible. As they rolled down the tarmac, try as he might, he could not keep from glancing over at her. He watched her biting her bottom lip, wringing her hands, and her eyes shut tight. She was obviously scared stiff. He knew it was against his better judgment to bridge the gap between them but his legs seemed to move involuntarily as he crossed the isle that separated them. "Molly, would you like me to sit beside you?" She opened her eyes and nodded. Doug sat beside her and immediately reached for her hand. "Why don't you hold on to my hand? Once we are up in the air, you will see how smooth the ride will be. Molly immediately reached for his hand and something thudded inside his chest. Her tiny hand fit so comfortably in his—that was until she began to grip it so tightly that he was sure she was drawing blood from the inside of his palm. *Man, her nails are sharp, beautiful but really sharp.* He looked at her and her eyes were closed so tight that her face was all scrunched up. She looked adorable.

Molly clung to his hand as a lifeline. It wasn't long when her hand began to relax—her breathing became even and shallow. She had fallen asleep. He couldn't keep from staring at her beautiful face. He wondered which he enjoyed looking at more, her beautiful long lashes or her mesmerizing eyes. He had to admit it gave him an opportunity to really notice her beautiful mouth: perfectly shaped lips and a perfectly shaped nose. *Is there anything about her that isn't perfect? Maybe her hips or her feet are too big. No, I would have noticed that. She's just perfect in every way. Well, don't even go there Douglas. What in the world are you thinking? She's your assistant.* Douglas got up and walked to the desk, hoping work would distract him from thoughts of his beautiful assistant. It wasn't long before Lisa swiveled the seat she had taken in front of him. He wondered how Lisa pulled today's flight. Then he remembered that it was Molly that had handled the flight arrangements for their trip. It was her first time doing this and he neglected to tell her he did not want Lisa as the attendant…. ever. It had been a couple of years since he had seen her and now was not a time or place that he wanted her presence. She was trouble with a capital T. *I shouldn't flatter myself so much, I'm sure she has gotten over me and has moved on.* There was a time he thought she was a good distraction after his breakup with Peggy. After one of their flights, he let her talk him into taking her out to dinner. After that one night, she was so bold and possessive—someone he had to run from. She was relentless in calling him, expecting him to take her out. He realized she was nothing but a gold-digger. And run he did. He insisted she was never to fly with him again. Eleanor was aware of this, but there was no way that Molly was expected to know. His pilot and copilot were always on standby but he used a service for their flight attendants. Eleanor always requested Philip; it was obvious Molly had no idea who to request. *Oh well, he would just have to make the best of it.*

"I've missed you terribly, Doug."

Doug felt her gaze boring holes into the top of his head and shoulders as he sat focused on papers. Not even looking up at her he said, "I really doubt that, Lisa. I can't imagine you ever missing anyone. In two years, I'm sure you have kept yourself busy."

"Why didn't you ever return my calls?"

"I didn't return your calls because the last time I spoke to you I told you things would never work out with us. I definitely did not want to be in any kind of a relationship." He wondered if this would be enough to keep her off his back. He contemplated what in fact he was looking for.

His eyes were immediately drawn to the beautiful form that lay asleep across the aisle from him and his heart stirred. Deep down he knew Molly would never be drawn to him. It was obvious she was intimidated by his gruffness, and he could be demanding at times. She kept him at a distance but then so did he keep her at arm's length. He was her boss and she knew his rules. *Dumb rules. If I don't follow them, how can I expect the other men to follow them, especially Jason.*

"I thought our time together was something special."

"I told you not to expect anything more. One dinner in London does not constitute a relationship." He really could not remember anything about her. It was so long ago... and meaningless. "Now do me a favor and find a blanket I can put over Molly." Her eyes glistened as she managed to push a few tears down her cheek. There was no way he would fall for her phony emotions. She hadn't seen him in over two years and he certainly did not need a scene. "Lisa, the blanket?"

"Oh, all right. I suppose she's the new attraction in your life." She said this as she tipped her head towards the sleeping beauty.

"There is no new attraction in my life, and it's none of your business if there were. Now stop with the phony tears."

Lisa stormed off to the rear of the plane grabbing a blanket that was stored in a drawer under the bed. When she returned to the cabin, she opened the blanket to cover Molly but Doug quickly snatched it from her and gently covered her himself. He couldn't help but notice the raised eyebrows Lisa gave him, but he really did not care what she thought. He couldn't say what he was thinking himself. All he knew was that he had such a desire to protect his assistant...at any cost.

Chapter 24

"**H**ONEY, YOU'RE AWFULLY quiet. What's troubling you?" Ed Edwards asked his wife as they sat in front of the fire together. They may have been married for almost forty years but they were just as much in love as the day they met.

Patricia Edwards looked lovingly at her husband. "I'm thinking of Douglas, Ed. He needs a wife. He's thirty-two and he's not getting any younger. And neither are we. I'm so ready to be a grandma, and you will make such an amazing papa."

"Honey, we have talked about this before, and we agreed to stay out of our boy's decisions when it comes to women. They both know how we feel, and how much we have instructed them to marry godly women. If they're not where God wants them to be, how can we expect them to look for a woman that would put God first in her life?"

"I don't think Doug would recognize a lovely woman if she literally plowed right into him on 5th Avenue. Our boys only seem to notice a woman if she's wearing a short skirt and has large boobs."

"Well, honey, I was a young man once myself and before I became a Christian that's what I noticed when I looked at a woman. They're healthy normal men that need to look for other qualities in a woman. And like I said, until God is first in their life, they're just being normal males. All we can do is keep praying for our boys."

"I know your right, love, but as a mom I can't help but long for a few grandchildren and a daughter-in-law that I could go shopping with and plan dinner parties with. I am praying for them and yet sometimes I wonder if God is listening to me."

"Sweetheart, of course he's listening. And what we are praying for is not out of His will for them. God certainly wants to see our sons in a relationship with Him first. And then bless us with loving, godly daughters-in-law. Waiting is hard, but not seeing any answers doesn't mean God isn't working."

"You're right. I need to be focused on a sovereign God who loves our sons even more than we do. I have to trust Him to do abundantly more than what I can even imagine. At least Douglas saw Peggy for what she was."

"That's my girl. I knew talking it out would get us both in agreement with what God wants for our boys. I'm sure that one day they will come around and realize their liberal way of thinking is not the answer."

"Ed, what was your impression of Doug's new assistant?"

"Now Patty, don't go matchmaking. You haven't done it so far and I'm not too sure you should start now."

"I only asked what you thought of his new assistant. I didn't ask if she would make a good wife for one of our boys."

"I think she's a beautiful young lady. I'm surprised she is so young. But from what Eleanor said, she is a very competent and lovely woman."

"I'm very impressed with her as well. I was also beyond surprised to see how young she is. After all, the "rules" that Doug has put in place would not allow for such a young assistant. I wonder what happened there?" There was no mistaking the gleam in his wife's eye. "Perhaps God has orchestrated this whole development after all."

"Now sweetheart, if this is in God's plan for one of our sons, then all we need to do is sit back and watch Him work it out… without your interference." Ed Edwards knew his wife only too well. If anything, she could be very persuasive and persistent.

"Of course, I won't interfere. I do wonder what her plans are for Thanksgiving."

With this comment, Ed Edwards almost choked on the coffee he was drinking. Catching his breath, he put his strong arms around his wife and brought her to himself in a warm embrace. "Patty, I love you so much. But why do I get the feeling your pretty little head has already been working overtime?"

"I love our two sons, and I only want to see them as happy as we have been. God has certainly blessed us, Ed."

"Yes, he definitely has. He has blessed me with you, and I don't know where I would be without you all these years. Now let's head up to bed." Ed Edwards stood and reached for his wife. She lovingly took his hand and immediately he put his arm around her as they headed for the stairs. He stopped and turned off the gas fireplace before they continued their walk up the winding staircase.

The staff had already retired to their quarters for the evening, so they were on their own for the rest of the night. They made sure all the lights were out as well as the fireplace. Their home was a beautiful mansion, but to them and their boys it was simply a home that they were blessed with. Their bedroom suite was massive…the size of many an apartment. The sitting room had an enormous marble fireplace on one wall, floor to ceiling windows with beautiful damask drapes. In front of the fireplace sat a love seat, couch, and mahogany tables. The colors in the sitting room and bedroom were both decorated in light blues and gold. The sitting room boasted of a sixty-inch flat screen television that hung from the wall over the fireplace. Patricia made her way to her bathroom suite to prepare for bed. After her nightly routine of brushing her hair, teeth, and facial creams, she put on her satin nightgown and robe and joined her husband in their sitting room. They sat cuddled on the couch to watch the news before going to bed. This was a nightly ritual Edward enjoyed immensely. Nothing would ever come close to sitting with his adoring wife of almost forty years. Yes, he was a very blessed man.

Chapter 25

THE CABIN LIGHTS were dimmed except for the light above Doug's desk. After what felt like a quick catnap, Doug once again sat and glared at the paperwork he had taken out shortly after their ascent. *Why couldn't he focus?* He knew why. He couldn't keep his eyes off his assistant. There was a rather significant matter that kept gnawing in his gut…what was the relationship Molly and George Bradley had? *Was he a past boyfriend, a current boyfriend, or perhaps a lover? No, I can't imagine sweet Molly ever having a lover. How can I broach the subject? If there's a way I can ask her about him, I will.* On any other overseas flight, he would have been sleeping comfortably in his private bedroom in the rear of the plane. He should have insisted that Molly sleep there but she was totally out in no time after taking Lisa's meds. *She couldn't sleep all the way to Europe, could she?* After ending a phone call, he walked forward to the cockpit; he wanted to know how close they were to landing. Looking at his watch he had a pretty good idea they were only a couple of hours out from landing at Heathrow. He needed to stretch his legs anyway.

After a brief conversation with the captain, Doug returned to the seat next to Molly—he wanted to be there when she woke. With his remote, Doug raised the cabin lights, not all the way, but enough to illuminate the cabin. He feared Molly would be in a panic once she realized where she was. Fear gripped Doug as past memories took hold of his thoughts. Molly was still in danger. They would return to the States in a couple of days only to be faced with keeping Molly protected and safe. *If only I could talk to Sergeant Malone.* His stomach tightened just thinking of Molly and his desire to protect her. That thought continued to haunt him, and why he felt so protective of her he had no idea. Never had a woman wrapped herself around his heart in such a way. He could let someone else, especially the police, handle this. *No, I'm in it and I'm not going back. I'll do all I can to keep her safe.*

Molly woke with a start…panic in her eyes as she realized she was still on the plane. Doug unconsciously took her hand in his. "Molly, we're almost there. Another hour and we should be landing at London's Heathrow Airport. Are you hungry at all? You've been sleeping soundly for almost the entire flight."

She looked into Doug's beautiful blue eyes and saw nothing but concern for her. Her heart gripped at his tenderness. This was so not like him. "No, I'm fine thank you. Perhaps some water would be good."

Doug got up himself rather than summoning Lisa. He wanted nothing to do with this flight attendant, and the sooner she was gone from being remotely close to him, the better. He returned with a glass of ice and a bottle of water.

Molly, still a little groggy, thanked him but told him she did not need a glass. She would simply drink from the bottle. Doug could not help but chuckle to himself as he watched her drink directly from the water bottle. Not many of the women he knew would dare drink right out of a bottle. *I bet she would drink a Coke right from a can too.*

Molly jumped the minute the wheels touched down. She had such a grip on Doug's hand that his fingers were blue. She realized what she was doing when she looked down at their clasped hands, "I'm so sorry, Mr. Edwards. I had no idea I was holding your hand so tight. Your fingers are blue." Doug simply chuckled at her comment as he flexed his fingers. "Thank you so much for sitting with me. You have no idea how much I appreciate this."

"I'm happy I was the first person you flew with after your horrible experience. I may not be able to ever use my right hand again but hey… I'm glad I was here." He wanted to keep the mood light as they taxied to the VIP terminal. He loved hearing her chuckle after making the comment about his blue fingers. Lisa had taken a seat behind them when they began their descent. Doug felt her eyes bore into the back of his head. If her eyes were lasers, he would have two permanent holes back there.

After securing the plane and the stairs were lowered, Doug helped Molly out of her seat. Her legs were a little wobbly, but she was thrilled with her accomplishment. How could she not show her excitement? She had made her first flight since the horrible accident when she was thirteen. With the biggest smile on her face she looked up into her boss's beautiful eyes. "Mr. Edwards, I made it. Thank you so much." Doug was thrilled to see her so happy. He reached down and brushed the stray curl, which had come undone from her hair clip. "Sorry, I must look a mess." He wanted to tell her she looked beautiful, but instead he told her she looked fine.

The copilot, Chip, helped with their baggage as they deplaned. When they arrived in the VIP terminal, Doug pulled Lisa aside. "I have arranged for you to fly back commercially on a red eye flight tonight. You will be paid for this entire trip and an extra five hundred dollars. I never want to see you again."

Lisa turned from Doug in a huff, but before he could stop her, she walked up to Molly. Eyes filled with jealousy and venom, she exploded with a snarky comment, "Good luck, Miss Sinclair."

Molly stood speechless. *Why the nasty comment and then to wish me luck?* Molly watched her walk out the automatic doors pulling her carryon.

Doug was quick to come alongside Molly. "Do you mind if I ask what she said to you?"

Her face had to be flushed and she wondered how she could repeat the snarky comment. "I have no idea what she was talking about Mr. Edwards. She wished me luck. Let's just leave it at that."

Doug held Molly's arm with no intent on letting this go. "She said more to you, and I want to know exactly what she said."

Molly took a deep breath, hoping she could repeat what was said, without complete embarrassment. "She said, 'I was sure Doug and I would have made a better couple than the two of you.'" Molly lowered her eyes shielding them from her boss's intense stare. He had to know she was embarrassed repeating this to him.

"Molly, I'm so sorry. Lisa is someone I cannot have as a flight attendant. She somehow thinks she has a hold on me when she is nothing but a gold-digger. I haven't seen her for over two years. I made arrangements for her to fly commercial back to the states. I guess she's not too happy having to fly back tonight."

Molly had a feeling there was more to it, but there was no way she would pursue the issue. "I'm so sorry Mr. Edwards. It's my entire fault. I had no idea you did not want her to take this flight."

"There's no way you would know, Molly. I should have told you. In fact, the agency should have known. I think I'm going to have to hire a full-time flight attendant as I have with our pilots." With a twinkle in his eye, he continued. "On our return flight, I will be your flight attendant, ma'am." With that, he bowed dramatically before her.

Molly could not hold back her laughter. This warmed Doug's heart. Her laughter was definitely contagious, and to Molly's surprise, her boss joined in. Their eyes met, and something unspoken stirred between them. Was it a spark, or a bolt of electricity? Neither acknowledged the moment—just as quickly, it passed, leaving the both of them wondering what just took place. Molly believed it really meant nothing, after all, he was her very wealthy, very irritating and demanding boss, and she his assistant. She saw a side of him on the plane that she never thought he possessed, and she had to admit she did enjoy how intimately he held her hand—even if it was only out of concern for her as his assistant.

Doug quickly escorted her out of the terminal to the waiting limo. The pilots also joined them as they were driven to their hotel. The ride to the hotel was quiet and Molly was thankful to have the pilots accompanying them. Doug, the pilot and copilot kept the conversation going.

Molly stood in awe taking in the beautiful suite. She never imagined anything so exquisite. It was massive and decorated to the nines. The furnishings were all French provincial...beautiful brocades covered the floor to ceiling windows. She could only imagine what her bedroom must be like. She never dreamed she would one day be staying in a five-star hotel suite in London. She realized she was gaping and immediately closed her mouth, hoping her boss did not notice. However, when she looked over at Mr. Edwards he simply stood staring at her with a big grin on his face. "Sorry, but I have never seen such a gorgeous place."

"That's quite all right, Molly. I don't mean to be laughing at you.

I just find you, well…. refreshing. I enjoy watching you, and I'm sure with your dread of flying you have not been to too many places." Doug walked to the bar and poured himself a drink offering one to Molly. She declined shaking her head. He wondered how smart it was of him to have a drink on an empty stomach. He would only have one.

"You got that right. I'm sure I have limited my world by not having the courage to take any adventures."

Just then Doug heard Molly's stomach growl. "You must be starving. We never did eat on the plane. There's a cute little café around the corner from the hotel. They have great sandwiches. Eleanor enjoyed eating at the café whenever she was with me." Lisa brought meals up to the pilots, along with plenty of coffee and cold drinks for them but he had made it perfectly clear he did not want her waiting on him for fear she would have expectations of spending time with him. When Eleanor traveled with him, they always ate on the plane; she only went to the café for their great pastries. He wasn't about to tell Molly that, fearing she would not want to venture out for a bite to eat. And he certainly did not want a starving woman on his hands.

Molly excused herself to go freshen up in her luxurious bathroom. Taking it all in left her breathless. She definitely had not experienced such luxury in her entire life. All the fixtures were gold and looked outlandishly expensive. *I can't wait until I can relax in the extra-large Jacuzzi. I don't care how late it is because that's exactly what I'm doing when we get back.* She brushed out her hair leaving it down for the evening. She could put it up but the clip had poked her head all day leaving it sore. She added some blush and lip gloss and was all set to go. When she arrived back in the living room, Doug was sitting on the couch waiting for her but it looked like he was dozing off. "Sorry to keep you waiting. Perhaps you would rather we stay in, that's certainly not a problem for me. You look exhausted."

"No, I'm fine. It's been a long day. It will be good to get something to eat."

"It's been a long day all right. And you babysitting me, I'm sure did not help any."

Doug could not help but notice how long and beautiful Molly's hair was. For a long time, she had been putting it in a low bun or a hair clip. Immediately the image of the woman that walked into him several months back played out in his mind. *She was a beautiful woman all right, but Molly cannot possibly be her. She is so efficient and smart, not some clumsy airhead.* He could not help but chuckle at the thought or even imagining them being the same person. He quickly dismissed that notion as he stood to help Molly with her coat.

Molly thoroughly enjoyed the light meal she had. The turkey and brie croissant was delicious and the French pastry for dessert melted in her mouth. Doug seemed to enjoy what he had but mostly enjoyed watching the healthy appetite his assistant had. He realized that all the women he dated ate like a bird, not wanting to overindulge in anything as frivolous as eating something they enjoyed. They returned to the hotel completely satisfied. She said goodnight to Doug and told him how much she appreciated him being there for her on her first flight.

After a nice long soak in the Jacuzzi, Molly was certain she would fall asleep immediately. However, sleep did not come and she attributed that to sleeping so many hours on the flight over. *Perhaps if there is anything in the kitchen, like some milk I could warm up. I'm sure this would help or I may have to order room service.* Her pajamas were a pair of boy shorts and a tank top. She was sure Doug would be sound asleep by now, especially with the meeting they had tomorrow. At least the meeting was scheduled for later in the morning and would extend to a lunch meeting. *Jet lag may have something to do with my insomnia.* She did not want to turn any lights on for fear it may disturb Mr. Edwards's sleep so she felt her way to the kitchen. She would turn the light on once she got there.

Wham! Molly walked into something that barely moved. *What in the world?* Her hands instinctively reached out only to feel hard abs and a thatch of coarse hair. A light came on and she found herself staring into a very hard, and a very beautifully defined manly chest. "Oh dear, I am so sorry. I did not expect to see…anyone…I mean you…up." She had to have turned a couple shades of pink to even red as she could only stare at Mr. Edwards's chest. No way was she going to look into his eyes.

He put his hands on her shoulders and she could tell he was just as shocked as she was. His eyes roamed from the top of her head to her bare toes. He couldn't help but notice that her toes were painted a beautiful shade of red. Immediately her eyes flew up to his face. "I'm so sorry. I'm just so sorry, Mr. Edwards."

"Molly, that's okay. I should have turned the light on when I came in the kitchen."

"I...I couldn't sleep and thought I would see if there was any milk or anything I could take that would help me sleep. Umm, I think I'll just go back to bed. I should be fine." She quickly turned making a dash to her bedroom leaving Doug with an amazing view.

It will be a long time before I get that picture out of my head. She's absolutely beautiful. He had to chastise himself for the thoughts he was having. She was an employee of Edwards and Sons, and more importantly, his assistant. Professionalism had to be maintained. He admitted that his rules were going to get the better of him. *Well, at least I proved my brother wrong. I don't have ice running through my veins. No, my blood is definitely hot.*

Sleep did not come easy to either of them. Doug could not get the image or the feel of Molly out of his head and Molly could not erase the way Mr. Edwards looked and felt. Doug lay with a smile on his face; however, Molly lay in complete humiliation. *How am I ever going to be able to face him in the morning? He's my boss for crying out loud...a very intimidating boss.*

Chapter 26

MOLLY WOKE WITH a start, panicking that she had overslept. She lay awake most of the night and was sure she would never get to sleep. Evidently, she was wrong. She looked at the clock and saw it was eight. Jumping out of bed, she quickly ran to the shower, grabbing her underwear as she flew past her suitcase. Last night she had hung up the suit she was going to wear along with the silk blouse. Mr. Edwards talked about leaving the hotel at nine giving them plenty of time to arrive at their appointment. To cut corners, she would have to put her hair up in a clip. Feeling confident in her appearance, she took one last look at herself in the mirror. She loved the navy pencil skirt, white silk blouse, and navy jacket. The jacket she could wait and put on just before leaving. The suit was wool and even with the London chill she would not need her leather coat that she brought along. She skipped putting on her 4" navy heels until after she had her morning cup of coffee. She looked at the time. *Whew, eight forty-five, I can't believe I made it.*

Doug was sure he never did sleep when he looked at the clock at seven thirty. He meandered into the kitchen making sure Molly was nowhere in sight. He couldn't wait for room service to bring him coffee, so he made a pot himself. He needed a cup of coffee…and bad. He ordered room service and not knowing what Molly would like, he asked for an assortment of Danish and croissants. It was obvious how embarrassed she was last night but she would have to come out of her room some time. These two meetings were very important and he depended on Molly more than she knew. *It's a very important meeting I have and both of us have to be on our game this morning. I cannot blow this meeting with James Schuster.* Doug headed to his room to shower.

Finishing in a matter of minutes, he put on a tailored white shirt, a red silk tie, and his expensive sterling silver cufflinks. Taking his suit out of the garment bag he recognized it as a suit he hadn't worn in months. He had taken it out of the cleaner bag only yesterday before packing for his trip. *I totally forgot that I had this suit. It used to be one of my favorites.* He put the suit pants on, his socks and shoes, and would wait to put the jacket on before they left for the meeting. He walked into the kitchen at eight-thirty expecting to see Molly. He heard the knock on their door and knew it was room service. He sat at the dining room table eating his croissant and finishing his cup of coffee when Molly sheepishly entered the room. Doug looked up from the paper he was reading and without a doubt he knew she was embarrassed over last night's encounter. Not wanting to humiliate her even more, he pointed to the breakfast items on the table, the coffee in the carafe and cup for her. Molly looked at him with hooded eyes and thanked him as she took a seat at the table. "Are you still planning to leave at nine for the meeting, Mr. Edwards?"

"Yes. I guess we should leave in about ten minutes. Are you all set?"

"I am. I went over the papers last night and unless you have any additions or corrections to the documents, we are good to go." After her encounter with Mr. Edwards, Molly spent much of her sleepless night going over everything needed for this morning's meeting.

Doug appreciated Molly's efficiency and he had to admit she was the best assistant ever. He hated admitting it because Eleanor was amazing, but Molly had learned so much about the company and the clients he dealt with that there seemed to be nothing she wasn't capable of. It was evident that what he didn't think of, she did. He wondered if he should say anything about last night or not. He certainly did not want any awkwardness between them. "Molly, about last night—"

"Oh, Mr. Edwards, I am so sorry about that. Believe me if I had thought you were up I would never have gone into the kitchen."

"Molly, please do not think anything of it. I don't want you to feel the least bit embarrassed. It's my fault for not putting any lights on. Let's forget it even happened. Okay?"

Does he even realize how awkward it was for me to walk in with what I was wearing? I was half naked—and he was absolutely gorgeous to look at. She never thought any man could look that good and she was failing miserably at erasing his image from her mind. "Okay." Totally at a loss for words there was nothing more she could say. Molly picked up their dishes and brought them to the kitchen placing them in the sink. The pastries she covered with some plastic wrap she found in a drawer. She was nervously trying to keep from thinking about last night.

"There's no reason for you to do any of this, Molly. Housekeeping will be in as soon as we leave and they'll clean up."

"Oh, you're right. I guess it's just habit for me to try and tidy up. I'll get my things and will be right out," she hastily left the kitchen.

"Yes, me too. I called for the car to be here in five minutes. Do you need any more time than that?"

"No, I'll be out in five."

Doug walked into his bedroom, quickly brushed his teeth, and slipped on his suit jacket. Molly had all the papers needed in her computer bag for the presentation. He looked good, and he looked confident. He did not anticipate any problems with today's meeting with Schuster and tomorrow's meeting with Jewels. He walked into the living room and waited a couple of seconds before Molly walked out to meet him. Taking one look at her took his breath away. Her suit was elegant and yet professional. Seeing her long legs and four- inch heels left him breathless. She looked the same most days in the office but seeing her come out of her bedroom looking this good got the better of him, *or was it because of how she looked last night? His mind was visualizing her in those boy shorts and tank top.* Whatever it was, he had to shake it off. He needed to be sharp for this meeting and focus on something other than Molly. His heart warmed at the thought of her sharing her greatest fear in detail. *That could not have been easy for her.* He was pleased that she trusted him enough to be so vulnerable in exposing her anxiety.

Doug slipped his hand to the small of her back guiding her out the door. Molly felt a zing race from her back down to her toes. *Well, that was weird.* She certainly was having mixed feelings regarding her intimidating, and very arrogant boss; *this is strictly business...I'm his assistant for crying out loud. How can I balance the juxtaposition of emotions I'm experiencing? He frightens me and yet he brings me calm, he's demanding and yet compassionate. I'm afraid of him and also comforted by him.*

The meeting went better than Doug had imagined. Molly was efficient in presenting the necessary documents; all without any corrections or additions required from the client. It was obvious Schuster was taken with not only Molly's efficiency, but with her looks and personality. Never had Eleanor received the attention that was given to Molly. And she was totally unaware of the effect she was having on Michael Schuster. Doug sat in the limo with a pleased smile on his face and hoped tomorrow's meeting would go equally as well as today's. And even though Jewels was a longtime family friend, Doug still had to prove himself worthy of his business.

"Molly, you didn't eat much for lunch and you must be hungry. Why don't we stop for dinner before going to the hotel?"

"That would be lovely." She welcomed the invitation, which meant she would not have to be uncomfortable sitting alone in the hotel room with her boss. He didn't say much about their meeting with Michael Schuster but she had a feeling he was pleased with the outcome. However, he did seem annoyed at the attention Mr. Schuster had given her. As far as she was concerned it was strictly his British manners that he exhibited, and no doubt he was taught them from his youth. Yes, he was a complete gentleman and definitely a ladies' man. Molly was sure he treated all women with such attention.

The limo driver dropped them off at a restaurant, walking distance to their hotel. Doug had eaten there many times and knew Molly would enjoy eating there as well. He could always count on a scrumptious repast at this famous restaurant. Getting a table without a reservation might be a problem but a hundred-dollar bill slipped to the maître d' spoke volumes. They were given a lovely table in a very private part of the dining room that looked out into a beautiful glass-enclosed English garden. The sun was just beginning to set, causing the flowers to glow in their vibrant colors. The sky with its pink and purple hue added to the breathtaking view. "Mr. Edwards, this is absolutely gorgeous. I have never seen such a beautiful scene, and I never imagined I would one day be sitting in London at such an elegant restaurant. Thank you."

"Molly, you are very welcome. I only wish I had known about your fear of flying. I would have been more prepared."

"No, you would not have. You would have insisted I stay back and not attempt the trip. You did say we could Skype the meeting and had we done that, I would never have made the trip. So, thank you very much."

Doug felt his chest expand with pride that he was able to help Molly get passed her fear of flying. "Have you talked to your mom since arriving?"

"No, I haven't. My cell phone is strictly for U.S. use. It's not international coverage."

"You should have told me and I would have had international coverage added to it. In fact, I want you to have a company cell phone when we return home. That way you will always have complete coverage. Why don't you use my phone when we return to the hotel? It should be morning in Connecticut by the time we make it back."

"Thank you. I think I will do that. I'm sure my mother is wondering if I made it without jumping out of the plane at thirty-thousand feet." She said this with the cutest giggle. "I still have to make it back to the states, don't forget, unless Michael Schuster can put me up some place." She of course was joking, however, the somber expression that came over Mr. Edwards's face wasn't without notice. "I'm only kidding. He just seemed very accommodating with his fine manners."

"Accommodating and fine manners my eye." Douglas said this under his breath hoping Molly would not catch the sudden jealousy that accompanied his words. She seemed unaware of his comment as she continued to peruse the menu.

"Mr. Edwards, why don't you order for me? I have no idea what to choose. I thought this was an English restaurant and yet I can't read anything on the menu."

Doug chuckled. "Molly, it's all in French. That's why you can't read the menu. I'll be happy to translate and order for you if you like."

"Well why didn't you tell me? I was having a horrible time trying to figure it out. You must have enjoyed seeing me unable to read any of it." She was embarrassed; *how could I be so naïve?*

"Molly, to be honest I really wasn't paying that much attention to you struggling to read it. You looked like you were simply having a difficult time deciding what to have. Here, let me translate some of the entrees for you."

She settled on a delicious sounding Dover Sole and insisted Mr. Edwards order for her. His French was exquisite. She sat transfixed listening to him order their meals. When a glass of white wine was set in front of her and a glass of red for Mr. Edwards, she was too embarrassed to ask him to order her a Diet Coke. Not experienced in drinking anything stronger than a soft drink, she would simply sip it as slowly as possible. She was not about to be embarrassed any more than necessary and a glass of wine certainly won't hurt. It may even calm her nerves. She only hoped Mr. Edwards did not see the sour face she made when drinking it. She had always heard it was best to have something in your stomach before having alcohol so she did not want to drink much prior to her meal. However, she discovered she had a lot of sips and her glass was almost empty by the time their meal arrived. She was thankful when the waiter brought their salads and bread—a welcomed sight as she was starving. By the time her meal was completed, she drank almost three glasses of wine and could tell she was talking way more than she normally would. *Note to self…do not ever drink. I talk way too much, and hopefully I won't stumble on the way back to the hotel.*

The hotel was only a block away but in her four-inch heels it may as well have been three miles. Her feet were aching when she finally got up to the room. It was only nine but she felt exhausted as she collapsed into the couch. She slipped off her shoes and laid her head back on the couch. Doug had to chuckle as he watched her a little uninhibited. *It was not like her not to be all prim and proper. She certainly wasn't inebriated but it still must be the wine. He should have asked her if she even wanted a drink and not assumed she would. He would know better next time.* "Molly, here is my phone. You need to call your mother before you head off to bed."

"Thank you, Doug. I think I'm just going to close my eyes for a few minutes. I'm exhausted."

She called me Doug. She hasn't called me Doug in a long time. It must be the wine talking. He walked to the kitchen thinking it would be a good idea to get a pot of coffee going. *She could use a cup before calling her mother. What would her mom think of him if she detected her daughter a little tipsy? That would not be good.* He waited for the coffee to finish brewing and poured a cup for Molly. When he returned to the living room she was sound asleep on the couch. She had curled up with her head on a couch pillow, her legs tucked to the side. He couldn't just leave her there to sleep. She didn't look at all comfortable. However, he could not help but stare at how beautiful she looked even as she slept. He reached down and removed the clip keeping her hair up. Her beautiful silky hair cascaded down to her shoulders. The color was beautiful, darker than when he first met her—something was different but he didn't know what. He walked into her bedroom and turned down the covers on the bed. He walked to the living room and carried Molly to her room, laying her gently on the bed. He was really getting used to how good she felt in his arms. Pity it was only when she was in distress, out cold, or asleep. Sleeping in her expensive clothes would not be acceptable either. *What if she planned on wearing the same outfit tomorrow? It would be a wrinkled mess.* Doug carefully unbuttoned and unzipped her skirt, gently removing it. Fortunately, she was wearing a slip. He carefully unbuttoned her blouse and was hoping she was wearing something under it besides a bra. He half hoped she would wake and undress herself, but he also hoped she would remain asleep so he could take in her beauty without her waking. *Oh good. She has one of those silky things under her blouse.* He pulled the comforter up to cover her sleeping form— then quickly exited the room. It was still early so he poured himself a cup of the coffee he had made for Molly and sat on the couch to watch a little British television. His phone lay on the floor by the couch. *It must have been right where she dropped it when she fell asleep.* He picked it up; he would make sure she called her mom in the morning. He watched TV until eleven and then headed for his bedroom. Their appointment with Jewels was earlier than their appointment with Schuster. He wondered if he would have to wake Molly up in the morning. He set his alarm for six and he would wake her around seven. Thoughts of his childhood began to bombard his sleeplessness. Things he heard in Sunday school and listening to sermons, but mostly the years he spent in youth group: thoughts of purity, walking the walk. *Did people really believe that today? His parents sure did but what about him? How could he have believed so strongly in those same values as a teenager? Once he got into college everything changed. His worldview was no longer a biblical worldview. He thought he and Jason were so much more liberated in their thinking... but were they?*

Doug was up, showered, and dressed, but there was still no stirring from Molly's room. He already had a cup of coffee and wondered if he should bring her a cup when he woke her. It was seven and he had no idea how much time she would need to get ready. After all, she was a woman. Her door was ajar as he left it the previous night so he gently opened it all the way. From where he stood, she was still sleeping. He quietly walked to the side of her bed. She looked like she hadn't moved from when he undressed her. Setting her coffee on the nightstand, he reached down and very gently pushed on her shoulder. "Molly, wake up. Molly, wake up." She sat up with a start looking bewildered and confused. Her hair looked no different than when he laid her down. *She must not have moved one iota.*

"What? Where am I?" She looked around the room, her eyes settling on her boss. "Mr. Edwards, what are you doing in my room?! How did I get here? I can't remember a thing. Oh no... my clothes! What happened to my clothes?!" She immediately pulled the covers up to her chin. "How did my clothes get off of me?" Her mind was racing with so many questions. This did not look good. *Could she be any more humiliated than she already had been? Note to self – don't embarrass yourself with any more questions. There has to be a perfectly good explanation.*

"Molly, you fell asleep on the couch. It didn't look very comfortable so I carried you to bed. And yes, I removed your clothes and hung them up. I didn't know if you would be wearing the same outfit as yesterday. I didn't think you would want them all wrinkled." He couldn't help but notice the obvious consternation clouding her beautiful face. "Don't worry I didn't take any liberties with you. As you can see you are completely covered. And thank you for wearing so much...stuff... under your clothing." Doug made a motion with his hands regarding her undergarments.

She noticed the smile on his face as he answered her embarrassing questions. *Is he making fun of me?*

"Molly, I take it you're not accustomed to drinking much alcohol."

"I'm not accustomed to drinking ANY alcohol. There's nothing wrong with it. It's just something I never felt the need to indulge in."

"You mean to tell me that you never got wild in college? Had a few too many beers or shots?"

"No. Never. I studied in college. I was there to learn. The parties were never my thing."

"Wow. I thought everyone partied in college. Maybe I got caught up in the wrong crowd."

Was he making fun of her and her innocence? "Maybe you did."

"What about Chief Bradley?"

"Who?"

"George Bradley. Police chief of Shepherd Connecticut."

Why would he bring up George Bradley? "Yes, I know who he is but I have no idea what George Bradley has to do with any of this."

"He just seems like someone you may have a personal connection with. It seemed like he knew you pretty well. I thought perhaps you met him in college and—"

"I knew George in high school…that's it."

From what Doug could tell, she was holding something back. *There was more to George Bradley than she wanted to admit. In time, he would find out.* "Hey, I woke you so you would have enough time to get ready. If you remember, our appointment with Jewels is at nine-thirty. I'll have a car pick us up at nine."

"Okay, that's fine."

"I brought you a cup of coffee. It's on your nightstand. I figured if you had a hangover some strong coffee would help."

"Was I that bad?" She asked sheepishly.

"No, I'm just giving you a hard time. But believe me it wouldn't have taken much more and you would have been completely wasted."

Molly could feel the heat from embarrassment flush her face. She couldn't be more humiliated than the day she walked right into him, spilling his Starbucks down his custom-made suit. She hoped that memory was erased from his mind, although it would never be from hers.

She got up and opened her drapes only to find the day was not sunny as yesterday. It was a typical London morning—foggy with a light mist. It looked cold and miserable. She was pleased she thought of packing her black rain coat. It was one she could roll up to fit in her suitcase. She could not understand how Mr. Edwards would even suggest her wearing the same outfit as yesterday. *It shows how much he really knows about women.* She showered and dressed in her red, raw silk, Chanel power suit, with a white lacy shell underneath. Her hair was up in a casual twist the same as yesterday. Looking for a second cup of coffee, she walked out of her bedroom and headed for the kitchen. Thinking of the cup of coffee Mr. Edwards brought to her room, made her blush. *It was sweet of him to think of me.*

Doug was back in his room finishing up and giving himself one last check in the mirror. Some meetings had to be perfect and this was one of them. It was not a problem for him to wear the same suit as yesterday…men did this all the time and besides, there would be all new faces in the meeting. He unconsciously slipped his hand into his jacket pocket. He never expected to find anything in it. To his surprise, he took out an envelope that had the dry cleaner's name and logo on it; he imagined it was simply a button or note from the cleaners. He tossed the envelope on the dresser and sat on the bed to slip on his shoes. He walked out to the living room and once again was taken aback when he saw Molly in a fantastic red suit. Trying to remove the memory of how she looked laying in the bed last night would be difficult. For that matter, he really didn't think he wanted to remove it. To his surprise, he quickly cleared his head of that thought. "By the way, how did you sleep last night?"

Was that a grin on his face? Oh, my goodness, he was thinking of last night. She felt her spine stiffen. She would not give him the satisfaction that she was totally humiliated over last night. "I slept just fine, thank you. And you?"

"I slept well." He was not about to admit that he lay awake most of the night trying to rid the image of Molly asleep in bed, or how soft she felt in his arms. Nor would he share the thoughts of his relationship to God that kept him awake until sleep finally overtook him in the wee hours of the morning. No, those thoughts he would deal with at another time. He looked at his watch and reminded her of the car that would arrive in ten minutes.

The rain that fell was a soft mist but with the chill it seemed much colder than what the temperature actually was. Molly was grateful for her raincoat. Doug however, seemed not to mind the inclement weather or the chill. They arrived in plenty of time for their meeting with Jonathan Jewels, an older gentleman with kind eyes and a warm smile. Molly could not help but be drawn to this likeable, fatherly man. He greeted them warmly and ushered them to his private conference room. Mr. Jewels introduced several other gentlemen around the table.

After Doug presented his offer, he sat back and allowed Molly to handle the details. She proceeded to offer the contracts that needed to be signed. Yes, he was very pleased with his assistant. She was poised, efficient, friendly... and beautiful. And from what Doug observed, Jonathan Jewels was very impressed with her as well. When everything was signed, Doug excused himself from the meeting stating he needed to make a phone call. The other men also rose and left the conference room along with Doug.

Molly remained with Mr. Jewels and their conversation became more intimate. A genuine camaraderie developed between them. They talked about family and life in London. He told her of his wife of fifty years and his six grandchildren. Molly told him of her father's illness and how close she was to her mother. She looked out his window to see the rain had stopped and the sun shining. "It's lovely to see the sun shining, Mr. Jewels. When I woke up this morning it was so gloomy. I thought we were in for a rainy day."

"It's certainly not unusual for us to have the gloom and drizzle the entire day, especially this time of the year. You are quite lucky, my dear."

"I only wish I could spend more time in your beautiful city, but I'm afraid we will be flying back to the states this afternoon."

"You are more than welcome to visit us any time. In fact, if you ever need a job I would love to hire you on as my assistant. Actually, I will be in need of one in a few months. My assistant will be retiring." Mr. Jewels had such a twinkle in his eye that Molly had to squelch the urge to give him a hug.

She could not help but think of the contrast between Mr. Edwards and Mr. Jewels. She was certain he would make a wonderful boss. "Mr. Jewels, what a kind offer. I will certainly keep that in mind. However, I don't think Mr. Edwards would be very agreeable to that." *Or maybe he would.* She never knew how Mr. Edwards felt from one moment to the next.

Mr. Edwards returned as Molly was collecting the documents and putting them in her briefcase. "I see you are all set to go, Molly. Jonathan, once again it was a pleasure doing business with you. I trust my assistant took care of the final details."

"She certainly has Doug. I was just telling her that should she need a job, I would be more than pleased to hire her as my assistant. Shirley will be retiring in a few months, and I have been most pleased with this young lady. I always enjoyed our phone conversations but meeting her in person has been a pleasant surprise."

"Molly won't be looking for other employment—or going anywhere, Jonathan."

"You are one lucky man Doug—better treat her well."

Doug cleared his throat but not before noticing the flush in Molly's face. Not wanting to embarrass her or himself, he reached out his hand to say goodbye to Mr. Jewels. "We best be on our way. Jonathan, as always it was a pleasure doing business with you. Be sure and greet Mrs. Jewels for me."

"I will do that Doug. You be sure and greet your mom and dad from me as well. We have had some great times together with them in the past. And you, young lady, my offer still stands no matter what this guy may say." Mr. Jewels took both of Molly's hands in his.

Molly did not know what came over her, but when he released her hands, she stepped forward giving him a warm embrace. "Thank you, sir, it was my pleasure to have met you. You have been most kind."

Mr. Jewels patted Doug on the back as they left the office and Molly got the impression that the two families had known each other for quite some time.

Chapter 27

As Doug and Molly stepped out of the building, Doug directed her to a waiting car. The driver stepped out, handing Doug the vehicle keys. Doug opened the passenger door for Molly which was on the opposite side than what she was accustomed to in the States. After Doug was settled, Molly's curiosity was too great to withhold. "Mr. Edwards, is there a specific reason that you have a leased car rather than the usual limo?"

"Well Molly, this isn't a leased car but one that I keep here in case I want to drive myself around."

"Ooookay. Are you telling me that we are not going back to the hotel right now?"

"I made the decision not to return to the States this afternoon but sometime tomorrow. I hope that's okay with you."

"Is there a reason we won't be returning today?" Teasingly she added, "Perhaps you're nervous about being the flight attendant and having to cater to my every whim?"

He loved seeing her smile and that she felt comfortable teasing him. *Man, she is not only beautiful but has a sense of humor. Never have I seen this side of her personality. Now I'm pleased with the spontaneous decision I made. I have never met a woman whose eyes smiled when she laughed. And those dimples are absolutely captivating.* He could not help but wonder how much more to Molly that there was for him to get to know. And at this moment he certainly wanted to find out.

Before she realized it, they were standing in front of the palace. Never in her wildest dreams did Molly expect to see Buckingham

Palace. It was a sight to behold. She remembered the movies she had seen with the guards at such rigid attention in front of it. "Mr. Edwards, they really do stand so perfectly still. This was truly a pleasant surprise. Thank you."

"You're welcome, Molly. The next time I'll have tickets for the tour." They walked around the palace taking in the areas that were open to the public. "When you have seen enough, we'll head for the car."

"Oh, I'm ready when you are." She was not about to admit that her feet were killing her. *What does he mean the next time? I guess he makes a lot of business trips to London.* Had she known they would be sight-seeing she would have brought a pair of flats with her. Doug kept his hand on the small of her back as he directed her to the car. The warmth from his hand and the sizzle that shot through to her very core was getting way too familiar. She tried walking faster but his hand never left her back. When they reached the car, he grabbed her elbow guiding her in. *Why does he have to keep touching me? I doubt he's even aware of it—it's probably a normal habit when he's with a woman... But it is unsettling.* Molly kicked her shoes off as soon as she sat down. It felt good to get them off even if it would be for a brief time.

Doug slid into the driver's seat but not before noticing Molly's high heels removed and her bare feet exposed. She was rubbing the bottoms of her feet. It didn't take a rocket scientist to figure out that her feet must be killing her. *And we have more walking to do.*

It wasn't long and Doug pulled into a parking place in front of several shops. "Mr. Edwards, what are you doing?"

"You can't very well go walking in those heels—as great as they look on you. We need to get you a pair of flats."

"I will be fine once my feet have had a little rest, and besides I really don't see any shoe stores."

"There's one across the street from here." He pointed in the direction of the exclusive shoe store.

"Oh no, that happens to be a Christian Louboutin shoe salon. There is no way I can afford any shoe they would have."

"Maybe you can't afford it but I certainly can. Now let's go. You cannot go walking in the heels you're wearing." Mr. Edwards came around to her side and opened the door for her. He took hold of her hand and pulled her out as she was getting her heels back on. One shoe was on and the other barely when she stumbled forward falling forward into Mr. Edwards's, very familiar, rock solid chest. He caught her and held her tight…perhaps a little too tight.

"I'm so sorry Mr. Edwards. Thanks for catching me."

Suddenly Mr. Edwards wondered why it had suddenly become so warm when it had been a rather chilly day. "Hmm, it's not your fault. I should have noticed you weren't ready." He stood her straight and took hold of her hand once again guiding her across the street.

Spending time in a Louboutin salon was exhilarating for Molly. Never in her wildest dreams did she imagine herself shopping in such an upscale store. Of course, she couldn't find a pair of shoes under five hundred dollars. Not even on the sale table. Leave it to Mr. Edwards to pick out an adorable red flat, perfectly matching her suit. "Oh, this is perfect!" She slipped it on and it was the most comfortable shoe she had ever worn. She took one look at the price and immediately put it back. "I think I'll keep looking."

Mr. Edwards told the sales clerk that they would take the shoes. Out of the corner of his eye he saw Molly eyeing a beautiful pair of heels. Her hand glided over the shoe as if it were satin. He noticed her sigh as she placed the shoe back onto the table. Doug looked at the sales clerk and asked that she discreetly get the shoe in Molly's size. "That shoe is called a Sharpstagram 100 pump and is one thousand, seventeen dollars, sir." It was a beautiful crisscross, black patent leather pump with the signature red sole. It would be well worth it knowing Molly would probably wear the shoes to the office one day. The clerk ran his credit card and Doug signed without blinking; over a thousand dollars for one pair of shoes would give Molly a heart attack but for Doug it was chump change. With the boxes put in a bag, Doug once again took Molly's hand as they returned to the car. He took the one box out, the one with the flats; he exchanged the heels that she wore for the flats, and quickly slipped the bag into the rear seat. She was none the wiser. Doug could not help the smile that curled all the way to his eyes. He felt like a little schoolboy with a secret he couldn't wait to share. But wait he would. He would surprise her with the heels later that night.

Molly was speechless as she slipped her new flats on. When her voice returned, she asked where they were headed. Mr. Edwards was once again tight lipped and was not about to tell her. She was getting a little frustrated, but she realized he really liked surprises. She sat as patiently as was possible for her as he wove through the streets. He parked the car and once again came around to her side and grabbed her hand to help her out. "We have a little bit of a walk but with your new shoes you should be just fine."

As they walked a couple of blocks, Molly could see their destination and she squealed. "It's the Tower of London and Big Ben! Oh, my goodness. I can't believe I'm actually going to be standing right next to it. It's huge and way more than I would have imagined. It's not just a big clock but the building around it is massive. Mr. Edwards, you must get a picture of me standing next to it."

Doug took great pleasure in watching Molly awestruck with her mouth agape. "I will. And Molly will you please stop calling me Mr. Edwards. That makes me feel so old."

"Oh, all right… But you are my boss."

"You may call me Mr. Edwards in the office and at meetings but when we're together having a good time, call me Doug."

"I'll try but I can't guarantee it won't slip out. You know what they say, old habits die hard."

"I sure don't want to be an…old habit."

Molly giggled and was practically skipping up to Big Ben. "My mother is going to be so excited when she sees the pictures." She was pleased he had taken pictures of her at Buckingham Palace and now at the Tower and Big Ben. What she didn't know was that he had snapped a picture of her practically swooning over the pair of shoes he planned to surprise her with that night.

They saw the famous River Thames and stood at the iconic Westminster Bridge. Her enthusiasm was certainly contagious and Doug could not believe he was having as much fun as Molly. He had seen the sights many, many times but never had he been this excited. *It's seeing them with her that's making the difference.* And that's when it hit him. Molly was becoming more than his assistant. He was falling for her…and hard. He felt his chest squeeze. *Who am I kidding? This cannot be good. She wants nothing to do with me other than to be my assistant. I know she thinks I'm arrogant, rude, and harsh. I should never insist that she call me Doug. Why would she even want to? Besides, I'm a confirmed bachelor.* He felt himself letting go of her hand… He immediately missed the warmth from her hand in his—the connection lost.

Molly could walk no more and Doug asked if she was ready to go. Molly nodded and grabbed Doug's hand as they walked back to the car. This sent a warm thrill straight to his heart. He wondered if she was even aware of what she was doing. No way would he ask.

She had no idea where they were headed and knew better than to ask. She was convinced Mr. Edwards would refuse to tell her anyway. As they drove past the London Eye, Doug asked if she wanted to go for a ride on the giant Ferris wheel. Looking into Doug's mischievous eyes she said, "I'm a little fearful of heights—I think I'll pass." He chuckled and gave her a wink as he patted her hand.

Before she even realized it, they were circling Piccadilly Square when he spotted a little bistro. Piccadilly Circus was another one of the most iconic locations in London. Doug could not imagine that Molly's eyes could get any larger than they already were, but to his surprise they were not only beautifully wide but shone like crystals. Watching her brought such tightness in his chest and a longing to spend as much time with her as possible. How could he feel this way? He had no intention of another serious relationship…but the emotions, he did not want to analyze, welled up in his chest. Once was enough. And besides, nobody married anymore…at least not before they lived together. Try and buy was the new way. He believed in his heart of hearts that his assistant was not that kind of a woman. No, maybe Jason would fall for the marriage trap but not him.

As they circled Piccadilly Square, Molly came to her senses, realizing Doug did not take her hand when they left Big Ben. *How presumptuous of me to think that he would want to continue holding my hand. He is my boss and there can't possibly be anything more to it.* As soon as the car stopped Molly had her door opened and started to exit, but before she was able to stand, Doug was quickly at her side. Although he did not take her hand, she did not take his either. He did however keep his hand on the small of her back as he directed her to the outdoor bistro. She really wished he would not do this as she could not control the sensation that surged through her entire body each and every time. It made her feel awkward and uncomfortable, and yet it had to be his excellent manners and something he did with every woman he was with. Once again Molly was pleased they were seated at a restaurant, thus eliminating a lot of time together at the hotel.

It was late when they returned to the hotel, and for this Molly was grateful. She had called her mom to let her know that they would be returning sometime Saturday. Mr. Edwards never told her their exact time of departure. She would pack that night and be up early and ready to go in the morning. Molly thanked Mr. Edwards for an amazing day. One she never expected to have. She hesitated as to shaking his hand or giving him a casual hug. She chose the latter and was pleased that he casually hugged her in return. Doug held her in his arms and he wished the feeling could last forever. *Did she have any idea what she was doing to him?* It was a simple thank you for the day but his breath caught before he could answer. "Molly, you're very welcome. Before you head for bed I have something to give you."

Molly searched his face with those magnificent eyes of hers. "What on earth could you possibly have for me? This day was perfect in every way."

Doug picked up the bag he had left by the door and brought it to her.

"Oh, I forgot I had my heels in the bag. I better get them packed, thank you."

"Molly, your shoes are in there but there is another box for you."

Molly carefully took her shoes out that were in the Christian Louboutin box her new flats had been in. She noticed another box underneath. "Mr. Ed…." Hearing him clear his throat she continued, "Doug, what in the world?" She was puzzled as to what could possibly be in the other shoe box. Her hands were trembling as she proceeded to remove the lid from the extravagant box. As she removed the tissue her eyes began to water, and with trembling lips that matched her shaking hands, she removed the beautiful pair of patent heels she had fallen in love with at the store. "Mr. Edwards, there is no way I can accept these from you. They are way too expensive. I don't think I can wear them in good conscience."

"Molly, they are a gift from me to you. And I can afford them. I couldn't help but notice how they caught your eye and I wanted to surprise you with them."

Molly had to admit she always had a weakness for beautiful shoes, and had a closet to prove it. She removed her new flats and stroked the soft leather before putting on the beautiful pumps. They fit like a glove. Immediately Molly stood up and began walking around the room. To her embarrassment, Doug had not taken his eyes off of her.

"I think you like them, Molly."

"Oh, I do. They fit perfectly. I don't know what to say. Thank you so much." Molly once again embraced Doug giving him a smile that reached his heart.

"Seeing you smile like that, made it well worth every penny I spent." It was difficult letting her go. *I could hold her in my arms forever.* He wondered where that thought came from. The feelings he was having for his assistant should not be happening. He could not, and would not allow it, but before he released his hold on her, his hand gently stroked her back.

His arms wrapped around her felt so good however, Molly pushed herself away knowing this could become dangerous. She thanked him once again and excused herself to go pack. She looked forward to a long soak in the Jacuzzi after she packed. This would benefit her nerves and her aching feet.

As she walked to her room, Doug told her they would be leaving after breakfast in the morning, around nine. She nodded and continued on to her room.

Doug's emotions were definitely on high alert as he entered his bedroom. As he ran his fingers through his hair, he wondered if buying the shoes for Molly was a wise decision after all. *She was certainly thrilled with the gift, and I sure enjoyed seeing her so elated, but would she get the*

wrong idea? Who am I kidding? I had the wrong idea when I bought them. I have loved seeing her in her beautiful shoes. He began unbuttoning his shirt and then sat on the bed to remove his socks. When he looked up, he noticed the envelope still on the dresser. The envelope had the dry cleaner's logo, and was sealed. He reached for it and knew by the feel of it that it did not contain a button which was his first thought when he took it out of his pocket that morning. He opened the envelope and removed a slip of paper. As he unfolded the paper, to his astonishment was the name Molly Beaumont and a phone number. *This Molly Beaumont… is… my…Molly? But why didn't I know that when I first met her at the office? And does she know I'm the guy she so unconsciously walked into?* Running his hands through his thick hair, he had no idea how he should handle this information. For now, he would hold it tight to his chest. At the right time, he would tell her. But when the right time would be he had no idea. He was certain that his Molly was not some air head that unconsciously walked willy-nilly into everyone on the street.

Doug had another restless night of sleep. Molly was an enigma. The feelings that were growing in his heart he could not explain to himself or anyone. Molly stirred feelings in him that he thought were long ago dead and buried. There was no way he could allow these feelings to become any more than what they were. In fact, he had to work on squelching what was there.

Chapter 28

MOLLY'S TREMBLING SUBSIDED, somewhat, once she was settled in her seat. She was not about to admit to Doug how nervous she still was at the thought of flying back to the States. As he took the seat next to her, she looked longingly into his eyes but insisted she would be fine. However, one look at her and he knew better.

"I don't mind sitting with you until we're up in the air." He reached for her hand and she gently slipped it into his. It felt good to hold her dainty hand once again as he wove his fingers with hers.

Once they were in the air, she pulled her hand out from his. "Thank you. I appreciate you holding my hand. I'm fine now. Go do what you need to do." Molly gave him a slight smile as she waved him off.

"Okay then. I do have some work to do. May I get you anything to drink?"

"No thanks. I'm fine. I'm going to do some reading if you don't mind, unless you have work for me to do?"

"No. No work for you. You go right ahead and read. The galley is just behind us so help yourself or ask me for anything at all."

"Okay, I will." Molly reached in her bag and took out her Kindle. She had no idea how long she read, but soon her eyes became too heavy to keep open. Sleep took over and she was unaware of her Kindle hitting the floor. She slumped awkwardly to the side sinking into the plush leather seat.

Doug sat at his desk but had barely taken his eyes off of Molly the whole time he tried to get some work accomplished. When her Kindle hit the floor, he couldn't help but notice the awkward position she was in. He was up in a flash and quickly at her side attempting to make her more comfortable…carrying her to his bedroom was not a good idea. He reached for a pillow and tucked it against the window and gently moved her head to rest on the pillow. Doug walked to the bedroom and got a blanket to put over her. After he covered her, he reached down on the floor and picked up her Kindle. It was still opened and he wondered what she could have been reading. It was her Bible and it was opened to Ephesians 5 in the New King James. He began to read verse 22, "Wives, submit to your own husbands, as to the Lord." He read verse 25, "Husbands love your wives, just as Christ also loved the church and gave Himself for her." He continued reading on to verse 26, "So husbands ought to love their own wives as their own bodies; he who loves his wife loves himself." It hit him as if someone knocked him over the head with a 2x4. *Why would God be so specific about husbands loving their wives if His intent and purpose wasn't for man and woman to marry and be one? God never intended for man and woman to live together outside of marriage or to have multiple relationships. He was living and believing a lie. His dad loved his mom like this for almost forty years. They had it right, not him, and not his brother.* He was ashamed for how he had been living. He thought he had it right, but he was so wrong. He noticed that her Kindle had multiple translations and he went to *The Message*. He had heard it was a modern paraphrased translation. Wondering what *The Message* was like he kept reading Molly's Bible on her Kindle and felt the tears trickle down his cheeks. He began reading from Ephesians 1 but when he came to Ephesians 2 in the Message, he had to reread verses 1 through 3 over and over: "You let the world, which doesn't know the first thing about living, tell you how to live. You filled your lungs with polluted unbelief, and then exhaled disobedience. We all did it, all of us doing what we felt like doing, when we felt like doing it, all of us in the same boat." *That's exactly how Jason and I have lived since our college days. We have certainly been fooling ourselves. The world doesn't know the first thing about living.* He finished reading to the end of verse 6. "Instead, immense in mercy and with an incredible love, he embraced us He took our sin-dead lives and made us alive in Christ. He did all this on his own, with no help from us! Then he picked us up and set us down in highest heaven in company with Jesus, our Messiah." Doug sat in the seat next to Molly and poured his heart out to God asking for forgiveness. *God, thank you for not giving up on me; I certainly do not deserve your love and grace but you freely give it. Thank you.* The tears continued but they were good tears—tears that washed and cleansed his very soul.

The remainder of the flight was smooth and when Molly awoke Doug gladly played the role of flight attendant bringing meals to the cockpit, and a salad, steak and baked potato to Molly. She was totally impressed and enjoyed eating such a delicious meal with Doug. He wanted to pour his heart out to her and what had taken place while she slept, but he could not. Not at this time.

The limo and driver were waiting to take Doug and Molly to her apartment by early afternoon. She was thankful for the time change. Doug grabbed Molly's suitcase and carry-on and walked her up the stairs. She was anxious to see her mom, but taken aback when she entered her apartment. Her mom stood at the door with her suitcase ready to leave.

"Mom, where are you going?"

"Why I'm going home, dear. George was kind enough to come down here to pick me up. I had no idea what time you would be coming home. I'm so glad I was still here to see you." Mrs. Beaumont leaned forward and gave her daughter a warm embrace. "I can't wait to hear all about your trip."

George walked out of the kitchen with a couple of water bottles. "Oh, I didn't know you were home, Molly. How was your trip?" He eyed Doug suspiciously before reaching out to give Molly a warm embrace himself.

She stepped back taking in the scene. "Mom, why are you leaving? I thought you would stay until I could drive you home."

"I was going to wait, but when George called this morning he insisted he come down and get me. He thought it would be quite late before you came home and of course you would be too tired to make the trip to Shepherd."

"Mom, there is no way I'm too tired, and even if I was, I could take you home tomorrow morning."

Doug was watching the interaction but finally got tired of it all. "Hey, I have no problem driving Molly and her mom up to Shepherd, or I could have my driver take Mrs. Beaumont up in the morning." He never once took his eyes off of George. *Who was this guy anyway?* He realized he never did get an acceptable answer from Molly.

"That's quite all right. George drove all the way here and I think it best I get home to your dad today anyway. You two can relax and have a quiet evening."

George grunted and did not look the least bit pleased with the outcome. He was hoping to play the hero here, not push Molly and her boss together. "Well, okay then, babe, I'll get your mom home safe and sound."

Babe, what on earth was he trying to do? Molly cringed but did not want to make a scene. She gave her mom a tender hug and told her to call when she got home. Next week was Thanksgiving and her mom would be back before then.

Dolores returned her hug and told her how pleased she was that she was able to get over her fear of flying. She thanked Doug for the beautiful pictures he had sent to her phone. Mother and daughter had talked in length on the phone when Molly was in Europe so there wasn't much else to say about her flying experience. Although Molly thought it would have been exciting to sit with her mom and tell her all about her trip. Disappointment set in but she tried not to let it show. After all, it was a business trip and not a vacation.

Doug extended his hand to George but George ignored it, instead he picked up Mrs. Beaumont's suitcase and the two water bottles. Mrs. Beaumont, oblivious to the scene, hugged her daughter once again and then left with George.

Doug was on his phone telling his driver to park and wait for him. He turned to Molly and pointed to the couch. "Molly, something's been bothering me and I know it's probably none of my business but... who is George Bradley—is it possible you're in a serious relationship with him?"

"I told you. I went to high school with George."

"And?"

"And… I am not in any kind of a relationship with him… Not anymore."

"He gives me the impression that there is more to it…babe."

"Oh, all right. I did date George when I was in high school. I broke up with him and I don't think it was something he ever got over. Now I think he has hood-winked my mom into believing he's this great guy and he can get to me through her."

"Well, can he?"

"Can he what?"

"Get to you through your mom?"

"Not at all. That train has already left the station."

Doug had to chuckle at that comment. He would drop the issue, but still had a feeling that there had been more to their relationship. *Why should it bother him anyway? He had a company to run and she was his assistant.* He wanted to take a quick ride out to his folks. He was anxious to tell his mom and dad what happened to him on his flight home. "Well, I better head out. Will you be all right tonight?"

Molly gave him a questioning look. "Why wouldn't I be all right?" Just then it hit her and she remembered what her life was like before her great trip. "It isn't over, is it?"

"I'm afraid not. I have had a car watching your apartment while we were gone and I'm going to make sure we have a police car out front at all times, or I'll keep my own PI car here."

Molly was overwhelmed at her boss's concern for her. The heaviness of the situation and the realization that it continued, hit her. Her eyes were beginning to fill with moisture but she refused to cry. She certainly did not want Mr. Edwards to think she was some needy ninny.

Chapter 29

"**M**OM, DAD, ANYBODY home?" Doug rushed into his childhood home almost bypassing the housekeeper that came to the door. Sophie, the Edwards's housekeeper for as long as Doug could remember, came to his side giving him a warm embrace.

"Mr. Doug, it is so good to see you. I can't remember when you or your brother have been here last. How have you been?"

"Sophie I've been good. In fact, I couldn't be better. Are my parents at home or are they out?" He was sounding anxious but he could not wait to talk to them.

"Both your mom and dad are out on the back patio."

"Thanks Sophie." Doug took off in the direction of the back patio. As he entered the massive kitchen, the smell of fresh baked cookies got his attention. His nose took him to the cookie sheet sitting on the marble counter next to the oven. He grabbed a sugar cookie before heading for the French doors that lead to the patio and the meticulous grounds beyond. Doug spotted his parents sitting together and obviously enjoying each other's company. It was chilly so they sat with warm jackets on, holding hands and enjoying the beginning of a beautiful sunset.

"Hey Mom and Dad."

Together they looked up at their handsome son. "To what do we owe this surprise, Son?" Ed Edwards rose from his chair to embrace his son.

Doug's mom started to rise but was stopped immediately. "Please, Mom, don't get up." Doug bent and gave his mom a tender kiss on her cheek. "It's a beautiful evening, isn't it?"

"It certainly is, and your mother and I know we won't have many more evenings like this. So, we like to sit out here and enjoy the sunset."

"Honey, I didn't think we would be seeing you, or your brother, until Thanksgiving next week. Is everything all right with you?"

"Mom, things couldn't be better. I have something to tell you that I'm sure will please you and Dad."

"I take it your trip to London went well. Did you get the contracts signed?"

"Great trip, Dad, and I got all the contracts signed. But that's not what I came to tell you."

Of course, his mother went in a totally different direction. She could not help but notice the joy in her son's face and the gleam in his eyes. "Oh Doug, are you telling us you have a new woman in your life?" She tried desperately to not show disappointment that her son would once again be drawn to another woman like Peggy. She silently prayed that this was not the case.

"No Mom, there is no woman in my life." He felt a deep stab to his heart. *My assistant is the only woman in my life. And where had that thought come from?* "I came to tell you what happened to me on our flight home."

"Oh dear; I certainly hope no one got ill."

Doug chuckled before pushing on. "No, no one got sick, but I did have an experience that practically brought me literally to my knees. You know my assistant Molly?"

"Yes of course, she is such a dear sweet girl. She did so much for Eleanor's farewell party."

"Honey, our son has something to tell us…let's give him a chance, shall we?"

"Sorry Dear. You know how carried away I can get. Please tell us."

"Molly happened to be reading on the plane, and when she fell asleep, her Kindle slipped off her lap falling to the floor. She looked so uncomfortable all scrunched up that I couldn't help but go over and put a pillow under her head and cover her with a blanket." Doug could not help but notice the excitement in his mother's expression. "Mom, let's face it, I'm now a confirmed bachelor so don't get your hopes up." He continued to push on how he sat there reading Molly's Bible that she had on her Kindle. "She not only had the *New King James* but *The*

Message. I could not stop reading. Do you have any idea what Ephesians 2:1 says in *The Message*?" Doug noticed the unshed tears in his mother's eyes. He reached for her hand and held it as he continued on. "It says you let the world, which doesn't know the first thing about living, tell you how to live. I first read Ephesians 5 about husbands loving their wives as they love their own bodies. That's exactly how you love Mom, Dad. It hit me hard that God never intended for us to go from a one-night stand to another, or to live together before marriage. Marriage is a serious commitment. Jason and I were both fed a boatload of lies in college. And not only college but society: movies, TV, magazines, colleagues, it's all around us. That's what the world even boasts about. We actually bought into the whole package that you and Dad are old fashioned when you have been nothing but the best example Jason and I could have had. Don't you see? We let the world tell us how to live and the world has no clue." Doug wiped his eyes with the heel of his palms. "I thought I could have it both ways: believe in God like I did when I was a kid, and live my life my way...my rules."

After that confession, all three stood, wrapping Doug in the biggest embrace possible. "Welcome home Son." Mr. Edwards hugged his son, and he too had tears of joy rolling down his cheeks. "You know we have loved you no matter what your choices, good or bad, but this has given us joy unspeakable."

"Thanks Dad. And thanks for your patience with me."

"I knew there was something special about your new assistant."

Doug looked at his dad and rolled his eyes. "Mom, you can be so persistent...and I love you so much."

Chapter 30

MOLLY WAS LOOKING forward to her mom driving down for Thanksgiving. She planned to arrive early Wednesday morning and together they would volunteer at Help You Stand. The center had much to do to get ready for the Thanksgiving dinner they would be serving. In fact, they had three seating's planned. Molly had been working every night since Sunday helping with food preparations: peeling apples for apple pie, peeling potatoes and carrots, fresh green beans had to be cleaned. Anything that could be done ahead of time was done. It was Tuesday and she was already exhausted; two more nights to go and hopefully there would be a lot of volunteers to serve the meals on Thursday.

Molly was at her desk when Mr. and Mrs. Edwards walked in; she was pleased to see them. Patricia told her husband to go on in to visit with their son, while she remained with Molly. "Molly, it's so good to see you again. I heard your overseas trip went well."

Molly was a little aghast wondering how much Mrs. Edwards knew of her fear of flying. *Would Doug share everything with his parents? Some things really were personal.* "Our trip was great, Mrs. Edwards. I never expected to see Buckingham Palace, the Tower and Big Ben, and even Piccadilly Square…and so much more. It was quite unexpected and an amazing experience."

"I'm glad you were able to do more than just sit in some boring old meetings."

"I thought the meetings were far from boring. I so enjoyed meeting Mr. Jewels."

"He and his wife Sarah have been friends of ours for many years. We have many fond memories of special times shared with them. I'm sure he enjoyed meeting you as much as you did meeting him." Mrs. Edwards hesitated wondering if she should be so bold but did not want to ignore the prompting deep within her spirit. "There is something I would like to ask you before I forget why I wanted to talk to you. I don't know what plans you have for Thanksgiving but we would love to have you join us."

Molly was all set to tell her that they would be volunteering at the shelter on Thanksgiving, and before she could do so, Mrs. Edwards continued, "We celebrate on Friday at our house rather than Thanksgiving Day."

"Oh, that's wonderful because I could not make it on Thursday. However, my mom will be staying with me for a few days after Thanksgiving."

"Well we would certainly want your mom to join us as well. Dinner is planned for two o'clock. Please say you will come."

"Thank you so much. That's very kind of you. Actually, we have no plans other than some volunteer work. Please let me know what I can bring."

"Great. I will email directions to our home this afternoon. Thank you for asking, but there is nothing for you to bring. I'm just so pleased you will be able to join us." Patricia was relieved Molly accepted her invitation. *She really wasn't matchmaking…was she?*

"Thank you."

Mrs. Edwards gave Molly a hug and headed for her son's office. She turned and gave Molly a warm smile and told her she would be looking forward to Friday.

Molly didn't know what to make of it. After Doug left on Saturday, her boss had hardly spoken to her. He had cocooned himself in his office and only spoke to her when necessary. It was very unsettling, and she wondered what she had said or done to cause such strange behavior. *I wonder how pleased he will be having me sitting at his family's Thanksgiving dinner table on Friday. I must have said something on Saturday, but I have no idea what.*

Doug sat at his desk trying desperately to ignore the feelings he was having for his assistant. Ignoring her all yesterday and this morning was not wise. Just the site of her left his heart pounding and his palms sweaty. *I need to get over this. After all, I'm a confirmed bachelor for crying out loud.* At least he was trying to convince himself of that. He had a company to run and all he could think about was his assistant sitting in the other office.

To Doug's surprise, in walked his dad. "Hey Son, your mom and I thought we would stop by and see how you and your brother are doing. We need to remind Jason of our plans for Thanksgiving and dinner on Friday."

"Has anything changed, or will it be our usual Thanksgiving?"

"No, nothing has changed. Your mother and I will volunteer at Help You Stand Thanksgiving Day, and then, as usual, your mom is planning dinner on Friday. It really works out well for all of us. The household staff gets to celebrate with their families on Thanksgiving Day, and then be with us on Friday. It's perfect, and your mother and I love volunteering at your place."

"Good. I'm glad to hear that. I haven't spoken to Kevin to find out if he has enough volunteers but he always seems to manage. Where did you say Mom happened to be?"

"Oh, she's visiting with your assistant. I think those two have really hit it off." Just then Patricia came in. She had a huge smile on her face and a definite bounce in her walk. It was making Doug nervous and he wondered what his mom was up to now.

Patricia embraced her son giving him a peck on his cheek. "Before I forget I better scoot down to your brother's office and remind him of our Thanksgiving plans. You know how he purposely forgets and ends up committed to something else. Or so he says."

"Yeah, okay. Dad and I will just visit for a while. After you talked to Jason, you can come back here."

Patricia Edwards walked out of her son's office and noticed Molly was on her cell phone. She certainly did not intend to eavesdrop but could not help overhearing Molly tell a Lieutenant Barlow that she looked forward to meeting him after work. She sounded excited and Mrs. Edwards wondered what that could be about. She was unaware of all the turmoil that had ensued the past few weeks. She walked over to Molly's desk and mouthed that she was heading down to Jason's office and would be back. Molly nodded and continued her conversation. "I should be able to get off early. I'm happy to meet you at The Diner on Wilson, Lieutenant Barlow. No, that's all right, it happens to be on my way home. Thanks so much for calling, Lieutenant." Molly waved to Mrs. Edwards as she ended her phone call.

Before Molly left for the day, she washed out the coffee pot and mugs in Doug's office, and informed him she would be leaving early. Since Mr. Edwards never even looked up from his desk but simply grunted, she quickly left his office. She had planned to tell him about her phone call from Lieutenant Barlow but changed her mind when he was so preoccupied and obviously ignoring her.

Chapter 31

MOLLY ENTERED THE Diner at five and immediately looked for the Lieutenant. He waved her over to a booth he had been occupying in the back of the diner. He stood when Molly came to the booth and slipped in next to her. She was taken aback with his forwardness, but then thought perhaps he wanted his information to not be overheard by anyone. "How have you been, Molly?"

"Just fine, thank you. Do you have some good news for me?"

"Why don't we have a bite to eat first and then we can talk."

Molly really wanted to know what was going on but thought it best to do things on his terms; either he had good news or bad, and by the look in his eyes she assumed it to be the latter. His eyes were dark and foreboding—even a little frightening.

"Would you like something to eat, Molly?"

"No thank you, I'm good. I think I'll just have a cup of coffee."

"That sounds good to me too." He called the waitress over and ordered two cups of coffee. "I'm sure you want to know what is going on with your case?" Not waiting for an answer, he continued. "How certain are you of testifying against McGee?"

"I don't even have to think about it. He's evil and he needs to be off the streets."

"What about your mother? Does she feel that strongly about it as you do?"

"Yes, I'm sure she does. We already told you that we would testify, so why the questions now?" Molly was starting to get a very uneasy feeling as she sat so close to this man. *Is he even with the police department?* Their coffee came and Molly had a hard time trying to swallow, even a couple

---

of sips. Something deep within her spirit told her she needed to get out of there. She looked at her watch and immediately told the Lieutenant that she had to leave. She had an appointment at six o'clock that she had to be at and had only ten minutes to get there. "I absolutely have to leave, so if you'll excuse me—" She tried scooting out of the booth, hoping the Lieutenant would get the hint and get out of the booth first.

"You're not going anywhere right now, Molly." He pushed her back down and pushed her into the corner of the booth.

"What exactly are you doing, Lieutenant?" She started to protest by raising her voice. To her shock, he immediately shoved something hard into her side.

"If you say one word, I'll have you on the floor so fast— everyone in this place will just assume you're under arrest. I have a badge don't forget. Let's finish our coffee, and I think I'll order a piece of pie. How about you?" He waved the waitress over and ordered a piece of pecan pie with ice cream. The less conspicuous they could be the better. He had been in this business a long time.

Molly shook her head. There was no way she would, or even could, eat a thing.

"Molly, drink your coffee." His voice was demanding. Her hands trembled as she raised the cup to her lips. She swallowed, but the coffee tasted bitter. The sudden lump in her throat would barely allow it to go down.

The waitress delivered his pie and ice cream and he immediately began devouring it; not taking his eyes off of Molly for one minute. Several times he reminded her that his gun was pointed right at her side and she had better behave.

They sat like this for a good thirty to forty-five minutes. She wondered what was taking him so long. She had a horrible feeling that he had something planned and he needed the time before they could leave. After finishing his pie and ice cream the waitress came with the bill and he handed her a twenty-dollar bill. With a wink, he told her to keep the change. "Molly, when I get up, I want you to slowly slide out of the booth and walk towards the door. One false move and I will have you on the floor so fast you won't know what happened. Got it?"

Molly gave him a nod. "You certainly will not get away with this.

I was expected someplace at six o'clock and they will certainly miss me when I don't show up." Molly looked at the elderly couple seated by the window and gave them a pleading look. She mouthed the word "help" and hoped they noticed.

"Oh please. If you think you're going to scare me, it won't work. Now quietly walk out the door and to my car. It's the first black SUV in the lot."

Before he pushed Molly into the car, the Lieutenant quickly slapped handcuffs on her. Thankfully he did not force her hands behind her back. Her legs wobbled and her hands trembled as she labored to get into his car. She felt her eyes begin to moisten but tried with all she had to keep from crying. The air felt considerably colder than when she had walked into the diner. *Could it be shock or had the temperature actually dropped?* With the cuffs on it made it impossible for her to wrap her arms around her waist, which was her first instinct. "Where are you taking me?"

"Don't ask. First, we're going for a little ride. Just sit and keep quiet. I'm really not a conversationalist."

Molly prayed, *"Lord, you rescued me before and I know your eyes are on me. If you know when a sparrow falls from a tree, you certainly know where I am. Please bring someone to my rescue. If possible, please bring Doug."*

As Doug walked out of the office, he remembered Molly saying something about leaving early. She was already gone. Disappointment hit him when he saw her empty chair and computer turned off. *How can I be such a fatuous person? She means more to me than she can possibly imagine.* Jason was waiting for the elevator when he reached it. "So, did Mom fill you in on the Thanksgiving plans?"

"Yeah, I told her not to worry. I even told her I was planning on volunteering this year. That seemed to make her day."

"You know, Jason, when we have a chance to talk, I would like to tell you about last week and something amazing that happened to me." Just then his phone chirped; he didn't bother to look at the screen, but immediately took the call. "Edwards here."

"Hey Doug, this is Kevin. Do you know if Molly is still at the office?"

"No, she left early. I really couldn't tell you what time she left. I only remember her telling me earlier that she needed to leave early." He felt a pain in his chest thinking how he had ignored her the past two days.

"She was coming to help out here. She's been coming in every night since Sunday. I was sure she said she would be in by six if not sooner. It's almost six-thirty and it's not like her not to show."

"Wait, you mean she is still volunteering there? With all that has happened these past weeks?"

"She insisted she come in to help with all the food prep we have going on. She's been a tremendous help. I know she was looking forward to tonight too. Alice was going to show her how to make the rolls for Thursday's dinner. She said she couldn't wait to learn how."

"Hey, I don't know what to tell you. I'll try and contact Mrs. Brackenburg, perhaps she went home for a nap or something."

Jason looked at his brother. "Do you even have her phone number?"

Doug brought up Molly's cell number and simply shrugged his shoulders. "It went to voicemail. She's not answering. Let's head to her apartment. I think I remember how to get there. I really don't have a good feeling about this."

"I'll go with you. We seem to work well together when it comes to finding Molly." Jason patted his brother on the back as they got in the elevator. It was a long quiet ride down to the garage. Doug had driven his Mercedes to work...it was fast but not quite like his Porsche. The ride to Molly's apartment was just as quiet. They both noticed the chill in the air and Doug's thoughts immediately went to Molly. He hoped she was warm and safe.

They arrived at Molly's apartment, and Doug took the front stairs two at a time—his urgency evident. Mrs. Brackenburg was quick to answer the door. She could not help but notice the apprehension in their eyes. "Hello boys. Is everything okay?"

"We're concerned about Molly. We were wondering if she came home early and took a nap or something. She was supposed to be at Help You Stand at six this evening and she never showed up."

"Oh no. I have not heard anything from her. I only noticed when she left this morning."

As they were talking, Doug's phone chirped. "Edwards".

"Mr. Edwards, this is Sergeant Malone."

"Sergeant Malone. I have been trying to contact you!" The excitement in his voice was without notice. "Lieutenant Barlow said you were on leave from the department."

"I guess you could call it that. It was really a forced leave. I wasn't ready to give up this case but the Lieutenant insisted I take a leave. I'm back on the case thanks to your attorney."

"My attorney? I know I asked him to find out where you were and how I could reach you."

"He was able to reach me. I'm afraid it wasn't too easy for him. We know we have a mole in the department and even though I have been on leave, I have tried to do some undercover work. The captain called me in. How can I help you?"

"To be perfectly honest with you, I have no idea how you feel about your Lieutenant…" Doug was having a difficult time confiding in the Sergeant.

"Go on."

"I guess he has taken over the case, and like I told my attorney, I don't feel comfortable with him. There is something unsettling about him and I can't seem to put my finger on it. Call it a gut instinct."

"That's interesting. In fact, he is someone we are investigating internally. I probably shouldn't be telling you this but since you are invested in the Beaumont case, and someone I have already spoken with, I'm going to go out on a limb here. We have a tail on Barlow."

"Something has come up that has us concerned. Molly left work early today and was going over to Help You Stand to volunteer. She never showed up."

"Maybe she just got a little waylaid and forgot, or had an errand to run."

"My cousin, Kevin, at the shelter, called looking for her. She was to have been in at six. He said she was looking forward to going over there tonight; something about Alice teaching her how to make some kind of rolls. This may sound silly but knowing my assistant, she follows through on everything she says she is going to do. It's not like her to blow something like this off. Another concern…she hasn't answered her cell phone."

"Maybe she went home for a nap."

"That thought already crossed my mind and my brother and I are currently at her apartment. Her landlady has not seen her since this morning. I don't know how to tell you this, but I have had a couple guys keeping an eye her."

"Hey, that doesn't bother us if you have a couple of bodyguards tailing her. Was she aware of this?"

"No, I didn't want to scare her. I'll give them a call. I can't imagine why they didn't call me with anything suspicious."

"Call them, and get back to me."

"Will do. And Sergeant. For what it's worth, I'm glad you're back on the case."

"I'm glad to be back too. Keep in touch."

Doug quickly called one of the bodyguards. "Hey Josh."

"Yes boss. How can I help you?"

"Have you been following Molly today?"

There was a sheepish sigh on the other end. With a shaky voice, Josh had to admit they followed her to work in the morning but were not prepared for her leaving early. "She always leaves at five-fifteen like clockwork. We got a call that we could leave and come back at five."

"Who called you?"

"We thought it was you, boss. So, Mike and I went for a cup of coffee and returned about ten to five and waited for her to leave the building."

"You mean you never noticed her car gone?"

"We did when it got to be about five-thirty and she never came out. We have been driving around all this time trying to get a tag on her or her vehicle. Sorry, boss."

Doug had all he could do not to call them a couple of morons. "Keep looking. She never showed up at Help You Stand and I'm getting worried something has happened to her." Doug's stomach clenched and he felt so helpless. *I need to find her. I love her. Wait, did I just admit to*

201

loving her? I thought I was a confirmed bachelor. Well what do you know…I love her. I really love her. I can't lose her. "Jason, I love her! I really love her!"

His brother looked at him in utter confusion. "What are you talking about, man?"

"Don't you get it? I'm in love with Molly! I couldn't admit it until now! We have got to find her…and I'm afraid it might be too late."

Doug's phone chirped as he and Jason said goodbye to Mrs. Brackenburg. He looked at his phone hoping it was Molly. To his dismay, it was not. His voice filled with frustration. "Hi Mom, what can I do for you?"

"Doug, what's wrong?"

He could never fool his mother as much as he tried to show calm. "Is it that obvious, Mom? We can't find Molly."

"What do you mean, you can't find Molly? I spoke to her this afternoon in the office. She seemed fine."

"She left early to go volunteer at Help You Stand and never showed up."

"Oh honey, I heard her on her cell before I went down to Jason's office. I'm trying to remember who she was talking to. I really was not eavesdropping. I couldn't help but hear her say she would be willing to meet someone—but who was it?"

"Mom, please try and remember. I need to find her."

Patricia Edwards could not hold back the smile at the tone in her son's voice. "I think it was a police officer from what it sounded like. Is this a boyfriend of hers?" She asked sadly.

Doug immediately thought of Chief Bailey and his stomach roiled. "Mom does George Bailey or Chief Bailey sound familiar?"

"No, I can't say I recognize that name at all. But I do believe it sounds like it. I think she said Lieutenant somebody."

"Lieutenant Bradley, does that sound familiar? Mom, think… please."

"Doug, I think that's the name she said on the phone…yes, Lieutenant Bradley. That's it I'm sure."

"Anything else, Mom? Anything at all will help."

"I'm pretty sure she talked about meeting him at some restaurant. Let me think."

"Mom, please try to remember. We're afraid something bad may have happened to her."

"She mentioned a diner... and I think she mentioned Wilson or something. Like I said, I really did not want to eavesdrop. I was waiting to tell her I was going down to Jason's office."

"Mom, I love you. I have to go. And Mom? Please pray."

"Oh honey, I certainly will be praying. You be careful."

Chapter 32

MOLLY SAT CONFINED to the back seat of Lieutenant Bradley's black unmarked SUV. With handcuffs on her wrists, she desperately tried the door handle but it would not open. She realized it only opened from the outside. There was no way she could make a run for it. When he got in the driver's seat he immediately got on his cell phone. "Yeah, I got her. I'm heading there now. My ETA is probably about forty-five minutes; maybe an hour at the most…depends on traffic. Yeah, no doubt she's going to testify. So is her mom. We can take care of her later. Oh, she's fine. The sooner this is over with the better. You better have my twenty-grand or you're toast. After her mother—she's the last one I deliver to you."

Molly could not imagine where they were headed; she only knew they were going north. He was probably taking her to some backwoods location and she could only imagine what he had planned for her. She would not allow herself to even think about it. The voice she kept hearing was the voice of God saying, "Trust Me Molly — Trust Me." Knowing she had a long ride, she sat back and tried closing her eyes. Her fear of flying was a distant memory. *If only Doug were here, he certainly had a way of comforting me. I could never let him know how much he means to me. A man I feared for so long has become my rock. Oh, I know God is my Rock and my Fortress but Doug has become my earthly rock.*

Doug and Jason drove to The Diner on Wilson hoping they had the right place. It was not that far from Molly's apartment. Sergeant

Malone said he would meet them there. They arrived just after six-forty-five and saw Molly's car in the parking lot...to their relief. This had to be the right place. Doug silently thanked his mom for the information. Upon entering, they searched the diner looking for the Lieutenant or Molly. They hoped they would still be there. They asked the waitress if she had seen a man and woman together only a short time ago. She said she had and showed them where they had been sitting. She told them it was strange and that the man only ordered pie and ice cream. She thought the woman looked uncomfortable. "I always remember big tippers and the man gave me a twenty for pie and two coffees, and told me to keep the change."

"Did you see where they may have been headed?"

"No, I did not. I was busy, and once they left the restaurant, I really didn't pay any attention...sorry."

Doug's frustration was evident. After running his hands through his hair, Sergeant Malone walked in. Doug walked over to Malone and shook his hand. "Sergeant, this is the right place. Her car is still in the parking lot."

The couple seated at the window could not help but overhear the conversation taking place. The husband was the first to speak up. "Excuse me, but I couldn't help but overhear your conversation. My wife and I were sitting here when the couple I believe you are talking about left the restaurant. The woman tried motioning us with her eyes that she was in trouble and then mouthed the word "help". We were discussing what we should do when you folks walked in. It was a bit unsettling as to what to do as I'm sure he had to be a cop."

"Did you happen to notice the direction they were going when they left the parking lot?" Sergeant Malone asked, after showing them his badge.

"The guy made sure she got in the back seat of a black SUV. It looked like a plain wrapper. I think that's what you guys would call it." He said this as he looked at Sergeant Malone.

The wife could no longer keep quiet. "She is such a beautiful girl. I hope nothing bad happens to her."

Her husband continued. "It looked like they left here heading north on Wilson." North on Wilson indicated they were on their way to the Interstate.

"Thanks, you have been a big help." Sergeant Malone reached for his phone that was clipped on his belt. "You still have that tail on Barlow?" He asked who was on the other end of the phone. "Good, how far out are they? Keep following. I really want to know where he's taking her." He ended his call and motioned for Doug and Jason to follow him outside.

"My guys have a tail on Barlow right now. I'm heading that way. I really want their final destination."

"Are you serious? You know they are going to kill Molly as soon as they have a chance. I can't, and I won't, sit back and allow her to be bait for you guys." Doug's blood was boiling and his brother had to calm him down.

"Mr. Edwards, I can assure you that we will not let anything happen to Miss Beaumont. Our guys are following and I'm on my way."

"My brother and I are going to be right behind you."

"You guys sure have a way of getting into my business. As I recall, you were insistent on entering the McGee house." He did have a semblance of a grin on his face.

"Yes, we were. And you know if it wasn't for us she would have been found dead in that horrible rat-infested basement."

"Okay then, follow me. I have your cell so if I lose you, I'll give you a call."

"Oh, believe me, you will not lose us."

Molly was aware of the car leaving the highway and onto a dirt road taking her further away from civilization. *Where in the world is he taking me?* Another turn and another dirt road and a cabin came into view. The sun had already lowered into the horizon leaving it dark and dank outside. She squinted as she tried desperately to peer out the side window. The windows were so heavily tinted that all she could make out of the landscape was nothing but trees and overgrown brush. If it were not for the lonely cabin, the place looked desolate. *This must be the place*

where he plans on killing me. She noticed another black SUV sitting in the gravel drive. She realized someone else was involved in all of this. Her heart was racing as the car came to a stop and Lieutenant Barlow exited the car. He came around to her door. He opened it with such force she thought he would rip the handle off. He told her to get out as he reached for her arm. She asked him to please take off the handcuffs as they were digging into her wrist…reluctantly he did so. His grip was forceful as he dragged her from the vehicle. Molly felt the sting of tears as they escaped her watery eyes. *I cannot allow him to see my fear—or my tears.* She took several deep breaths hoping this would prevent the tears from gushing out. *I will not cry,* she kept repeating to herself. Lieutenant Barlow pushed her up the two steps to the cabin door. Before he could knock, the door swung open. A seedy looking man motioned them to enter.

"Anyone follow you?"

"Of course not," grunted Barlow. "I'm a detective remember." His condescending reply evident. The cabin was dark with only one lamp that was lit. Another man in a business suit sat in a chair next to a rather disgusting couch. He sat puffing on a huge cigar. "Have a seat Miss Beaumont." He motioned to a threadbare couch that appeared to be bug infested. Reluctantly Molly sat. She had no choice as Barlow gave her a push towards the couch. "Thank you for joining us." His smile was sardonic as he tapped the arm of his chair. "The Lieutenant tells me that you have every intention of testifying against McGee? As you can imagine, we can't have that."

"What are you planning to do to me? You know you will never get away with murder?"

"Oh, my dear. We already have. A couple more won't make one bit of difference."

"Should I go pick up Mrs. Beaumont?" asked Barlow.

"I have someone else taking care of that. They're on their way now."

"Well, I did my part, so if you would just give me my twenty-grand, I'll be on my way."

"Not so fast, my boy. Do you really believe you're going to walk out that door?"

Lieutenant Barlow's face paled as he quickly tried to compose himself. "For two years I have worked for you; doing everything you asked of me. I did all but kill for you."

"You didn't do any of it for me, Barlow. You did it for your own greed. I paid you plenty." The man's voice was raised as he gave Barlow one of his sardonic smiles—evil evident in his beady eyes.

Molly wondered who this man could be. He was dressed in a very expensive looking pin-stripe suite, polished black shoes, and coal-black hair slicked back around his ears. She intently tried to listen to any name given him, but his name was never mentioned. Just then there was a knock on the door. The seedy looking guy stood to answer the door. When he opened it, Molly saw her mother standing beside a very brutish looking man. He was quite tall, very large in stature, and wearing sunglasses even though it was now dark outside. Molly's breath hitched as she saw her mom looking so frail and weary. "Mom", Molly gasped. She longed to hold her mother in her arms and comfort her. The huge ghoulish-looking man pushed her mom into the room. Molly immediately stood and began reaching for her mother wanting to cling to her. The ghoul stopped her immediately.

"Get back to your seat," he bellowed at Molly, as he shoved her mother down onto the couch.

Molly took her mother's hand as she sat down beside her. Dolores sat down so hard that she bounced wincing in pain. Molly's eyes glistened as she felt her mother's pain. The two women locked eyes as Molly discreetly raised her mom's hand to her lips. She whispered, "I love you, Mom." Dolores gave her daughter's hand a comforting squeeze.

Lieutenant Barlow reached for his gun aiming it at the beady-eyed kingpin in the chair. "Lazzio, I will shoot your boss if you so much as remove your gun from your belt. That includes you too Shooze." Both men looked at their boss as he waved them off. "Just give me my money and I'll be out of here. What you do with these two is up to you, but I'm not gonna take them out. Murder was not in our agreement."

"Murder may not have been in our agreement, Barlow, but what's the difference between actually pulling the trigger, or the one that covered up the murder? And besides, do you actually think I carry that kind of money with me? You'll have to come to my office." With that the kingpin nodded to the two guys. They both pulled out their weapons and Barlow got off a shot at one of them before he collapsed to the ground. He was shot but he was not dead. Barlow reached for his gun and shot again missing the huge man. Again, he tried shooting, aiming at the kingpin. The man named Lazzio was not wounded and came up behind Barlow taking aim at the back of his head. Suddenly the door burst open; Sergeant Malone and two other officers stormed the room with guns drawn. One officer shot Lazzio before he could get a shot off at Barlow. Lazzio fell to the ground joining Shooze who had already been shot by Barlow.

Molly and her mother clung to each other shaking and in shock as the scene unfolded before them. Relief washed over Molly as soon as she recognized the Sergeant and the other officers. They were there to help. Sergeant Malone kept his gun aimed at the kingpin. "Well what do you know? We finally got Vince Langusto. You have the right to remain silent. Anything you say can and will be used against you in a court of law…"

"You know I'll get out of this."

"Not this time, Langusto. We heard it all. And you, Barlow, you're under arrest. You have the right to remain silent. Anything you say can and will be used against you in a court of law… Take them away boys."

Molly sat shaking, paralyzed in fear, the whole time clinging to her mother. Her eyes remained closed at the scene that had played out before them. A familiar voice, with the unmistakable timbre she knew so well, quietly spoke to her. It was Doug. He knelt on the ground in front of her. He lifted her chin up with his finger, so he could look in her beautiful eyes. "Molly, everything is going to be fine—you're okay. I won't let anything happen to you." Doug reached over to her sweet mother and squeezed her hand. "Are you okay, Mrs. Beaumont?"

"Yes. Thank you. I was certain one of those bullets would have been for me or Molly."

Doug helped Molly stand. He put his arm around her waist and held her close to his side. It just felt right having her nestled beside him. Jason helped Mrs. Beaumont up from the couch. Understandably, she too was shaking and unsteady as she walked out the door.

Sergeant Malone came up behind them. "Are you folks going to be all right? I need to ask you a few questions for my report, but if you prefer, I can meet you at the station tonight."

Molly looked between Doug and the Sergeant. "I think it best we go to the station."

"I can take you in my car."

"No. Molly won't be driving in any police car. I'll drive her and her mom in my car. Fortunately, I drove my Mercedes today."

"Suit yourself. I'll meet you there in about an hour." He instructed his officer to call the coroner to come for the two bodies. Barlow only had a flesh wound and was taken to the ER by the other officers.

Chapter 33

IT WAS QUITE late when they finished at the police station. Molly was exhausted and it was obvious her mother was just as weary. Doug asked Molly for her car keys and told her not to worry about her car; he would have someone drive it to her apartment tomorrow. "Oh, and Molly, I think it would be okay for you to take the rest of the week off. With your volunteering at Help You Stand, not to mention the last couple of days you had, I think you deserve the rest. Doug could no longer resist the temptation as he enfolded her in a warm embrace, tenderly placing a kiss on her forehead. "Molly, I was so afraid I was going to lose you today." He was so choked up and the lump in his throat prevented the words from coming out. All he could do was hold her tight. *I want to hold her in my arms forever.* As she pressed her head against his chest, she could hear his heartbeat. Something indescribable passed between them at that very moment, leaving the both of them to wonder if the other felt the same. Feeling a bit self-conscious, Molly also had a difficult time with words. "Thank you, Mr. Edwards." *What else could she possibly say to this man?* She had to reexamine the feelings she had for him. No longer did she feel intimidated by him. However, it did not change the fact that he was her boss and if he ever found out who she really was...how would that change things? She could easily be out of a job. Words could not describe what was happening to her. Doug bent down and kissed the top of her head. He gave her a tight squeeze and told her to sleep well.

Molly and her mother arrived at Help You Stand at seven-thirty on Thanksgiving morning. The turkeys were in the ovens and the smell of roasted turkey was already permeating every room in the facility. Alice had to have been there way before sunup to get the turkeys in the ovens. She had told Molly that she would have plenty of help getting the turkeys prepared. They did not put the stuffing in the bird so it would go much quicker. Molly and her mom immediately got to work preparing the stuffing and putting it in very large aluminum pans. Neither Molly nor her Mom had ever prepared food for so many people. It was a bit overwhelming but they had Alice there to give them careful instructions. The first seating would be at eleven. Alice said others would be coming in at ten to help serve the food.

With the tables set, and a small but very pretty Thanksgiving decoration placed on each table, they were all set for the servers to arrive. Kevin had been in early and Alice made sure he was kept quite busy. Without question, Alice was quite capable of handling such a daunting task as feeding a couple of hundred people.

At nine-forty-five Mr. and Mrs. Edwards arrived. Kevin greeted them immediately, giving his aunt a warm embrace and kiss on her cheek. He shook hands with his uncle and told them both how pleased he was to have them volunteer another year. Mrs. Edwards asked if he would be having Thanksgiving with them on Friday or going to his mother's in upstate New York. He said he would be leaving that evening after cleanup and driving up for the weekend. "Well, you know you are more than welcome to have dinner with us tomorrow," said Mrs. Edwards.

"Thank you, Auntie. I know, but I promised my mom I would come up there this year." Kevin's mother, Katherine, and Patricia Edwards were sisters.

"Be sure and give her our love. I know it has been a difficult year for her without your dad. Will Jess and Josh be there for Thanksgiving this year?" Jess and Josh were Kevin's younger siblings. Kevin's dad had passed away suddenly earlier in the year and they did their best to spend time with their mom.

"Yes, we will all be together tomorrow. Mom is quite happy about that."

"I'm so pleased to hear that. Let your mom know that if she ever wants to come here for a visit we can send the plane for her. I know she hates to fly but it is so much quicker."

"Thanks, I'll tell her."

Just then Mrs. Edwards noticed Molly setting a huge basket of rolls on one of the serving tables. "Excuse me Kevin, but is that Doug's Assistant over there?"

"Yes, it is. That's Molly Beaumont. She has been volunteering here for about a month now."

"Well, I certainly have to say hello to her before the rush starts." She walked over to the table and reached for Molly giving her a warm embrace. "Molly, it is so good to see you, dear. I did not expect to see you here. We were all so worried about you. How have you been?"

"Mrs. Edwards, it's good to see you too. I'm doing well and thank you for your concern. I had no idea either that you would be here today." Molly returned her embrace genuinely pleased to see her. "Mrs. Edwards, I would like you to meet my mom." She immediately took her hand and directed her to where her mom was working in the kitchen. "Mrs. Edwards, I would like you to meet my mom, Dolores."

"Please call me Patricia. That goes for you too, Molly. It's a pleasure meeting you, Dolores. I hope you are still planning on joining us for dinner tomorrow?"

"Thank you, we're looking forward to it. That was very kind of you to invite me and my daughter to your Thanksgiving dinner tomorrow. You must tell me if we can bring anything." Just then Alice called Molly away from their conversation. It appeared the two women hit it off famously. Molly was confident her mom and Mrs. Edwards were very much alike.

Molly was placing the last of the dishes on the serving table. It happened to be a huge aluminum pan of mashed potatoes. She no sooner set it down when she felt a sturdy arm wrap around her waist. She was shocked as she looked up into Doug's beautiful blue eyes. "Oh my, what are you doing here?"

Doug chuckled. "Molly, Help You Stand happens to be the charity I founded several years ago. Remember, you were at the fundraiser?"

"Of course, I remember. I just never expected you to be this involved in feeding the homeless."

Doug looked a little offended that Molly would think it beneath him to volunteer at his own organization. "Oh Doug, I'm so sorry. I certainly didn't mean anything by my comment. It's just that…oh never mind. I'm certainly making things worse. It's good to see you."

"It's good to see you too." Doug had a hard time removing his arm from her waist. *She belongs by my side. I'm sure of it. But how do I convince her of that?*

Just then Alice came out and began directing everyone to their specific stations. She had Doug serving the turkey and down at the opposite end was Molly serving up the pumpkin slices for dessert. Doug did not like this arrangement one bit. He wanted to have her by his side.

His mom, who happened to be serving the mashed potatoes beside him, noticed him looking over the table; she had no doubt what her son was thinking – Or was it *who* he was thinking about. "Doug honey, why don't I switch places with Molly?" She gave him a wink as she quickly walked down to the far end of the table. Doug had no idea what his mom was saying but Molly didn't hesitate to look at Doug and give him a nod before heading down.

"Your mom asked that I take her place and dish up the mashed potatoes. I guess your mom wants to visit with my mother since she happens to be putting the whipped cream on the pumpkin slices. The two of them seem to have hit it off."

"Yeah they have. I think they have a lot in common."

Just before the crowd started, Jason walked in. Molly noticed how pleased Patricia was to see her son. From what Molly could gather, it was not uncommon for Jason to be "missing in action" when it came to volunteering at Help You Stand.

It was a long day and by the end of the night, both Molly and her mom were exhausted. Kevin did not hesitate to give Molly a warm embrace as he thanked her for all her work. This did not go without notice from Doug. *What does he think he's doing? He certainly does not have to hold her that long.* Doug was at her side immediately. He patted Kevin on the back, breaking his hold on Molly. "Hey Kevin, have a safe drive tonight and be sure and greet your mom from me."

Kevin turned to thank Doug, giving him a firm handshake. "You bet. Thanks for everything, Doug."

As the two men continued to talk, Molly and her mother quickly said their goodbyes and were on their way. When Doug turned to look for her, his heart sank… She was gone.

Chapter 34

MOLLY AND HER mother arrived at the Edwards' home at two o'clock for Thanksgiving dinner Friday. They were both in awe at the mansion that stood majestically in front of them.

"Molly, are you sure you have the correct address? I have never seen anything so massive."

Molly looked at the address in her hand and the address on the gate. "Yes Mom, it's what Mrs. Edwards gave me." She noticed the intercom but before she could push the call button, the gates parted. Molly followed the circular drive and parked in front of the house. "Mom, am I dressed okay? I suddenly feel a bit underdressed for this place."

"You look fine, dear. I'm the one that is underdressed."

"No, I'm sure you're fine. I have no idea how many people will be here, but it's a little late to worry about how we look." The two women approached the door and could hear the beautiful chimes ringing from inside the house. It wasn't long before a butler came to the door and welcomed them in. Dolores gave her daughter the tray of cookies she had been carrying before the butler helped to remove their outer wraps. He then showed them to the living room. Before they sat, Mrs. Edwards entered and gave them both a very warm embrace. Molly sheepishly gave Patricia the plate of homemade cookies. "Mom and I did some baking on Wednesday and we thought we would share some with you."

"Oh my, they look delicious and I totally recognize the krumkaka. I don't believe this, are you Norwegian?"

"Yes, I am", said Dolores. I know with the last name Beaumont no one would think that but my maiden name was Olsen."

"And my maiden name was Hansen. Ed is also Norwegian. His

surname was Edwardson but his grandfather changed it to Edwards when he came to America. His grandfather was Edward Edwardson. His parents named Ed after his grandfather. People always look confused when they hear his name, Edward Edwards, but there is actually a story behind the name. The cookies will definitely be a treat for the both of us. It's been a long time since we had any krumkaka. And I know the other cookies are sunbuckles. I can't imagine how you ever found the time to make all this?"

Molly spoke up, pleased that they brought something they would enjoy. "Since Doug, I mean Mr. Edwards, gave me Wednesday off, Mom and I spent our free time baking. I find it very therapeutic. Mom brought her krumkaka iron and sunbuckle tins with her last week just in case we had a chance to do some baking. I certainly hope you and Mr. Edwards enjoy them."

"Oh, you can be sure we will." Mrs. Edwards rang for Sophie giving her the tray of cookies. "Sophie, be sure and include these for dessert. And say nothing to Mr. Edwards. It will be a surprise."

"Yes ma'am. I have never seen such cookies. They look fragile. I will take special care of them."

Sophie no sooner left and Mr. Edwards entered the living room. He gave Dolores a warm handshake but Molly he engulfed in a tender embrace. "I am so pleased you ladies were able to join us for our Thanksgiving dinner. The others should be here shortly." The words barely left his mouth when Doug walked into the living room. His eyes were immediately drawn to Molly and his lips turned up into the most becoming and yet mischievous smile. He noticed the beautiful patent heels Molly was wearing and memories of London quickly danced in his thoughts. *She is the most beautiful woman I have ever seen.* His heart must have skipped a beat as his blood pressure had certainly increased.

"What a pleasant surprise. Mother, I had no idea that Mol—I mean Miss Beaumont would be here."

"Oh piff. You don't fool me for one minute. I'm sure it's fine with Molly that you call her by her first name."

Doug greeted Molly with a wink and tight embrace. He immediately walked over to Dolores and gave her a hug. He also turned to his mother to give her a hug and kiss on her cheek. It was obvious to all that they were not quite the same affectionate embrace he gave Molly. *Is my mother playing matchmaker?* If she is, he was not about to show any resistance.

Jason also arrived totally unaware of the greeting that just took place. He too gave Molly and her mom a warm embrace. Jason was one to never feel inhibited—he never stood on formalities. To Molly's delight, Eleanor Larsen and her husband also arrived completing the guest list.

Immediately following introductions, beautiful hors d'oeuvres and drinks were served allowing the guests to chat before dinner. Sophie announced that dinner was served and they were escorted to the formal dining room. It was magnificent with the most elegant setting Molly had ever seen. However, the warmth and atmosphere were so welcoming that both mother and daughter did not feel the least bit intimidated. There were beautiful engraved place cards by each place setting. Molly was seated between Doug and her mom. Eleanor was seated opposite, between Jason and her husband Jim. Doug was the perfect gentleman holding the chair out first for Mrs. Beaumont and then for her. There was no way it could get more perfect than what it was. That was until Mr. Edwards prayed for the meal. His deep voice and heartfelt love and thankfulness for his family and God made his prayer earnest and undeniably powerful. There was no lack of sincerity. Molly was taken aback. She had no idea they were such a godly couple. *I wonder if Doug and Jason share the same faith as their parents obviously have. It would certainly be a surprise. Oh, I shouldn't be so cynical.*

Before dessert was served, Doug's phone chirped. He looked at the screen and excused himself from the table. He returned only a few minutes later with the biggest smile on his face. "That was Sergeant Malone. Barlow is turning state's evidence and confessed to the several crimes Langusto was involved in, and Tommy McGee is locked up and will be going away for a very long time…probably life without parole. It looks like we can all relax and sleep a little easier now."

Molly's eyes glistened. She could not keep the tears from escaping. Doug reached for his napkin and gently wiped her tears away. Oh, how he wanted to wrap his arms around her and hold her tight. He found himself reaching for her hand as he whispered in her ear – "Molly, it's all over. Everything is going to be just fine."

She nodded and thanked him for all he had done for her and her mom. She wondered if Doug would distance himself from her, and their relationship would return to employer and employee as before. After everyone's emotions settled, Sophie came in with the desserts: pumpkin pie, pecan pie, and apple pie. She followed with the beautiful tray of cookies that Molly and her mom had brought. To Mr. Edwards's surprise, he never expected to see krumkaka and sunbuckles. "What in the world have we here? These are two famous Norwegian Christmas cookies!" Looking at Molly and her mom, he asked if they made them.

"Yes, we did. We made them on Wednesday. Mom brought her iron and tins with her last week when I was gone—just in case there was a chance we would have time to make them." Molly didn't think anyone could be more excited over a tray of cookies.

"My dear young lady, do you happen to be Scandinavian?"

"Yes, my mom is Norwegian."

"Did my lovely wife tell you that we are also?"

"Yes, she did. We are so pleased we were able to bring something that you would enjoy."

Doug and Jason merely sat taking in the entire conversation. It meant nothing to Jason but to Doug it was the icing on the cake. Not only was Molly a woman of strong faith but her being Scandinavian was an extra bonus as far as his parents would be concerned.

When they had finished eating, Patricia asked Dolores if she would like to see the house. "Of course, what woman would not love to get a tour of this grand mansion," exclaimed Dolores. They excused themselves and the first room they entered was the massive kitchen. Dolores was taken aback at the enormity of the room.

Doug leaned over to Molly and asked if she would like to go for a walk. "It's a beautiful day and we could get a little fresh air."

"That sounds lovely, Doug. It wouldn't hurt to walk off some calories after that fabulous meal." He moved her chair out from her and immediately took hold of her hand. Molly felt her hand swallowed up in Doug's and for some reason it felt right.

Doug kept his hand on the small of her back as he led her out the kitchen patio doors. A shiver went through her body at his touch. He asked if she was cold and offered to go inside for a wrap. The air was crisp but not too cold. "No, I'm fine thanks." She wanted to tell him the shiver was from his hand on the small of her back. It brought back memories of their business trip to London when he took her sightseeing and the beautiful shoes she happened to be wearing... certainly a memory she would never forget. *I wonder if he has even noticed the shoes I'm wearing today.* They walked side-by-side down a beautiful path. The leaves on the trees had not completely let go of their bright colors of red, orange, and yellow. It would not be long before their branches would be completely bare of any leaves and snow covered. Molly thought how beautiful this walk would be covered in snow and the both of them bundled in heavy coats, gloves, and even snow boots. She marveled at God's creation and the beauty all around her. Lost in her own thoughts, she felt Doug slip his hand in hers as he led her on to a walking bridge. "Doug, this is absolutely gorgeous." He pointed to the waterfall that fed into the pond and stream that they were standing over. "I take it this is all your parents' property?"

"Yes, the grounds are quite large. Over to the right are the tennis courts; to the left the outdoor pool, spa, and bath house. They also have an indoor pool attached to the east side of the house."

"Well, I'm totally impressed. It's absolutely beautiful."

"It's the house Jason and I grew up in so we have never known anything else. As beautiful as it is, my parents never really spoiled us. We had chores to do as kids, even if it was simply feeding the dog and cat. We had to have our rooms picked up all the time. My mother would not hear of Sophie picking up our clothes and toys. My parents insisted that we go with them to the mission to serve meals on the holidays."

"Wow, that's amazing. Is that why you started the foundation and Help You Stand? I would have imagined that you and your brother were two very spoiled boys."

"I'm sure a lot of people have thought that. But to answer your question, yes that's probably one of the reasons. I have always felt the need to give back to the community when I have been given so much. I'm sure that attitude is from my parents."

Molly stood there impressed with Doug's passion—the pull on her heart was almost overwhelming. Before she even realized it, Doug had closed the gap between them and gently had his arm around her. She instantly felt the heat that radiated from him. She could not help but be drawn into his beautiful ocean blue eyes. *Is he going to kiss me?* She didn't know how it happened but she found herself lifting her head as he lowered his and sweetly covered her lips with his. "Oh my, that was unexpected."

"I'm sorry, Molly. I should not have done that." He had kissed plenty of women in his day, but this woman had totally wrapped his heart in a knot.

"Oh please, don't be sorry." She did not know what came over her to say such a thing. Molly knew she had to be blushing and felt the heat rush through her entire body. Her heart was pounding and she was sure Doug could hear it from where he was standing.

Doug took both her hands in his as he gazed into her eyes. "Molly, I have to admit, you do something to me that I can't explain. I never thought I could ever feel this way again—"

"What do you mean by again? I don't understand."

"I was in a relationship for three years—it ended over five years ago. I mean…it was a serious relationship for three years." He unconsciously slipped his hand in his pocket.

"Okay." Molly did not really know how to respond to this revelation, but then it was five years ago. She could not help but notice the slip of paper he fiddled with while talking to her. What in the world? It looked too familiar.

"What's the paper you have in your hand?" Molly reached for his hand and opened his fist that he had closed the moment she pointed it out. To her consternation, she found the slip of paper with her name and phone number. "You have known who I am all this time?" Doug noticed her eyes were no longer the beautiful aqua blue but now looked like a raging sea.

"Molly no. Let me explain."

"No explanation is necessary. I'm sure you've had a good laugh at my expense this entire time. I have never been more humiliated or embarrassed in my whole life!!" Her eyes began to glisten with unshed tears. "And to think I was falling in love with you!!"

Doug reached for her but she pulled away. The hurt and anger in

221

her eyes were piercing. She started to walk away but abruptly stopped. Bending over she took off her shoes and walked back to him.

"And Mr. Edwards, I cannot accept these. I'm sure you will have no problem finding someone else to give these shoes to...maybe even what's her name...Lisa!" Doug stood with his mouth agape, not believing what was happening. "Oh, and Mr. Edwards, I will no longer be able to work for you. I quit!"

As Molly walked away, she never heard his whisper, "Molly, I love you."

Molly could not run away fast enough. The tears were falling and there was nothing she could do to control them. After wiping her tears, she entered the house and immediately looked for her mother. She saw her in the parlor with Mr. and Mrs. Edwards, Jason, and Eleanor and her husband. She was so hoping to find her mom alone. Dolores was completely puzzled as she took one look at her daughter standing in the entryway. Obviously, she had been crying. She immediately came to her but not without asking, "What in the world happened to you, dear?"

"Mother, we have to go. Please, let's just get our coats and leave." Of course, she noticed her mother's bewildered expression. "I'm sorry, Mom, I can't stay here any longer. I will explain in the car." She was practically hyperventilating as she tried desperately to catch her breath.

Mr. and Mrs. Edwards were by their side in a heartbeat. "What is wrong, dear?" Mrs. Edwards had her arm wrapped around Molly which only made matters worse.

"I'm sorry, but we have to leave. Thank you so much for a lovely... dinner." Molly's voice kept hiccupping as she tried desperately to hold back the flood of tears.

The butler was quickly at their side helping them with their coats. Mr. Edwards looked at Molly's feet. "But dear, you have no shoes on your feet."

"Your son will have to explain why." With that said, Molly and her mother left the Edwards' home.

Jason, still seated but not unaware of the conversation and turmoil taking place in the hallway, took his leave to go look for his brother. His brother had some explaining to do.

Jason found Doug still standing on the walking bridge staring into space. "Hey bro, what happened? Do you feel like talking about it?" Doug unfolded his fist showing Jason the paper he had found in his pocket. "So, it has Molly's name and phone number. I'm confused. What's that supposed to mean?"

"Jason, Molly is the woman that ran into me all those months ago. Remember when I walked into the conference room with a coffee stain down my suit jacket? It's her, and she thinks I have known who she is all this time."

"So, what's the problem? You and I both know she is not some kind of ditz or klutz. She's a very efficient, capable, and I might add, a very beautiful woman." Doug glared at his brother. Jason continued, "What. Do you think I haven't noticed just how beautiful she is? I'm not blind but maybe you have been."

"What's that supposed to mean? I already told you that I love her."

"Yeah, you have, but have you told her? All your company rules and all the barking at her have probably made her gun shy."

"I don't think it's just that. She said she was embarrassed and humiliated to think that I had known all this time, and honestly, I only found the note in my suit jacket just before we left London."

"And still you didn't say anything?"

"No, of course not. I was waiting for the right time. I thought this was it."

"You know what? Your timing stinks. How come you're holding her shoes? You know she walked out barefoot."

"They're shoes I bought for her in London. I had noticed her practically drooling over them at the Louboutin shoe salon and surprised her with them that night. I knew at that time I had to keep my distance from her— My heart was getting too involved."

"And now what is your heart telling you?"

Doug gave a strained laugh. "Now my heart is telling me what a fool I have been. Jason, she not only walked away feeling humiliated and embarrassed but...she quit."

"She quit?"

"Yeah, quit." Doug did not know how much he should confide in his brother, but then he had nothing to lose. He ran his hand through his hair and down his face. "Jason, I told her about my three-year relationship with Peggy— But I also told her it ended five years ago."

"Are you crazy? Why would you go and tell her all that?"

"You won't understand."

"Try me."

"I wanted to be as open and honest with her as possible. I wanted her to know everything about me…I'm not a perfect man. I really don't deserve someone like Molly. I wanted her to know who she was getting if she married me. Jason, I've wanted to tell you what happened to me on our flight home from London." Doug began telling Jason how right he was about Molly's fear of flying and finished telling him about Molly reading her Bible on her Kindle. It was a perfect opportunity for him to share what God had done in his heart that day and how different he felt. "You know, Jason, Mom and Dad totally have it right when it comes to love and marriage. They've been committed to one another for almost forty years. That should tell us something. I'm convinced more than ever that we have allowed the liberal world view to control our hearts and minds." Jason nodded but it was obvious to Doug that for now Jason did not share his conviction. He told him how he had surrendered his heart to God on the plane. Jason just nodded and Doug knew that all he could do was to pray for his brother. With a slap on his back, Jason turned and walked away telling him everything would work out. Hearing this did not change how badly Doug's heart ached.

Chapter 35

MOLLY CONVINCED HERSELF that taking her mom home on Sunday was for the best. Dolores offered to stay with her, knowing how devastated she was. Molly ached all over and was exhausted from all the tears shed. It did not matter that Patricia had told Dolores about Doug's commitment to Jesus Christ. She was happy for him but it made no difference to her. She was too hurt and angry. She was relieved and yet disappointed that Doug never came after her. Oh, she had some text messages from him…at least fifty of them, but she could not even bring herself to read a one of them. Molly finally turned her phone off. She was convinced her heart would never heal from this hurt.

She had to do something about a job and her future—wallowing in her grief and anguish would do nothing in solving her dilemma. At first, she struggled to pick up the phone but she was determined to wipe the tears, grit her teeth…and call Mr. Jewels. Oh, moving to London would be a real stretch for her, but the farther away she could go the better. *And Mr. Jewels kind of offered me a job as his assistant.*

Her call was immediately put through to Mr. Jewels. "Hello, Mr. Jewels. This is Molly Beaumont. How are you, sir?"

"Molly, it's so good to hear your voice. I'm very well, thank you. How are you my dear? I certainly hope you had a chance to enjoy our city before your flight home?"

"Yes, sir, I did. We did not return to the States until Saturday and Mr. Edwards showed me some of the sights of your great city." Molly had all she could do not to let her emotions show as she was desperately trying to keep the tears at bay. Just the mention of Doug's name hurt deeply.

Mr. Jewels, however, recognized the sadness in her voice. Something was making this call very difficult for her. "Is there something I can help you with, Molly?"

Taking a deep breath, she pushed on, "I was wondering if Shirley will still be retiring shortly and if there is a chance that your offer still stands for an assistant. If that is a possibility, I would appreciate the opportunity to apply for the position."

Mr. Jewels' voice brightened to think he could have this beautiful and competent woman as his assistant. "Why yes, Molly, in fact Shirley will be leaving a little sooner than anticipated. How do you feel about working across the pond though? Do you think this is something you would really like to do?"

"Yes, sir, I really think I would."

"Well then, I would definitely like you to fly over for an interview and an opportunity for me to show you our firm before you make a decision."

"That sounds wonderful. When would you like me to be there? I'm free all this week." *Well I'm really free for a whole lot longer than this week. How about the rest of my life?*

"Why don't you fly over on Wednesday? I'm free all of Thursday to show you around. I will have Shirley book your airline ticket and hotel for two nights. I'll have your return flight scheduled for Friday morning. Will this arrangement work for you?"

"That sounds wonderful. Thank you so much, Mr. Jewels. I promise, you will not be disappointed."

"I'll have Shirley make all the arrangements and she'll e-mail your itinerary this afternoon." Mr. Jewels definitely had a twinkle in his eye and a smile on his face when he hung up the phone. Something was not right and if it meant he had to play cupid, so be it. *Those two young kids are meant for each other. Anyone can see that.*

"Thank you, I'll be looking for Shirley's e-mail." Her heart sank at the thought of moving to London and leaving her mom and especially her dad but she had to make a clean break. Every time she thought of Doug, her heart ached. She thought of his kiss as they stood on the bridge; his tenderness as he wrapped her in his arms to comfort her fears. He was always there for her. She couldn't even think of their trip and how he held her hand without even wincing at the pain she inflicted on him. *Where was he now? Probably having a good laugh at how he was able to fool her into believing he really did care for her. And all the time, he no doubt had been laughing at the klutz working for him.* She really was the fool in telling him she was falling in love with him. *Why did I have to tell him that?* Molly curled up on her couch. She would have to tell her mom and Mrs. Brackenburg about London…but not right now. She would tomorrow.

Doug was going nuts. Molly would not answer any of the texts he had sent all weekend. Her car was never at her apartment and he felt like a stalker driving past it so many times. He was sorry he released the bodyguards he had hired to follow her. He made a call to retain them and they already had another assignment. *But even if they found her what would he have them do? Tie her up and force her to come back with them? She probably went to her mother's. Well, I have a business to run and I can't simply drive all over the place.* Sometimes the pain in his chest was so great he was sure he would have a heart attack. Why couldn't she understand, he loved her.

Wednesday, the third day without Molly in the office; is this how it would be each day from now on? Counting the days and being miserable? His family tried to help but right now he couldn't face anyone. The only way he was getting through each day was reading his Bible every night—praying for an answer. *What did God want him to do? He would do anything to have Molly in his life, even if all she wanted was to be his assistant. Why, he would even take that…at least he would see her five days a week.*

He could not bring himself to even open the blinds. Jason, being the great brother that he was, brought him a Starbucks each morning but left as soon as he put it on his desk. His brother didn't even want to talk to him. The office phone rang, and rang, when he finally realized no one was there to answer it other than him. "Edwards and Sons." The voice on the other end of the line was a little difficult to make out—the connection not the best. The caller had an accent or something. Finally, the connection cleared up.

"Douglas my boy. Jonathan Jewels here. How are you, Son?"

"Oh, Mr. Jewels. I'm doing well, sir. How have you been?" Doug was puzzled as to why this man would be calling him. *Was something wrong with the contract they had signed? Or was he backing out of the deal?* The way he felt right now he really didn't care what the reason was.

"I'm doing very well, thank you. How is that assistant of yours? I hope you're taking good care of her."

Doug cleared his throat before confessing what had happened. "She quit last week, Mr. Jewels, so I really can't tell you how she is doing."

"Well I'm sorry to hear that. But pleased that I will be the one gaining a new assistant shortly."

Doug froze in his chair. *Molly was going to go work for Jonathan Jewels? In London? How could she?* "She'll be a wonderful asset to have working for you, sir."

"Yes, I have to agree. By the way, she will be leaving JFK this morning at ten. She'll be on a British Airways plane, Flight 560. I'm looking forward to our interview and giving her a tour of our office on Thursday. I just thought I would pass along that information, Son. It's up to you what you want to do with it."

"Yes sir. Thank you, sir. I appreciate the call." *What was he going to do with this information?* Doug looked at his watch, it was already nine o'clock. *Could he make it in time?* He had to try. He took his passport out of the safe and was on his way.

Doug flew out of the office; the elevator couldn't get there quick enough. As soon as he hit the garage floor he jumped into his Porsche. He was really thankful today for his fast car. He called his brother once he was on his way. He just had to make it before the plane took off. *British Airways, British Airways, okay it was at the International Terminal.* He flew into a parking spot and ran into the terminal. He looked up at the board and saw the plane was leaving on time, *just my luck. Why couldn't it be delayed?* He had twenty minutes to get to the plane. There was only one way he could get through security. He ran up to the counter and purchased a ticket to London's Heathrow Airport on Flight 560.

The agent looked at his passport, "Mr. Edwards, do you have any bags to check?"

"No. No bags. Just one ticket and make it one way."

He was given a very skeptical look. No doubt she thought him to be a terrorist or something. "Look, I just need to make that plane." His pleading eyes revealed his heart.

"Good luck, sir. I hope you make it." She had a smile on her face as she handed him his ticket. Looking into such desperate eyes, it was obvious his reason for making that flight.

"Thanks."

Doug took off running down the concourse to the gate. *If only people would get out of my way. No doubt, it's the last gate possible.* He felt his lungs burning and was sure they would burst by the time he got there. His heart sank to the bottom of his stomach when he saw the jetway door already closed. The agent was still at the counter. He pleaded with everything he had in him. He had to get on that plane.

"I'm sorry, sir, but as you can see the jetway has already pulled away."

"No. That can't be! There is someone on that plane that I have to get to, it's important." He couldn't cry in front of this agent but his heart was breaking.

"Sir, is it a woman you are looking for?"

"Yes, it is. She's a very beautiful woman and...I have to tell her that I love her." *Was he really telling a stranger this?*

"Sir, there's a woman sitting over by the window. She got all the way to the gate but then she would not walk down the jetway. She simply said, 'I can't fly without him.' And then she walked away. She has been sitting there watching the plane back out."

Molly sat staring out the window. Tears streamed down her cheeks like rivulets. She was a mess. *What am I to do?*

As the woman was talking, Doug turned in the direction she had pointed and saw the back of Molly's head. It was her. It was his Molly. "Yes, that's her. Thank you." He leaned across the desk giving the attendant a quick kiss on her cheek.

Doug's heart was beating so fast he thought it would burst out of his chest. He ran to her and fell on his knees in front of her. He enveloped her hands in his. "Molly, you can't leave me."

"Doug, what are you doing here?" She could not believe this handsome man was kneeling in front of her. *He came for me after all.*

"Molly, I need my assistant."

"Excuse me?" Her disappointment was evident as she desperately tried to remove her hands from his. "I'm sure Eleanor would be more than happy to come back as your assistant." She could not believe what he was saying.

With the pads of his hands, Doug reached over and wiped the tears from her cheeks. "No Molly. I love you and I want *you* to be my assistant...only you."

"You love me?"

"Yes Molly. More than you know. I think I have loved you from the first day I walked into that conference room and saw you standing with my brother. You took my breath away."

"But the note with my name and number—you knew who I was the whole time?"

"No, Molly. I never knew until the morning we were leaving to return to the States. I had no idea how to tell you. I actually thought it was kind of cute to have found it. Then when you saw it in my hand, I tried to explain—"

"And I wouldn't let you. Doug, I am so sorry." Her arms twined around his neck and she pulled him closer. Her fingers reached up and automatically stroked his hair as she gave him the most passionate kiss he could have ever imagined.

"If that's how we'll always apologize, it's fine by me." Doug pulled her up and into his arms. He returned her kiss with so much passion she was sure her toes curled. "You're the only assistant I have ever wanted. I love you, Molly."

"And I love you, Mr. Edwards."

They were married on New Year's Eve in a quiet but lavish ceremony in Molly's home church in Shepherd, Connecticut. Of course, Jason was best man and Molly's best friend, Lauren, was her matron of honor. She and Lauren had been friends all through high school and college.

The highlight of the ceremony was having Molly's father attend as he walked her down the aisle. His walk was stiff and gated but his mind seemed clear and vibrant as he looked at his beautiful daughter. When they reached the front, Dolores was quick to come to her husband's side directing him to the pew she was seated in. The tears flowed freely as everyone looked on. Even Pastor Riley choked up as he began the ceremony. The service was brief as they did not want Mr. Beaumont to sit in a lengthy service. Doug and Molly had written their own vows which were touching and personal giving everyone an insight into their amazing love for each other. As soon as Pastor Riley told Doug, "you may kiss your bride", the applause erupted immediately when their passionate kiss finally ended. Molly felt the blush rise to her cheeks but all embarrassment vanished when she looked up into her handsome husband's eyes.

A beautiful reception was held at a local country club that was every bit as perfect as if held in one of New York's finest private clubs. After greeting all the guests, Doug excused himself and Molly as he anxiously pulled his bride off the dance floor. "Sweetheart, we have to leave. I certainly hope you like the honeymoon I have planned for us."

"Doug, you're still not going to tell me where we're going?"

"Nope, you know how much I like to surprise you."

Their plane landed and Doug was just as excited as Molly as the limo whisked them away. The honeymoon suite at the beautiful Disney Hotel was the beginning of their honeymoon destination. Molly's eyes were like saucers as she realized they would be spending the entire day at Disneyland. Doug announced they would be also going to SeaWorld and Universal Studios. Molly's heart was warmed by her husband's thoughtfulness. *He remembered that I never made it to my thirteenth birthday destinations.* "Doug, I love you so much. This is absolutely perfect."

"And perfect is what you are, Molly. I can't believe God has blessed me with the most beautiful woman in the world."

Doug had all he could do to keep another secret from her. She never made it to the beach for her thirteenth birthday and to surprise her, he bought her a beautiful beach home in Malibu. It would be a three-week grand finale to their honeymoon spent in luxury on the beach. But his wife would have her own beach whenever she wanted to visit. It was just the beginning of all the adventures Doug had planned for his wife who had missed so much. He was there to rescue her time and again, but the truth was—she had rescued him.

The End

Thank you for reading *Rescued*. I hope you enjoyed reading it as much as I enjoyed writing it. I always get so caught up in the characters and the story, that I find myself teary-eyed. It's a message from my heart and I trust it touches your heart. God's love for us is amazing and unconditional. He is always in pursuit of our heart no matter our journey. Jeremiah 31:3 (NIV) "...I have loved you with an everlasting love; I have drawn you with unfailing kindness.

This is a work of fiction. Names, characters, places, and incidents are products of the author's imagination or are used fictitiously and are not to be construed as real. Any resemblance to actual events, locales, organizations, or persons, living or dead, is entirely coincidental.

The origin of Mr. Ed Edwards's name, however, is not fiction. It happens to be the true account of my maternal grandfather's name. When he and his brother, Tom, arrived from Norway in the late 1800's they both changed their surname from Edwardson to Edwards. Thus, my grandfather was Edward Edwards. It was fun weaving in a little bit of my ancestry into the story. I am thankful that I've had the privilege of visiting the towns of each of my four grandparents in Norway.

Watch for the sequel: *Innocent Deception* (The Edwards Brothers – Book 2). Jason Edwards also has a story of God's grace and forgiveness that I think you will enjoy.

Made in the USA
Lexington, KY
29 January 2018